EDGE OF NOWHERE

FELICIA DAVIN

ISBN-13: 978-0-9989957-3-1

If you don't need content warnings and prefer to avoid spoilers, skip this page.

Warnings: This book has explicit sex scenes in it, and there's a scene where two characters accidentally get high and almost have sex. A main character is an orphan, and there are a few references to abuse by bad foster parents in that character's past. There are mentions of starvation (as part of a horrific science experiment). There is also a scientist/research-subject sexual relationship, which is portrayed as unethical, between two supporting characters. There is also some discussion of prejudice (against people who can teleport, mostly, but there are a few references to real-world prejudices against characters who are not white, not straight, and not cis).

Tags: M/M, bisexuality, sex pollen, accidentally high, trapped in a closet, huddling for warmth, pining, friendship, found families, goofy made-up sports, goofy made-up physics, sinister corporations, teleportation, space

To Lis and Kristin

CONTENTS

[1]
CATS

Months of strange incidents at Quint Services Facility 17, and it was the cat that had done it. Emil wished he'd just let the poor thing wail for his dinner, but there'd been no telling when Lange would return to feed him. So he'd walked to the lab in the middle of the night. He'd never regretted a kindness more. Emil had spent twelve years in the Orbit Guard—eight years active duty, four in the reserves—but somehow twelve weeks at QSF17 had landed him in more trouble.

He didn't sigh. He kept his tone even. "As I said in my report, I was standing in the hallway when the lab door blew off and hit me. It knocked me unconscious. I don't know what happened in the lab before or after that."

Emil's interrogator was some higher-up at Quint Services, but not the billionaire himself. He'd given his name as Kristian Auer. Black suit, short grey hair, judgmental expression. He stared Emil down across the table and said, in a voice that could preserve corpses, "You were found *inside* the lab, Mr. Singh."

Because the Nowhere doesn't follow the laws of physics. Emil knew better than to say that. He waited for a question. If

Auer wanted to accuse him of some wrong, he'd have to make that accusation in words.

"If something caused the door to blow off and hit you while you were standing in the hall, then why were you found inside the lab?"

"I don't know how I ended up there, sir. I was unconscious at the time."

Auer had laid a pen and an old-fashioned paper pad on the table at the beginning of this meeting, but he hadn't touched either. The first page was still blank. Emil had known this interview would be useless—he knew so little, and he'd already written a report—but Auer's hopes had been higher. Or maybe he was using his unnatural stillness to creep Emil out. "Did you know Dr. Lange well, Mr. Singh?"

"No, sir." Emil's bruised face still ached. They'd given him stitches to close the cut through his right eyebrow. The black eye needed more time to heal. Contusions purpled his arms and legs. And the rest of Emil was still reeling. They'd transported him to Franklin Station and de-orbited a pod to get him to this interrogation, worried that a trip through the Nowhere would cause him further distress. Re-entry in the pod hadn't exactly been buckets of fun, but the space elevator would have been far too slow.

Not that Quint Services cared much for Emil's time. He'd been recovering in a featureless room for four long days, forbidden from looking at screens, supposedly because they were worried he had a concussion. He'd been hit in the head pretty hard. But still, his alleged concussion had been a convenient reason to keep him from communicating anything to his team about what had happened six days ago, or why he'd been whisked back down to Earth for questioning without a word.

Emil still wasn't sure what he'd witnessed before the door hit him.

"You and Dr. Lange lived in the same isolated facility together for months."

"It wasn't really possible to know him, sir. He kept to himself." The Orbit Guard had had its share of grouchy assholes, but none of them held a candle to the head scientist at Quint Services Facility 17. Emil had never met a more cantankerous recluse than Dr. Solomon Lange. Not even Chávez and Beck could get him to smile, and everybody liked Chávez and Beck. Emil's team avoided Lange, which meant Emil was the one who always got stuck telling him to go lie down, or eat something, or feed his damn cat.

"And yet you were in the lab with him on the night of the incident," Auer prompted.

"I was passing by, sir. Sometimes Dr. Lange needed to be reminded to eat and sleep. On that particular night, Dr. Lange's cat was crying for food. I went to tell him."

"Are those not the actions of a friend?"

"As I've said, sir, we weren't friends. I was keeping him alive. I knew he was crucial to the mission. And Dr. Lange's room is right next to mine. His cat's yowling was keeping me awake."

The fucking cat was named *Niels Bohr*. When Emil's team had first arrived at QSF17 and found that famous physicist Solomon Lange was a cat lover so passionate that he'd refused this post unless his cat was allowed to accompany him, they'd been charmed. Niels Bohr himself was a charming creature, a plump, dapper tuxedo cat who was always ready to give and receive affection—unlike his owner. After learning the cat's name, Dax had laughed and asked why, if the cat was going to be named after a famous physicist, Dr. Lange hadn't gone for broke and named him Erwin Schrödinger? Lange had given Dax a stare that promised violence. For one long, fraught moment, Emil had wondered if his first act at QSF17 was going to be breaking up a fistfight. The whole team had breathed a sigh of relief when Lange had simply turned on his heel and walked away.

Emil didn't share any of that with his interrogator. It wasn't relevant. He didn't want to find out if Auer's disapproving frown could get any deeper.

Auer didn't drum his fingers on the table or fidget in any way. Emil was beginning to wonder if the man ever blinked. "Do you have any notion of what Dr. Lange was working on at the time of the incident?"

"Only in the most general terms, sir. I know he studied the Nowhere and that he wanted to... open a door, I think, was the metaphor that one of the other scientists used to explain it to me. A way into the Nowhere for people who weren't born runners."

"Which other scientist?"

"Dr. Heath, sir. She's working on the runners, on what biological differences make it possible for them to go into the No—"

"I am aware of Dr. Heath's work with Dr. Winslow, Mr. Singh," Auer said, his voice even crisper and more clipped than usual. "Do you believe that Dr. Lange was trying to open this door on the night of the incident?"

"I don't know, sir. As I said, I was just passing by. I was knocking on the door of the lab when I heard this loud, ripping sound. I thought Dr. Lange was in danger but the door—"

"The details of the incident are in your statement, Mr. Singh. There is no need to repeat them here. Let me rephrase my last question. Based on what you saw in the aftermath of the incident, do you believe that Dr. Lange succeeded in opening a so-called door?"

"There wasn't... there wasn't a *hole* in the lab, if that's what you're asking. It didn't feel like the Nowhere." Emil repressed a shudder. He would have noticed that. But he couldn't explain how he'd ended up inside the room after the door had blown off its hinges and thrown him backward into the hallway. He wanted to say *I think it was both an explosion and an implosion*. Then Auer would ask him why he thought so, and he didn't have an answer except that he'd ended up inside the lab. Some force had propelled him there, since the lab door had still been half on top of him when he'd woken. If Emil said that, they'd be right back at the beginning. "It just looked like an explosion had happened. Everything broken or flipped over. The walls were still intact."

"Thank you, Mr. Singh. Now, regarding your statement, I'm still unclear on a few things. Did you see Dr. Lange die?"

"I don't see how a human being could possibly have survived an explosion like that, sir."

"But did you see him die?"

"No, sir. It was impossible to see anything. As you can see," Emil gestured at his black eye and his stitches, "my injuries are consistent with my statement."

"And after the incident, did you find his body in the wreckage?"

There had been a blinding light, a burst of pain, and then blood rushing into Emil's right eye. An instant of unconsciousness. Emil had woken up to emergency alarms blaring and Dr. Heath and Dr. Winslow rushing into the lab, both in their pajamas, lifting the door off his body and dragging him out. Emil could remember the sight of the lab in disarray, smashed tables and broken glass on the floor, but he couldn't remember seeing Dr. Lange's body. Maybe he'd blocked out the sight. "No, sir."

"Dismissed, Mr. Singh. You'll be sedated for transport back to QSF17 tomorrow. For now, you should report to medical for your regular treatment."

[2]

AND DOGS

THE TRICK TO MAKING MONEY WAS NEVER ASKING questions. Clients didn't pay him to talk. They paid him to transport parcels thousands of miles in an instant. Kit could navigate the Nowhere with ease and he didn't worry about what exactly he was delivering. That had won him a reputation as the most discreet and reliable runner out there.

Unfortunately, today's parcel had an attitude. Kit had to break his own rule.

"You didn't sedate her?" Kit held the squirming dog at arm's length. For a tiny thing, she had a lot of fluffy white fur. And sharp claws. Kit never feared crossing the Nowhere, but this yappy little dog would put his leather jacket and pristine black-and-silver t-shirt in serious danger. Animals—and most humans —reacted badly to the trip. Kit was one of the rare people who didn't.

He felt sorry for the dog, but he was more worried about the clothes. The t-shirt was programmed to shift its abstract silver pattern every few minutes and was one of his favorites. He'd bought the jacket in Tokyo. It was designer, for fuck's sake. He'd saved for months and made a special trip and it was the perfect shade of bright green to clash with the Virulent Violet dye in his artfully tousled hair.

"Arielle has an all-natural diet," Carl said. The dog's delicate name sounded funny in his deep, scratchy, tough-guy voice. Carl Akins was a local mob boss whose mistress lived states away in Inland New York, and their long-distance relationship was making Kit richer by the week. The mail and regular delivery services were slow, fraught with corruption, and subject to scrutiny by state police. Like any criminal with two brain cells to rub together, Carl didn't want to expose his business to that. Since he could afford Kit's fees, Kit's talents as a Nowhere runner had become essential to his underworld empire and his personal life. There were no border patrols or customs agents in the Nowhere. Kit just wished Carl's preferred love trinkets tended more toward diamonds and less toward sending Miss Tallulah an entire menagerie.

At least the parakeet had been in a cage.

"*Arielle*'s gonna all-natural yarf on my jacket and it'll cost you extra," Kit said.

"There won't even be time for that." Carl waved his hand dismissively. "You'll be there in two seconds."

Kit resisted the urge to roll his eyes. "It doesn't work like that. Time passes differently in the Nowhere." In truth, Nashville to Inland New York only required a few minutes traveling through the void, but a few minutes was more than enough for Arielle's special diet to end up on Kit's favorite distressed-to-perfection fitted black jeans and limited-edition red sneakers.

"What's with you today? You never talk this much. I don't pay you for physics lessons, kid."

"Not a kid." Kit was twenty-one years old and most days, it felt like a lot more. "Seriously, Carl, this poor animal's gonna have a rough time in there. You sure you don't want to sedate her?"

"And send my Tallulah a sleeping lump of a dog? And have her message me shrieking about *chemicals* and *toxins* and whatever the fuck else? I don't think so. Do your damn job and bill me when you get back—which should be four seconds from now, if you get going already."

Like most people, Carl hadn't ever been in the Nowhere. And if he had, he wouldn't have wanted to go back.

Kit wasn't most people. He could feel the Nowhere all around him, no matter where he was, currents of tension in the air, pulling him closer. All he had to do was focus for a moment and he could step right into the void. He'd been able to since he was eleven years old and it came so naturally that he had a hard time believing other people couldn't. It was *right there*. You just had to want it.

One second he was standing in Carl's warehouse arguing, and the next, he and Arielle the dog were soaring through the airless black of the Nowhere. Kit propelled them forward, feeling powerful and free. Arielle yelped and scraped her claws down his face and chest, shredding his t-shirt. Then, as predicted, she vomited.

"Fuck," he muttered, glancing at the wet mess on his t-shirt. Poor dog. No more live packages—at least, no more live packages that weren't sedated.

It was the easiest kind of trip, going to a place he'd been before. The Nowhere was directionless, a pulsing expanse of darkness, so runners navigated by feel. Most people worked the same routes over and over again, but Kit didn't like to limit himself. If the price was right, he'd go anywhere.

The remaining moments of his trip through the Nowhere weren't as carefree and weightless as he wanted them to be, since he was feeling sorry for the dog and for his clothes. But the trip was short for him and shorter for everyone on the outside, since he arrived in the lobby of Miss Tallulah's high-rise apartment building only one second after he'd left Carl in Nashville.

The doorman eyed his disheveled state and gave him a dirty look. *Yeah, fuck you too, buddy.* "Delivery for Miss Tallulah," Kit said. She had a last name—Miller—but it was too mundane for her career as a famous spiritualist and she'd once squawked at Kit for using it. She was real stuck-up for a goddamn scam artist, but her criminal boyfriend was paying for Kit's rent and his taste in clothes, so he kept his mouth shut.

The doorman nodded and accepted Arielle as gravely as anyone could accept a motion-sick lapdog. He messaged Miss Tallulah—of course she wasn't waiting in the lobby for her delivery, no matter how instantaneous—and a minute later, the elevator dinged and she exited in a flutter of floral-printed silk bathrobe and hair curlers. A blindingly pink cocktail sloshed out of the glass in her right hand. It was three o'clock in the afternoon.

Kit could have appeared directly in her apartment. Depending on the parcel, sometimes that kind of privacy was necessary. But Miss Tallulah claimed he emanated "negative energies" and would throw a fit if he showed up at her door, so he used the lobby. She was probably right about him, in a way. Kit put off all kinds of negative energies when she was around.

She squealed at the sight of Arielle, took the dog from the doorman, and kissed her head. "Oh, but what's that smell?" she asked, cradling the dog in one arm and the cocktail in the other. When her gaze landed on Kit, she scrunched up her sharp features in disgust.

He wanted to ask if her cocktail was *all-natural*. He didn't. Kit could sometimes get away with rolling his eyes at Carl, but if he so much as blinked wrong in Miss Tallulah's presence, he'd lose this very lucrative line of commerce. So he said, as neutrally as possible, "Arielle didn't enjoy the trip."

"Oh, poor baby," Miss Tallulah cooed, pressing her nose to the dog's. "Well, we'll get her settled, won't we? Yes we will! Oh, sweet thing, come up here with Mama..."

She went back to the elevator without a thank-you or a goodbye. Kit did roll his eyes then, and the doorman caught him, but the man was too dignified to respond with anything other than offering Kit a tissue to wipe up the dog barf.

"Thanks." It didn't help much, but the thought counted for something.

Before the doorman could say goodbye, Kit was back in Nashville, awaiting payment and trying to look as steady as possible. Even two quick trips through the Nowhere left him drained.

Carl frowned at him. "Guess you were right about Arielle."

"Yeah," Kit said, holding out a hand, expectant. "You owe me five percent extra for damages."

"The fuck I do," said Carl. "Your fee's high enough as it is, you little freak. Five percent! Jesus. You'll bleed me dry."

"Five percent extra or our arrangement is over," Kit said. Carl didn't usually insult him like that, but it wasn't the first time he'd heard it. The law-abiding world feared runners, a class of people who couldn't be caught or imprisoned, and sometimes the criminal world did, too. The only difference was that Carl needed him.

Carl sighed and handed over a stack of cash, dollars as green as they'd ever been, even if commerce between states had been more difficult since the institution of border patrols. Tight border security was great for Kit's business but bad for everyone else. Kit counted the money and nodded, satisfied.

"You comin' in on Monday?"

"Of course," Kit said. Monday would be a regular re-up for Carl's stash of out-of-state medicines. An inanimate parcel, no sedation required. "See you then."

He walked out of the warehouse to his bike. Technically, he could have been home in an instant, but only if he wanted to collapse on the floor as soon as he got there. Three jumps in a day was a lot, and it had been a long week. He needed food and rest. His stomach was already rumbling.

Besides, the bike looked cool. He had his priorities.

He'd always loved to get away, to go fast, to come as close to flying as possible. Lots of kids were fascinated by motorcycles and cars and planes, so at least in that sense he'd been normal. Most kids didn't channel their need for speed into learning to teleport, but then again, most couldn't. No one knew exactly why some people could jump into the Nowhere at will. The speculation was that it was a rare genetic mutation. People like Kit were such a tiny fraction of the population that it was hard to study them. Sure, there was an official corps of Nowhere runners working for the federal government—making deliveries to the space stations that needed to get there faster than the elevators could and whatever else they were tasked with—and they all had to give blood samples and shit. But there were only a few dozen of them, and Kit stayed far away from that. He'd rather mix with Carl and Miss Tallulah than some faceless, soulless government agents. As a rule, he didn't join things. He was just a courier, but he had enough money to do what he wanted and he was nobody's lab rat. Kit was free.

He took the ramp up to the freeway and accelerated until it almost felt like he was flying through space again.

———

KIT PARKED his bike in the alley behind Zin's bar and walked in through the kitchen. A pot simmered on the stove. Lime and Thai basil wafted through the air. He was starving.

"Is that you, baby?"

"Yeah, be right there," he called, then forced himself to hurry up two flights of stairs so he could dump his disgusting jacket and t-shirt into the hamper and change into something clean. He stuffed the cash into the hole in the wall where he kept the rest of his earnings, then shifted a pile of clothes until it was hidden from view. He pulled out another black t-shirt, this one with diagonal slashes across the chest. Slashes of color, that is—intentional ones, not terrified-animal-claw ones. The t-shirt was made of smart fabric, and the slashes subtly changed color in response to heat. Right now they were neon green.

When he came back down, his legs were already beginning to shake with exhaustion. He paused at the bottom of the stairs to catch his breath, but he ran his hands through his hair to make it look like he was messing it up just right. Zin was sitting in one of the booths in the back corner of the long narrow bar, smiling at him. "So vain."

"I learned from the best," he told her. She beamed. The green in his t-shirt clashed magnificently with the brilliant walls of the bar, one of which was yellow and the other a different shade of green. Zin loved color as much as he did.

He went into the kitchen and collected a bowl of pho from the giant pot on the stove. At least once a week, on a day she knew he was coming back from a run, Zin ordered it special from a restaurant down the block. They probably thought she was hosting a party. Kit scooped some sprouts and cilantro into his bowl and went to join her in the bar.

Too hungry for conversation, he sat down and shoveled the entire bowl—noodles, brisket, herbs, bean sprouts, and broth—into his mouth.

"The way you eat, boy, I swear," Zin said. "It doesn't make any sense. You oughtta be my size at least."

Zinnia Jackson was gloriously fat. Her gorgeous, unusual combination of brown skin, freckles, and red curls—not to mention her ample breasts and hips—had won her brief pop stardom in her youth, but money hadn't followed fame. Now she ran this bar in the undercity with her wife Louann and made it her hobby to keep Kit alive. They'd known each other since Kit was eleven years old. He'd lived here as an adolescent, then moved out after he started earning enough to pay for his own place, then moved back into the third floor apartment last year when Zin and Louann had needed a tenant to stay afloat.

"Running makes me hungry," he said between mouthfuls of pho. "You know that."

"You can know a thing and still not understand it," Zin said. "And Laila's fat and she's a runner."

Kit made a noise with his mouth full. That was true, and he couldn't explain it, but Laila had run out on him and he wasn't going to talk about her.

"You gonna tell me what happened to your face?"

"Dog," Kit said. Eating was more important than words.

"Not sedated, I take it," Zin said. "You do get into some trouble."

He shrugged and kept eating. Louann came down the stairs carrying a toolbox. She nodded at Kit, which was about as talkative as she ever got, and then disappeared into the basement, no doubt to fix something structurally essential to the crumbling building.

"Hello to you too, sweetie," Zin called. She was grinning.

Louann had an effortless, stoic butchness to her. She kept her greying brown hair buzzed and she always had an oil-stained bandana somewhere on her. She'd never worn anything designer in her life and she thought Kit and Zin were endearingly silly for caring about clothes, and yet somehow she was still the coolest person Kit had ever met. Louann was quietly competent at everything, whether it was plugging leaks or propping up doorways or repairing Kit's bike or coming by his apartment with groceries and medicine when he was sick. Louann did all that without ever being asked, and Kit was grateful. Zin would have come for him, but she'd have been melodramatic about it.

"I worry about you," Zin said, which was exactly the kind of thing Louann never said, thank fuck.

"Well, stop."

"You don't tell me what to do, *Christopher*," Zin said. As far as either of them knew, his real name was Kit, but Zin had taken to calling him Christopher as a private joke whenever she scolded him. "I will worry about whatever I damn well please, and if it happens to be about how you work these wild, quasi-criminal jobs all the time, wearing yourself down to the bone crossing some unknown void full of fuck-knows-what, and you don't ever see another soul—"

"It's not full," Kit said. "It's a void."

"You hush when I'm scolding you. I don't care what's in there. It's not good for you to run all the time like you do. Every time you come home starving—and mauled by animals!"

"It's a scratch, Zin. From a lap dog."

"Don't back-sass me when you're supposed to be listening. You need something in your life that's not work. Go out and make friends! That young runner Aidan hasn't been here this week, and he comes by all the time—did you hurt his feelings?"

"I can only hope." Kit hadn't done anything. He didn't know why Aidan had stopped showing up, but he wasn't one to look a gift horse in the mouth. However it had happened, he was grateful that Aidan Blackwood had finally gotten the message that Kit didn't care about his stupid crusade. Kit would rather take a trip through the Nowhere with an un-sedated alligator than have a conversation about *comradeship*. He'd never joined anything in his life and he wasn't about to join a runners' union.

Zin made a disapproving noise, then continued. "I haven't

seen Laila, either, and she's just about your only friend. Or I guess there's that other one, the tall, handsome one you work with sometimes, but I haven't seen him either. But anyway, there's the sweetest little waitress at the pho place and she always asks after you. And a young woman who does those fancy light-up manicures down the street. They're *magged out*, so I hear—"

"No one has ever said that," Kit interrupted, ready to tell her that no one even said *mag* anymore unless they were being ironic, but she waved him off and kept going.

"Well, they seem like exactly the sort of thing you like, and besides, my point is you could go get yourself one and get to know her."

Instead of responding, Kit got up and went into the kitchen for a second bowl. He didn't want to meet anyone new. Laila had flaked on a job this week, as well as their standing post-run appointment at Winfield's barbecue joint—Kit knew because he'd waited in a booth by himself for an hour—thus proving once again that friends were a waste of time. She hadn't answered any of his messages or the door of her Detroit apartment when he'd knocked. He'd jumped into her living room, too, but she'd been out and none of her roommates would tell him anything. Kit wasn't going back for more humiliation. He and Laila were done.

And if Zin happened to be right that "tall, handsome" Travis Alvey wasn't around, Kit wouldn't be the one to tell her. She wouldn't approve of his arrangement with Travis, one where they appeared directly in each other's bedrooms if either of them had an itch to scratch.

"Oh, you are so difficult," Zin said. "For the record, I'm not bothering you to get a girlfriend. Just a regular friend. And how am I supposed to know what you like when you never talk to anyone or go anywhere unless you're getting paid?"

Money was reliable. Things were reliable. People let you down and got you hurt.

Kit came back and ate his second helping while Zin talked.

"Anyway, if you don't want women, you know that won't bother me. Why don't you get on Elevate and message that nice boy who delivers the booze, Kit? What's his name? Antonio or something. He always smiles at you."

He stopped slurping down broth for a second so he could say something. "No girl or boy, no matter how nice, will make me any money."

"Money's not everything, Kit."

He looked at her, mouth pulled to one side, and raised his eyebrows.

"Sure, it makes life a lot easier," Zin said, gesturing at the cracks in the plaster, the taped-up windows, and the rips in all the upholstery. "But it won't make you happy."

Kit shrugged. "Who says I'm not happy?"

It was Zin's turn to raise her eyebrows at him. He didn't want to deal with that, but he did want more food, so he went in for a third bowl. As he was dipping his chopsticks in, Zin said, "If you're running yourself ragged to pay rent on that room, I just want you to know that you don't have to."

"Zin." The question of rent always made them argue. Zin and Louann had convinced him to move back in by saying they needed a little help. An understatement. They were deep in debt, and so was he. Kit owed them for years of his life. The least he could do was pay rent. "I'm not strapped for cash, you know that, right? I work because I want to."

And the money made him feel safe.

She tried and failed to hide her frown. "Okay, baby. Like I said, I just want you to know."

He shook his head. "I'm fine, Zin. I have you and Louann and enough work to buy whatever I want. I don't need friends."

Once, he'd had a few, but they'd all up and vanished. Aidan only came around to bother Kit about his stupid union and Travis only showed up when he wanted sex, and now neither of them was around. He'd thought things were different with Laila, but he'd been wrong. He shouldn't be surprised. That was what people did. Everyone except Zin and Louann, anyway. He didn't need to meet anybody new—he already knew how it would go.

———

KIT WENT UPSTAIRS to check his messages in private. His third-floor apartment was a studio with a kitchenette along one wall and a mattress taking up most of the rest of the space. He almost never used the kitchen to cook, since Zin and Louann were only one flight of stairs away and they were much better at it than him and always willing to feed him if he washed dishes afterward. But he couldn't live without food nearby, so all his cabinets were overflowing with snacks. Louann would never have said so, but Kit knew she was horrified by the amount of processed junk in his apartment. She was always quietly heaping vegetables on his plate when he went down for dinner, and she never listened when he explained that he ate vegetables all the time, because he ate *everything* all the time, because he was a runner and he was always hungry. Zin always laughed and told him he was "like a little animal storing food in its den." Kit always rolled his eyes at her fox joke, but it was true enough. He'd been hungry a lot in his life. Keeping his cabinets well-stocked made him feel safer. He'd even started keeping the gross candy that Laila and Travis both loved—chocolate-covered wafers called Zings that looked good on the outside but contained some kind of red-dyed, cinnamon-and-cayenne-flavored syrupy goo that made your mouth go numb—but he supposed he could throw them away now.

Food wasn't the only thing he saved. Every spare corner was stuffed with clothes. There were two free-standing racks forming an L-shape around his mattress and piles of folded and unfolded clothes everywhere. He knocked some aside, flopped onto the bed, and looked up at the ceiling.

He flicked his wrist and a display appeared above him in large print. He checked Elevate first, not for social purposes like Zin wanted, but for business proposals. Elevate was too public and easily surveilled for real business, but Kit liked to keep track of who was messaging him there. Incompetent criminals and, judging from the misused slang in one message—almost as cringeworthy as Zin saying *magged out*—at least one undercover cop. Kit deleted those unanswered. The cops couldn't hold him without resorting to sedation or starvation, both of which were currently illegal, but still in practice. This cop was probably after Akins and associates, and if Kit led him to them, he'd never work again.

More reliable proposals came in through an encrypted messaging service he used. There were twenty-two messages in his inbox, and the display scrolled with the motion of his eyes. He sorted through them and began to dictate his responses. Ten of them he rejected outright. Kit was running a business and he didn't have time to be fucked with. Those people would come back with a real offer if they were serious. There were six offers he immediately said yes to—clients he knew, small parcels, short distances, easy money—and arranged his schedule accordingly. There were a few more that required some thought.

And one very strange request.

It was from a new client, which was always tricky. Kit preferred to meet people before he agreed to work for them. It was a common-sense precaution, since his work often led him to skirt the law. Or break it, if you were dead-set on getting technical. But this client, some company called Quint Services, wanted him to show up for a job tonight. That was unusual, too, the short notice. And the address was somewhere far out of the city. No details on what he needed to carry, or their final destination.

But the offer was enticing. No—arresting. Jaw-dropping.

It was a buy-yourself-a-personal-spaceship kind of offer. A silk-sheets-and-champagne-for-the-rest-of-your-life kind of offer. Or more realistically, a pay-Zin's-debts-and-go-the-fuck-on-vacation kind of offer. Although the silk sheets sounded like his kind of indulgence, come to think of it.

Kit normally played it safe and kept to one job per day. Zin might worry about him getting ambitious or greedy, but he wasn't a complete fool. Preserving his health was an investment. It made working six or seven days a week possible.

That offer, though.

He ran a quick search for Quint Services and almost nothing came up. Some kind of private research firm. It was the latest venture of a billionaire named Oswin Lewis Quint. He was white and cookie-cutter handsome in the promotional photos. Nothing too scary. Come to think of it, he looked vaguely familiar. Kit scanned the search results again. There were a few brief, friendly profiles of him, all talking about how he was going to *change the world*. No details. These tech companies were just secretive, that's all.

If he was going to make it on time, he had to leave now. Kit was sitting up and grabbing for his helmet before he'd even finished replying to the message.

[3]

A QUALM OR TWO

HE RODE OUT OF THE UNDERCITY AND UP ONTO THE freeway, past blinking, chirping ads for everything orbiting the sun. Normally, if you were alone on the road, the ads changed if they recognized your buying history, so you had to drive past personalized billboards hawking whatever shit you'd bought last. Kit kept all his communication encrypted and paid for whatever he could in cash, so even at night he saw the usual, rush-hour nonsense. He had to drive past a campaign ad for Dawson Ellerby, a local politician trying to pitch himself as macho, that said *the only thing that stops a runner is a bullet*. The slogan was probably effective with voters—it would be a lot less so if they knew that Dawson Ellerby was a regular customer of Carl's, which meant his addiction to real was effectively financing Kit's wardrobe.

Kit had to give the man credit, though. Real—the short name for a drug that was officially called *virtual reality enhancement*—could fuck you up, and so far Ellerby was keeping it together in public. Bigoted billboards aside, that is.

Kit passed another billboard with the face of a smiling, handsome man and the slogan *for a safer world*. There was a logo on it, one that looked like an O with a curlicue tail on its right side, and Kit was far down the road by the time he pieced together that it was meant to represent a Q entwined with an S. That face belonged to Oswin Lewis Quint. Kit knew his search hadn't been tracked—he was always careful—but a shiver went down his spine anyway. He couldn't say why. It was an innocuous enough slogan.

The sun set while he was riding. The city was awash in light all hours of the night, but an hour out of town and off the free-way, Tennessee was still dark. It was like driving two hundred years into the past. What the hell did Quint Services do out here? What was here except old barns?

He almost missed his turn onto a country road. He'd had to consult a map to get to this place, and it was a lot to remember even with his strong sense of direction. He could have programmed the coordinates into his bike, but he kept the guid-ance feature turned off. Too easy to track. And boring. He avoided self-driving cars for the same reason. Luckily, Louann specialized in old bikes, ones that weren't self-driving, and she'd fixed this one up for him.

The route rolled past tobacco fields and empty pastures. The hills loomed in the darkness and the increasingly narrow roads dipped and wound around them. Kit slowed down to take a curve, and realized he'd gone far enough now that he should be at his destination.

There was nothing out here. Just hills. And trees. How could this be the place?

He pulled off the road and killed his engine.

A second later, in a place he could have sworn was foliage, a massive door slid open. A square of black yawned in the hillside. It was foreboding and, Kit had to admit, kind of cool.

A man in a black suit appeared in the space. Kit could only really see the brilliant white of his shirt collar and the long oval of his face, as though they were floating in the darkness. His grey hair was short and styled like a helmet. He wasn't smiling.

"Kit Jackson."

Kit hadn't been born with that last name, and sometimes people looked at him funny when it came up. They stared at his face and tried to reconcile his name and his heritage. Kit never answered their questions, if they bothered to voice them. Never mind that he didn't know the answers. It was none of their goddamn business that he'd taken Zin's last name for himself. Zin had always guessed he was multiracial, because she was multiracial herself and it made her feel connected to him, but she'd never specified what she meant by that. Talking about racial or cultural background meant talking about family, and Kit didn't have one. Plus, Kit didn't know of any people on Earth whose eyes reflected light in the darkness like a cat's. He wasn't fool enough to take a DNA test, not when he suspected there were people out there who'd do terrible things to get biological samples from runners.

But the man in the suit didn't seem to care what Kit looked like or what his name was. Or if he did, it didn't show. Kit parked his bike just inside the secret door and followed the man down a long, concrete corridor. It sloped downward. They were heading underground.

Despite growing up in the undercity, Kit didn't like being underground. It was a silly fear, since he could escape at any time just by thinking about it. But still. It was different in the undercity, where it was just freeways above you and there were streets branching off in every direction and people everywhere and you could always find the sky if you looked for it. Out here in the country, going underground, Kit felt like he was walking into a tomb. He'd spent his whole life checking for exits. Maybe that was why it was so easy for him to get into the Nowhere.

The man in the suit wasn't talkative. He walked in front of

Kit, suit hanging off his wiry frame and his long legs carefully unhurried. What kind of salary was Quint Services paying him, and why wasn't he spending it on better tailoring? Kit didn't wear suits, at least not businesslike black ones, but if he did, he'd make sure they fit him better than that.

The concrete corridor ended in double doors that led into another corridor, fluorescent-lit and linoleum-tiled. The place felt like a high school or a hospital, but empty. And secret. And underground. What the hell was this job, anyway? Kit hadn't seen anything that looked like a parcel. The place was sterile, not an object in sight.

He could take anything he could carry into the Nowhere. Weight wasn't an issue, just volume. He had to be able to wrap his arms around whatever he was delivering, or at least get a really solid grip. A few times, he and Laila had worked together to deliver larger objects—usually fancy tech destined for the space stations, big electron microscopes or rovers or whatever, things one person couldn't really grab solo. But that was dicey, working with another runner. Laila had been his most reliable partner.

What did Quint Services want him to deliver?

The man in the suit stopped in front of a door. There was light coming out of the bottom, but the narrow rectangular window at eye level had been papered over, so Kit couldn't see inside until the man opened it.

What the fuck.

There was a man sitting on the floor, legs splayed, back leaning against one white cinderblock wall. He was blindfolded.

"He's sedated," the man in the suit said. It was the first time he'd spoken since saying Kit's name. "We understand that makes the trip easier. The blindfold is a precaution against disorientation, in case he wakes up during the trip."

"Yeah," Kit said. He didn't say *usually people sedate them-*

selves after *consenting to be transported somewhere.* The man in the suit made him wary. *Jesus.* This wasn't what he'd been expecting. The hairs on the back of his neck had been standing since he'd walked into this place, and now his heart was hammering. Hadn't he just promised himself no more live packages? *Think of the money.*

The man on the floor had at least one ugly, visible bruise on him. The purple tail of it was peeking out from under the white linen blindfold. What would it take to beat up a guy that big? Shoulders like that—Kit wasn't even sure he could wrap his arms around the guy. What had they used to sedate him? Horse tranquilizer? Fuck, this had gone way past weird. Kit should get out now.

Silk sheets. Champagne. Zin's mortgage.

But who was he? Where was Kit taking him?

Kit tried to figure it out from context, but the whole thing was too bizarre. The sedated man's clothes—a black t-shirt and sweatpants—gave no indication of who he might be. He looked more like he was dressed for bed than anything else, but he had on sneakers. White ones with no personality. So new they were shiny.

That was a strange detail. Had they never been worn? How had this man come to be here? He was fit in a way that made Kit think of soldiers, but his black hair stuck up wildly—maybe a result of the blindfold, but his haircut looked too long and uneven to be military. His skin was about the same shade of light brown as Kit's own, except for that bruise on his face.

Kit had been staring for too long. "Where are we going?" he finally said. It was a funny way to ask his usual question—*what's my destination?*—and he couldn't say why he'd phrased it in a way that emphasized the two of them. It wasn't like he felt any connection to this unconscious stranger. For all he knew, Quint

Services had knocked the guy out for being an asshole. Maybe they'd done him a favor.

At Kit's question, something happened to the man in the suit. His face moved in imitation of a smile. It didn't look happy or amused or natural, and Kit found it hard to look at. But he couldn't let that show.

"Up," the man said, his face still an uncanny mask of human emotion. He rattled off six coordinates, numbers Kit knew had to represent a location in space, but they couldn't possibly be in Earth's orbit.

Kit had been to both U.S. civilian space stations, Franklin and Sojourner, plus one U.S. military station and a dozen foreign ones. He was well-fucking-traveled. And those coordinates didn't mean a damn thing to him except *space*. That wasn't a place he wanted to go, so he had to break his rule and ask another question.

"We're not gonna end up as space debris, right? These coordinates go somewhere with pressure and breathable air?" Of course, if they did lead to the vastness of space, Kit could just jump right back. But then he wouldn't get paid.

"Yes," Suit Creep said, still with that plastic smile. Smarmy motherfucker. "Quint Services has a facility inside an asteroid that was deliberately drawn into lunar orbit almost a century ago as part of an experiment long since completed. I'm not at liberty to say much about it, and I must ask that you spend as little time there as possible. We chose you for this job because you have a reputation for making prompt, uncomplicated deliveries. You'll receive payment in full upon your return here."

Prompt, uncomplicated deliveries. Sure. Kit had a reputation for not having any ethical qualms. He was starting to think he didn't deserve it—he'd found a qualm or two tonight. Maybe he should have developed them along the way. Say, before ending up in this secret underground facility, taking orders from a creep in a suit, agreeing to deliver an unconscious man who seemed very much like a prisoner into some unknown location *in space*.

Then again, there was all that money.

———

GETTING the sedated man off the floor would probably be the hardest part of this whole job, Kit told himself. Sure, lunar orbit was a long run, but he could push himself. And if he collapsed when he got there, well, he'd just stay the night and they could dock his pay accordingly. They could take twenty percent if they wanted—he'd still make plenty.

The suited henchman watched in silence as Kit crouched next to the sedated man, leaned forward, and awkwardly wrapped his arms around the guy's chest. Jesus, where did this guy shop? You couldn't buy off the rack with arms like that. His poor t-shirt was stretched almost to its breaking point.

Yeah, okay, Kit, calm down. Not the time or the place to let his thoughts wander in that direction. Suit Creep was still watching. Kit could struggle to stand up while lifting a man twice his size, or he could just hold on tight and vault them into the Nowhere from right here on the floor. He picked option two.

He always thought of it as *stepping* into the Nowhere, or jumping, but he didn't actually have to move his body to get there. It was a question of mental focus. On a day like today when he was already tired, taking a physical step might have helped smooth out the transition from reality to void. But he didn't think he could haul Biceps McGee upright, and he wasn't in the mood to become Suit Creep's entertainment, so they had a rough takeoff. Even sedated, the man jerked in his arms as they entered the Nowhere, startling Kit and causing them to tumble head over heels into the black. Kit managed to flip the two of them upright again—not that it mattered, since there was no up or down. But he'd already been vomited on today, so he might as well keep this guy's body oriented in its usual direction.

Moving through the Nowhere was a little bit like swimming. That was the only thing Kit could compare it to, not being able to fly. He could feel the Nowhere pulsing around him like water—and not like water at all. He kicked his legs to go forward, although forward was just as much nothingness as backward, or sideways, or any other direction. There was almost no resistance. Moving wasn't strictly necessary, but just like a physical step could make it easier to focus on the mental step into the Nowhere, when Kit moved his body, it helped him channel his thoughts into finding the exit point.

The Nowhere wasn't alive. But Kit couldn't help but feel that it *wanted* things. It would push him in one direction or another. Once, Louann had asked him how it was that he'd never ended up stuck in a wall or occupying the same space as some other object, and Kit had only been able to shrug. He couldn't say it out loud to Louann, but when he was here, it made perfect sense: the Nowhere didn't want that. They had a cooperative relationship, insofar as a man and a void could have any kind of relationship at all.

Kit had never been anywhere in lunar orbit—Jesus, he was basically jumping to the fucking moon—but he knew the coordinates, and that was all he needed to feel it out. It would take longer to get to this secret Quint Services asteroid than it had to get to Inland New York this morning, but it was less a physical traveling through the Nowhere and more of a meditative few moments of nothingness. Kit only moved—kicked, swam, whatever—because it felt right to move. He concentrated on his destination. As exhausting as it was, it was often his favorite part of the day.

Or it would have been, except something huge and blindingly bright came zooming toward him. Kit dodged out of instinct, but the thing changed course to follow him without slowing down even a little. It crashed into him and an instant later, instead of whizzing through the Nowhere, Kit and his passenger were spit out and slammed into hard ground.

———

EMIL WOKE BLINDFOLDED with the sick wrongness in his bones that could only come from travel through the Nowhere. He ripped off his blindfold and found himself staring at the sky. It was daytime. He had no idea how long he'd been lying on the hard ground. The last thing he remembered was being sedated in an exam room at a Quint Services facility somewhere underground. He was still dressed in the clothes they'd provided.

There was an unconscious person on the ground next to him.

The person in question—short and slender, purple-haired, tan-skinned—was young and androgynous. Unconscious, but alive and seemingly unharmed, as long as Emil didn't count that eye-searing combination of color in the outfit as a form of violence. Logic told Emil this was the runner Quint Services had hired to take him back to QSF17.

The runner certainly didn't look like anyone else who worked at Quint Services Headquarters, given the hair, the tight black jeans, and the t-shirt with orange slashes across the chest. Come to think of it, the runner didn't look like anyone else Emil had ever seen. Emil studied the angle of the cheekbones and the small, rounded point of the nose as if they might offer clues. The runner had a nice face, but one that resisted categorization.

Who knew how Quint Services found runners? Emil didn't know many, but the ones he'd encountered usually lived on the fringes of society. Some would say that was their choice, but it was hard to get a normal job if anyone knew you could access the Nowhere. There was a general feeling of mistrust surrounding runners, a worry that they'd abuse their power to take you for all you had. A few high-profile crimes, like the Franklin Station Bank robbery, hadn't helped dispel that prejudice. Emil didn't subscribe to that bullshit, but he couldn't help feeling a certain curiosity and fear.

Maybe more curiosity than fear—the runner *was* pretty cute.

Emil shouldn't be thinking about that. He had problems to solve. They were in a desert unlike any he'd ever seen. Somehow the runner had brought them here, and more importantly, now they needed to get back.

Emil put his hands on the runner. "Hey," he said. "Wake up."

———

Two LARGE, strong hands gently gripped his face. "I need you to open your eyes," said a deep voice. "And tell me your name."

There was so much authority in that tone—so much command, such a promise of safety—that Kit didn't even consider blurting out his other questions, which were *what the fuck happened*, *where the fuck are we*, and *who the fuck are you*, in respective order of importance. *Who the fuck are you* was least important because when a man that gorgeous was touching his face, Kit left well enough alone. So instead of asking questions, with barely a thought in his head other than meeting that steady, dark gaze, Kit said, "Kit."

"I'm Emil. Are you hurt, Kit?"

He was lying on hard, sandy ground and the sun was so bright it hurt to look at anything other than Emil's beautiful, bruised face. The out-of-focus background was colored in reds and oranges. Even working with only a fraction of his wits, Kit could tell this wasn't a base inside an asteroid. And it had been nighttime when they'd left Tennessee. They'd missed their destination by a long way. Something had hit him. He ached all over. But that would heal. The exhaustion from too much time in the Nowhere in one day, though, posed a problem. How were they going to get out of here? Wherever *here* was? "No. Tired, hungry."

Even with Emil's hands on his face and Emil's eyes looking deep into his soul, Kit's eyelids threatened to shut. He was shaking a little. Not the look he wanted to achieve.

"Tell me about yourself," Emil instructed. "Full name, pronouns, birthday, hometown, that kind of thing."

"Kit Jackson. He, him." Kit pretended he hadn't heard the rest. "Same for you?"

Emil nodded. "I'm usually more prepared for survival situations," he apologized, a note of humor in his voice. The blindfold was now hanging around his neck. His long, disheveled bangs almost covered his black eye. "But we'll make do. Can you walk?"

Walk where? Kit blinked and squinted as he looked around. It was all sand and rocks as far as he could see. He tried to push himself into a sitting position to get a better view, but his vision spotted black. Emil grabbed his shoulders.

"Never mind. Save your strength," Emil said and scooped him off the ground. Kit would have complained, but it felt too good to close his eyes and let his head rest against Emil's chest.

The next time he woke up, he wasn't sure how much time had passed. He was propped up against a large rock, his legs extended in its long shadow. Emil was gone. Kit was so hungry his stomach felt like it might cave in. He couldn't possibly control a run through the Nowhere in this state. Especially not if something was going to slam into him like that. What the fuck had that been?

When Emil walked back into view, he was carrying something in a fold of his t-shirt, exposing his absurdly toned abdomen. His sweatpants were slung low enough that Kit could see the trail of dark hair leading down from his navel and the angled tops of his hipbones. At least if Kit had to die of starvation while stranded in the desert, Emil's beautiful brown hips could be the last thing he ever laid eyes on. A small consolation.

"I ate a handful of these about two hours ago as a test and nothing has happened to me yet," Emil said, kneeling in the vee of Kit's legs. He'd stretched out his t-shirt to hold a couple of pints of some unfamiliar berry. They were smooth and reddish-purple. "They don't taste like much, but I think they're safe. And you need the calories if we're going to get out of here."

"Where are we," Kit murmured, too sleepy to intone the question. "What happened."

"I don't want to alarm you, Kit, but I have to be honest. I don't know the answer to either of those questions."

"Oh." It didn't matter much that he didn't know where they were. Kit needed to know a destination when he jumped, but his origin wasn't important. He could get to the Nowhere from anywhere. Emil was working so hard to reassure him and keep him alive. Kit should tell him the good news. "Doesn't matter."

Emil touched his cheek. "You're pretty out of it. That jump really wrecked you, huh?"

Kit didn't want to answer yes to that question. "There was... a thing. In the Nowhere."

Emil nodded. "I thought I remembered... light. There isn't normally light, is there?"

Impressive that he remembered anything at all. He'd been unconscious. The collision must have jarred him awake. "It hit me," Kit said. It had *looked* like light, but it had felt solid enough when it ran into him. "And now we're here."

"We'll find our way out soon enough," Emil said. They'd only just met, but there was something in his tone that made Kit want to believe him. He sounded so sure. When Kit focused on him again, Emil was already nodding to himself. "I've heard that runners need to eat a huge amount of food to sustain themselves," he was saying. "I haven't found anything else around here that looks edible, but if this isn't enough, I'll take another look. Here."

A hand loomed in front of his face, a few berries nestled in the palm.

Kit must have stared a moment too long, because before he knew it, Emil was pressing a berry against his lips. *Feeding* him. The thought made his insides squirm. Was it shame or something else that he felt? It didn't matter. He'd already parted his lips. He chewed, swallowed, and tried not to think about it. As Emil had said, the berries were bland. A hint of sweetness yet to come. What kind of berry ripened so late in the fall? Or was it fall here? Kit didn't know.

Emil's hand returned mechanically, offering him more as he finished a bite. Every time those fingertips brushed his lips, Kit's urge to swallow more than just the berries got a little stronger. He wanted to lean forward and take two of Emil's long, thick fingers into his mouth.

Somewhere in the back of his mind, a mortified voice was screeching about how *inappropriate* that was. Just to get some quiet, Kit reached out and grabbed a handful of berries from Emil's t-shirt. Kit could feed himself. Then the temptation would go away.

Except it didn't. As he ate, his trembling subsided. It grew easier to guide his hand to and from his mouth. The berries diminished the hollow in his stomach, but he still felt hungry.

Emil was right there, watching. He never looked away. In Kit's vision, all the colors were too bright and all the edges blurred. Only Emil was in focus. That was fine. He was the only thing Kit wanted to look at—those brown eyes with a hint of amber, that strong jaw with its dusting of dark stubble. If he was this beautiful with a black eye and stitches tracking through his right eyebrow, how would anyone bear the sight of him when he was healed?

Eventually the berries were gone and Emil let his t-shirt drop back down over his stomach. Neither of them had said anything for long moments. Kit was no longer sure if time was passing. Was this a dream? He reached out and touched Emil's face to make sure it was real.

There was smooth, warm skin under his fingertips. Kit traced the shape of Emil's cheekbone and his eyebrow, careful to stay away from the bruised side of his face.

Emil blinked, smiled a little, and said, "Kit—"

He didn't finish the sentence, or maybe Kit's name had been all he intended to say. Distantly, Kit knew it was a funny thing to do to someone you'd just met, touching their face, but he couldn't seem to stop. Or he didn't want to stop. Did Emil want him to stop? He hadn't said so. He'd only said Kit's name.

Kit's fingers trailed down the angled ridge of Emil's nose and then over the bow of his lips. He pressed the pad of his thumb into Emil's bottom lip, just to feel that softness and watch his mouth open so pliantly.

How stupid, to do this with his hand when he could do it with his tongue instead. Kit clambered up until he could settle his ass on Emil's thighs, then took hold of his face and kissed him. Just as he had before, when it had been Kit's hand, Emil opened his mouth willingly. Kit angled his head and slid his tongue deep. Emil made the most beautiful, desperate, throaty little sound. Everything felt suspended and dreamlike except for the heat of Emil's mouth against his—that was real, and forceful, and overwhelming.

Emil brought his arms up and clasped them around Kit, crushing their bodies together. One of Emil's big hands splayed across his back and the other laced its way into Kit's hair, cupping his head and pushing him into another kiss. Kit sighed with pleasure and writhed against him. His stupid skinny jeans felt even more constricting that normal. He was already achingly hard. It was easy to rock his hips and rub up against Emil's body, where he found an answering hardness. God bless sweatpants. Kit slid one hand out of Emil's hair and stroked it down his side, waiting for the electric moment of contact when he lifted the hem of Emil's t-shirt and his hand met bare skin. *Fuck*, but that feeling made his whole brain light up. There ought to be a neon trail left behind where his fingers had swiped over Emil's stomach and found their way just beneath his waistband—

"Kit." A breath. "Kit. Stop."

Emil's hands were on his shoulders now, pushing him back just a little. Kit's whole body was throbbing.

"Why the fuck would we *stop*?"

"Kit. I don't think you're in your right mind. I made some kind of mistake and you're—*we're* feeling the effects of those berries."

"Who cares?" There were only inches between them. It would be so easy to duck back in and kiss Emil again.

"*I* care, Kit." Listening to Emil's steady, commanding voice, it was impossible to tell he'd been undone with lust only thirty seconds ago. He was still hard, for fuck's sake. Kit could see his cock straining against his sweatpants. Emil continued, "And you'll care when you're sober. We can't do this. It's unwise for a dozen different reasons—and probably unsafe. We don't know where we are, we haven't talked about what happened in the Nowhere, or how we're going to get out of here."

Somehow Kit found his hand stroking Emil's face again. His body had a will of its own. And so did his voice, which said, in a sultrier tone than he'd ever used in his life, "Can't we talk about that *after?*"

"No." Emil grasped his hand firmly and removed it, then pushed their bodies all the way apart. The loss of contact stung, but it did nothing to clear Kit's head, which was still a fog of *Emil Emil Emil*.

"You don't know me. How do you know I'm not in my right mind?"

"That's the problem, Kit. We don't know each other."

"People who don't know each other can fuck each other. It happens all the time in club bathrooms." Kit didn't know that from experience, but the truth would work against him right now. If Emil believed Kit was a person who fucked strangers, maybe he'd relent and let them finish. Kit didn't even care about this interlude ruining things. His body was still decidedly in the right mood. All he wanted was to touch Emil again.

"Not to me," Emil said, decisive. Fuck, but even that rejection was kind of hot. If Kit couldn't touch Emil, he could touch himself while Emil spoke to him in that voice. His hand was halfway down his underwear when Emil said, "I'm gonna take a walk for a little while. Do what you need to do."

And just like when he'd woken up to Emil asking his name, it didn't even occur to Kit to disobey.

[4]
DON'T THROW ME AWAY

Emil walked to the other side of the outcropping to give Kit some privacy. He clenched his jaw in an effort not to imagine what was happening—and not to regret his decision to stop things. He'd made the right choice. It was shameful he'd let things get that far in the first place. He might not have been totally sober himself, but he was a damn sight better off than that poor kid. Kit must have weighed about a buck thirty and he'd been shaking with hunger when Emil started feeding him some kind of intoxicant.

Jesus.

He paced another few steps, trying to push away the memory of how perfectly Kit had fit into his lap, or the sound he'd made when Emil had pulled him close.

He could take care of himself out here—it would only take a second—but he preferred to grit his teeth and will his arousal away. He was a dirty old man, taking advantage of Kit while he was high and then thinking about getting off on the memory. It was his job to watch out for people Kit's age—even if Kit wasn't a member of his team.

It would probably be a couple of hours before Kit was clear-headed enough to take them back to the Nowhere, but maybe they'd be able to talk before then. Kit just needed a little time to come down—and Emil couldn't go back over there until he was sure Kit wouldn't try to persuade him to pick up where they'd left off. He had a lot of self-control, but that was a test even he was bound to fail.

No, he'd wait over here within earshot. Close enough to protect Kit if he heard anything coming, but far enough to protect Kit from both of their regrettable urges. And when he did walk back over there, Emil would apologize again. He'd reassure Kit that there was nothing to be embarrassed about, while simultaneously not giving away how ashamed he was of his own behavior. What had he been thinking? Why hadn't he realized what was happening sooner? He was a little high—as different as it was from any of his previous experiences, he recognized the signs—but that was no excuse. He was supposed to be better than this. He'd promised.

He'd have to overcome his own reaction as fast as possible. They had to work together to get out of here. Emil could make that happen. He could speak the right words, strike the right note, get Kit to cooperate for as long as it took to get them both out. It was his job, after all.

He had to get back to the facility for his team. It meant walking—or jumping—right back into danger, but he couldn't leave them there. He had no idea what had happened in his absence and he didn't trust Quint Services to do right by any of them.

Emil let half an hour pass. He didn't hear anything from the other side of the rock, so he walked back around and found Kit curled up on his side on the ground, asleep. His purple hair was a wild mess—Emil blushed to think whose fault that was—and Emil had to suppress an urge to lean down and smooth it.

There was no evidence of what they'd done here earlier, but

somehow Emil could feel it in the air. He shoved the thoughts aside. He had to focus. "Kit."

Kit stirred, blinking awake and then pushing himself upright. When he saw Emil, he pushed himself back farther.

"I want to apologize for what happened earlier," Emil began. "I take full responsibility. I shouldn't have let it happen. I don't want you to feel at fault for anything. Please don't be embarrassed, either. There's nothing to be ashamed of. Still, we have to work together to get out of here, so I think we should put it aside for the moment and concentrate on the task at hand."

Kit rubbed sleep out of one eye. "It's just a high, not the end of the world. Calm down. Not like I've never done drugs before."

Emil's team wouldn't have responded to his tone that way, and it took him aback for a second. "I am calm," he said. "And I am treating everything as seriously as it should be treated."

"Oh, so *you've* never done drugs before," Kit said. "Got it."

That wasn't true, but it wasn't relevant, either. Emil cleared his throat. "As you know, we need to get to the Quint Services facility where we were headed."

"Wait, you still want to go back there? Aren't you some kind of prisoner?"

"There are people there who need me," Emil said.

Kit raised his brows. "Okay."

"Are you well enough to make the run?"

One side of his mouth turned down. He was so small and so fine-boned, with such quick movements and changes of expression. His fox-like nickname suited him. It made Emil want to smile, but if Kit asked him why, he'd have to say *because you're cute* and it wouldn't get them anywhere good.

Luckily, Kit was all business. "Not sure. Haven't really had enough food or sleep to do it right, but I don't think I'm going to get much more of either if we stay here. And it's a long one."

Emil choose to ignore the delicate subject of food. "A long run, you mean?"

"I've done Earth to orbit before, but lunar orbit's farther than that. I know I can, but..."

"You'd rather try it for the first time when you were feeling your best," Emil guessed. He didn't say *how can you be sure if you've never done it before?* because he couldn't let his own doubts contaminate Kit. They both needed to believe Kit could make it. "There's something I need to tell you, Kit. I wasn't completely honest with you before, when I said I didn't know where we were. I have an idea of where we are, but you were so out of it earlier, I didn't want to make things worse by freaking you out."

Kit held his gaze for a second. "You don't have to protect me."

I'm sure I don't know what you're referring to, Emil didn't say. He also didn't say *you already know that I do.* Instead he agreed, "Of course not," with an ease he didn't feel. "It's more that *I'm* a little freaked out, that's all. You see, I'm a botanist."

This made absolutely no impression on Kit.

"Well, really, I specialized in designing greenhouses for facilities in space, and that was after my time in the Orbit—" Emil was rambling. "Anyway, I know a lot about plants."

"Don't care."

So maybe Kit was feeling a little bit surly. Understandable. Emil could deal with that. "I've spent years acquiring a broad base of knowledge of Earth plants. I have a passing familiarity with a variety of ecosystems spanning every continent." Emil pretended not to see the bored expression on Kit's face. He took a breath. "And I don't see anything here that I recognize."

"So it's not Earth," Kit said, his tone far flatter than it should have been for such a revelation.

"Exactly," Emil said. "But we're breathing. And—as we know—there's life here."

At last, Kit's face lit up. "Holy fuck," he said, breathless.

Emil couldn't tell if he meant that in a good way or a bad way. He wasn't sure how he felt about it, either. "So, yes. If we ever make it back to Earth alive, we can confirm the existence of extraterrestrial life."

"So where are we, then? Which planet? It can't be..." Kit paused, and Emil could tell he was going through all the planets in the solar system in his head. Emil had done the same when he'd first had this realization—he'd gone through all the potentially habitable moons and all the exoplanets he knew about, too.

"That's where my knowledge fails me," Emil admitted. He wasn't supposed to tell anyone about Dr. Lange's research, even though he barely knew enough to explain it. But this might be life or death. "But there is—there was this scientist on the base. He studied the Nowhere. He believed it was a sort of... membrane between realities. That's why you can get to it from anywhere on Earth, or even in space. It's everywhere. It's what holds our universe together. He believed that we hadn't confirmed this hypothesis yet because most runners didn't know they could travel any further. Or possibly because most were only strong or skilled enough dip in and out to get around our world. He thought some day, deliberately or accidentally, a runner would break *through*."

Actually, Dr. Lange had been convinced that some runners already had. He'd once theorized that runners had originated somewhere outside of known reality. Their inborn ease in the Nowhere didn't result from a rare mutation in the human genome—strictly speaking, they didn't have human genes.

Emil kept those thoughts to himself. Kit might not want his protection, but the kid was already having a rough day. "So maybe the reason we don't recognize anything about this planet is because it doesn't exist in our universe," he concluded.

"Well," Kit said. "In that case, it's a longer jump than I thought."

It was impossible not to smile at that cocky smirk. Unfortunately, Kit's expression faltered a moment later.

"But I don't know what we'll do if that thing comes back," he said.

"We'll figure it out," Emil said. He had no idea how, but he needed to believe it. "And maybe it won't."

"We don't have a way to sedate you," Kit said. He got to his feet and brushed sand and dirt from the legs of his jeans. Emil recognized the deliberate movements of someone who wasn't fine, but who was working very hard to appear that way. "So don't throw up on me, okay?"

"You sure you're ready? You can rest a little longer—"

"There's no food here," Kit said, holding his hand out impatiently.

Emil took it, but stood up without putting any of his weight on Kit. He'd been in the Nowhere before without being sedated and he'd hated it. And that had been with Beck, who he'd known and worked with for years before they'd tried it, and who was huge and gave crushing bear hugs to his friends all the time. Emil trusted Beck. He'd never worried for an instant that Beck couldn't hang on. Hanging on was what Lennox Beck did best in life.

Kit, on the other hand, was willowy. And he had plenty of reasons not to want to touch Emil.

So it startled Emil when Kit clamped both arms around his chest in a fierce grip. The top of his head came up to Emil's chin. He tilted his head back, met Emil's gaze, and said, "Hang the fuck on."

Emil brought his arms up, and before he'd even wrapped

them around Kit's back, darkness enveloped them. It felt like someone had slid a hook behind Emil's navel and yanked him sideways, except he hadn't moved—he could feel the vise of Kit's arms just where they had been. There was no light and nothing to see but Emil closed his eyes anyway, as if that would make this less disorienting. The darkness of the Nowhere felt *thick* somehow, not just an absence of light and air but the presence of something heavy and alive brushing against his skin. It was every prickly contradiction of sensation at once, wet and dry, hot and cold, rough and smooth, and it made him feel like his brain was folding in on itself.

He and Kit held still within that darkness, but Emil felt like someone had strapped him in upside-down and launched him into the fastest, loopiest rollercoaster ride of his life. There was pressure bearing down on him from all sides. Everything was wrong. He couldn't—*shouldn't* be here, where there was no space for him. He was suffocating, hurtling through the Nowhere faster than he could comprehend and dying by slow, miserable increments. *Please let me pass out*, he begged, not sure if he was addressing his own body or the void itself.

There was a flicker of blue light. Kit squeezed him so hard their ribcages might get tangled. And then they were out.

———

KIT WAS ASHEN AND QUIVERING, breathing too hard to get a sentence out. "Sorry—the thing—I couldn't—"

Emil wasn't in a state to offer comfort to anyone. He wanted to heave or faint or curl up in the corner or lie down and black out for twelve hours. But years of training kicked in and he put on his *I'm in charge* voice and said, "It's okay. We're okay. Breathe. Calm down. Take your time."

It was good advice and it worked on him, too. He still didn't feel like himself, but a few deep breaths went a long way toward making him feel like he wasn't about to shake out of his skin. That was when he noticed they were still hanging onto each other. He didn't let go. They were standing on a mattress on the floor of a room that was barely bigger than that. The ceiling hung low over Emil's head. Three walls were a shade of neon green that might have made Emil flinch if he hadn't just been dragged through the Nowhere, and the fourth was an aggressive shade of purple. There were piles of clothes, some folded and some wrinkled, surrounding and encroaching on the mattress. The mess wasn't the haphazard mess of hastily discarded items, but the carefully curated, archaeological kind. It was more of a nest than a room. Emil would bet Kit could reach for any item in here and find it within seconds—and looking at the violet-haired, green-leather-jacketed young man in his arms, there was no doubt that this was Kit's room.

Outside the window, an elevated freeway roared by. What looked like morning light filtered through the roadway grime on the glass. They'd been gone all night.

"I saw it coming and I panicked," Kit said at last. "I couldn't focus on the coordinates. I just brought us to the first safe place that popped into my head."

Your bedroom, Emil's treacherous brain supplied. *More specifically, your bed.*

"I can't do another jump now," Kit said. "Regardless of everything else, I'm exhausted. But we're in Nashville, so you can get a car back to the Quint Services facility. They can hire another runner, if it's urgent."

As he spoke those words, Kit looked like he was eating something very sour. The prospect of another meeting with Kristian Auer made Emil feel the same way.

"I might not be able to for another day—not as far as you need to go, and not with that thing out there."

"We'll cross that bridge when we get there," Emil said, even though he knew Kit's suggestion was what the higher-ups at Quint Services would want, and therefore what he should do. Quint Services had been willing to pay for a runner to get him back to Facility 17. They wanted him returned as quickly and quietly as possible.

But of course, they'd also want to get their hands on the first runner to cross into another reality. Emil wasn't sure what they'd do if and when they found out, and he wasn't ready to think of that yet.

He still hadn't let go of Kit. More importantly, Kit hadn't let go of him. Emil was actually supporting most of his weight. He looked ready to collapse.

"First things first, let's get you some food—real food, I mean, normal food." *Shit.* He could feel the heat rising in his cheeks at the thought of their earlier encounter. "Is there somewhere around here we could do that?"

If he'd perceived that Emil was flustered and blushing, Kit didn't show it. More likely, he was too out of it to notice. "Bar, downstairs."

With one hand, Emil patted his pockets. He was wearing the clothes they'd put him in at Quint Services—his wallet was still at Facility 17, not that he had any need of cash or a driver's license when he was living on an asteroid. Damn.

This time, Kit had noticed what he was doing, and he looked amused. "We don't need money," he said. "It's Zin's bar."

That meant nothing to Emil, but when Kit made his way to the door, he followed.

———

It took all of Kit's concentration to get down two flights of stairs and into the bar. A little voice in his head kept pointing out all the convenient places he could stop and rest—in that landing, up against that wall, in Emil's arms. But if he stopped now, he'd fall asleep for hours. When he woke up, the hunger in his belly would be an even sharper pain. Better to eat now.

Kit was so focused on finding food and shoving it into his mouth that it didn't even occur to him that Zin would be in the bar until she dropped the broom she was holding and swept him into a hug.

"Kit! Oh my God, baby, I was so worried when you didn't come back last night, I'm so glad you're okay." She punctuated her sentences with kisses to his temple, which he normally sidestepped, but today he was too tired. Yes. Too tired. Not scared and in desperate need of comfort. "But look at you, you're all bruised and tired and dirty and wearing yesterday's clothes, where have you been? No, I don't care, I'm so glad you're safe, sit down, let me get you something to eat—and *who* is *this*, oh my God, Kit, when I told you to get a boyfriend I was trying to get you *out* of trouble, not *into* more trouble than ever before, Lord, you will be the death of me." Zin didn't so much stop hugging him as deposit him into one of the booths at the back of the bar.

Kit shook his head at her, but it was the most admonishment he could muster.

"Oh, and your tall friend came by earlier this morning," Zin said. "What's his name? I can never remember."

Zin could remember perfectly well that his name was Travis Alvey. She just didn't like him because he never made small talk with her. It was a stupid standard to hold him to. Kit never made small talk with anyone if he could avoid it, so in his opinion, it was a mark in Travis's favor. But why would Travis have come by early this morning? They weren't really friends. They worked together sometimes, and they had an equally transactional sexual relationship. Travis hadn't been in touch about any jobs. And before nine o'clock in the morning was a strange time of day for the *other* thing Travis usually called him about. Kit frowned and put it out of his mind.

Emil, meanwhile, was wide-eyed and gaping at Zin. It would have been adorable if Kit didn't know exactly what it meant.

"Hello, young man," Zin was saying. "I'm Zin."

"Zin," Emil repeated, awe coloring his voice. "Zinnia Jackson."

This was worse than getting knocked into another reality by some unknowable force of destruction. Emil was a *fan*. Kit's commanding, uptight, strong, masculine soldier-acquaintance-parcel-crush was into deeply uncool, cheesy pop ballads from twenty years ago. Kit might have been able to handle it if they'd been some other singer's work, but—Zin? It was too much. He didn't want to be embarrassed *or* endeared. He was too tired for feelings.

"That's my name," Zin said cheerfully, because she hadn't caught on yet. "What's yours?"

Emil tore his attention from her and turned to Kit. "You didn't tell me that 'Zin' was Zinnia Jackson."

Kit shrugged one shoulder. He'd had no reason to mention it. Honestly, he forgot sometimes.

"'Don't Throw Me Away' Zinnia Jackson. 'Soft-Hearted Fool' Zinnia Jackson. 'Love You All Night' Zinnia Jackson," Emil said to him, listing a few of Zin's more famous songs. "*The* Zinnia Jackson."

Zin clasped her hands to her chest, beaming. "Aww, Kit, you brought me a fan." Then she hugged Emil and rocked him side to side a few times. His face was caught between wonder and bewilderment. Zin held him by the shoulders and looked him up and down. "Well, you're handsome and you have good taste. What can I get you, mystery man?"

"Emil," he finally said. "My name is Emil Singh."

It was an unusual combination of names, but Kit wasn't sure he could ask about it yet. He didn't like it when people asked about his name. So he let Emil babble at Zin for another minute, before she directed him to sit down in the booth and went to find them both something to eat.

"Oh my God," Emil murmured to himself. He propped his elbows on the table and covered his face with his hands, spiking up his bangs.

"Calm down. She's just a normal human being."

"Are you kidding me? A normal human being with the voice of an angel and a criminally underrated musical career! This whole time, you were living with a legend and it didn't even come up."

"We were busy," Kit said, and if it had a dark edge to it, well, he couldn't be held responsible for that. He wouldn't be so irritated that Emil was being goddamn adorable if Emil hadn't rejected him earlier. And sure, yeah, Kit had been high off his ass and he was hellishly embarrassed about it, but his cards were on the table. He'd climbed all over Emil like an animal.

He wouldn't have done it sober. But it was done now and there was no taking it back. As mortifying as it was, in a way, it was a kind of gift. Kit hadn't needed to work up the courage to say anything. It had all just happened. And now Emil knew and it could be perfect—they could skip all the uncomfortable talking and go right to the good part—if only he'd let it.

But maybe Emil didn't want that. Maybe he really hadn't wanted to do any of it and he'd let Kit sit in his lap and kiss the ever-living shit out of him because of some kind of fucked-up politeness. It had been so easy for him to put a stop to it and walk away. He'd barely mentioned it since.

"Yes," Emil said, suddenly in command again. "We should talk about how we're going to get back to Facility 17."

"What do you mean 'we'? You wanna wait for me? As soon as I eat, I'm gonna crash. I'll probably sleep all day."

Emil nodded. "You might have gathered but—the situation is delicate, up there. I want to talk to my team again but I don't trust any communications channels. I have to do it in person."

"And you don't have any ID or cash on you, so you can't get back up there except with me."

"Well... yes."

Kit sighed. Would Quint Services even pay him for a job this late? Did he have the heart to say no? "It's fine. I'll do it. I just need time."

"Kit, there's something I should tell you. My team has been at that Quint Services facility for just over three months, preparing for a mission."

Kit didn't need to be told where that mission was headed. "You were supposed to cross the Nowhere into some other reality."

"Or failing that, another planet in this reality," Emil said. "I got into this because I wanted to explore. Not to colonize or exploit. Just explore. I thought if I participated in the exploration, maybe I could help ensure that it would be ethical. And the scientist who was in charge, Dr. Lange—I think he wanted to explore, too. But he's gone now and I don't know who will be in charge when I get back. But I'm a little unsettled by the way Quint Services has treated me, and I'm... worried."

"About your team."

"About you."

Kit fixed him with a look. "I can transport myself to a different continent with a thought. I'm not part of your team. You don't need to worry about me."

"If anyone there finds out that you're the runner who crossed through... there'll be questions, to say the least."

"Like I said, I can get by. I don't need your protection." Kit stared Emil down as he said it. Then Zin came back in with bowls of pho for both of them, and she pushed herself into the booth right next to Emil, which made him all flustered. Kit rolled his eyes and ignored their conversation—mostly Emil praising every obscure track Zin had ever recorded and Zin cooing over him—in order to eat as much as he possibly could. Three bowls later, he stood up. "I can't stay awake any longer."

Zin stood up and let Emil out of the booth. Thankfully she didn't ask any questions about where they'd been—probably because she assumed they'd had some kind of wild sex last night, which was both way too close and way too far from what had actually happened.

Emil said, "Let me help you."

Kit frowned. He'd made it down the stairs earlier and now that he'd eaten something, he could trudge back up on his own. Did Emil want to lie down with him? In his bed? He narrowed his eyes, but Emil's sweet, open expression wasn't giving anything away. Fuck that. Kit's bed was reserved for people who hadn't rejected him. If Emil liked Zin so much, he could sleep on her couch. "Zin, can you put Emil up until—I don't know, tomorrow sometime?"

Zin raised her eyebrows at that, and Kit was grateful that she didn't say anything. She'd joked about Emil being his boyfriend earlier and Kit did *not* want to return to that topic. "Of course. Sleep tight."

She put a hand on Emil's shoulder and said something to him that Kit didn't hear because he was already halfway up the stairs.

SUSPECT LOYALTIES

EMIL HAD BEEN STRANDED IN ANOTHER REALITY ONLY AN hour ago, and now his childhood pop idol was offering him a towel and a toothbrush. Zin—she'd insisted he use her nickname —lived above the bar in a long, narrow apartment that didn't show any sign of being inhabited by a world-famous pop star. No photos of her glory days on the walls. No awards decorating the shelves. It was painted in the same burst of colors as the bar below and Kit's room above, and from where Emil stood, he could see walls of magenta, orange, and piercing blue. The couch she'd offered him had probably once been bright green, but like the rest of the place, it was worn down. Not that Emil was complaining. He was tired enough to sleep on a hardwood floor, and if that hardwood floor belonged to Zinnia Jackson, it would be his honor.

Still. Somewhere above him, Kit was curling up on that mattress, in his little nest of blankets and laundry, and Emil had been very clearly disinvited. More worrisome than thinking about touching Kit was the fact that Emil was contemplating that room with anything but horror. A neat freak since the age of fifteen, Emil ought to have been overcome with the urge to organize. Instead, he'd been charmed.

He was being ridiculous and he had to stop thinking about this. Kit was upset with him, and he was perfectly justified in it, and Emil shouldn't wish for anything more. He'd behaved disgracefully. And now he was about to drag the kid into further danger, and who knew what would become of either of them once they got back to Facility 17.

As Emil walked into the bathroom to shower, he noticed something in the pockets of his sweatpants. He reached in and his hand came away sticky and red. *The berries.* He'd forgotten he had more stashed away. Guilt flooded him, but then his rational brain took over. They were biological samples from another reality. He had to bring them back and study them.

He walked to the kitchen—*Zinnia Jackson's kitchen*—and went hunting through drawers until he found a plastic bag. Not many of the berries had survived the trip intact, but he was able to scoop out his pockets and bag the contents. He tucked the plastic bag away for later.

Emil showered—in *Zinnia Jackson's shower*—and brushed his teeth—with *Zinnia Jackson's toothpaste*—and changed back into his clothes. Winslow and Heath would probably confiscate them and try to study whatever particles remained from that other place. He might end up in quarantine. This wasn't the way the mission was supposed to go. He should have been with his team. They'd been preparing for months now.

He settled onto the couch, which was just a little too short for his full height. He'd have to sleep with his knees up. He drew the throw blanket, a blue-and-beige plaid wool that didn't go with anything else in the apartment, down over himself.

What had happened to his team in his absence? Had Heath and Winslow told them anything? Did they think Emil had abandoned them? What did they know about the incident—and Dr. Lange?

Dax would be suspicious. They were a smart kid. Miriam would be furious no matter what anyone had told her. Chávez and Beck would be worried, but they'd follow Dax's lead. And McCreery... well, Jake was so tough and stoic it was hard to tell how he'd react. He was a good team member, always got the job done right, but he held himself apart. The weirdest thing about Jake was that sometimes, Emil could swear the guy had a soft spot for cranky, acid-tongued Lange... weirder yet, sometimes Emil could swear the feeling was mutual. If so, Jake would be upset about the incident.

Emil hadn't harbored any affection for Dr. Lange, and *he* was upset about the incident. Had Dr. Lange died? If he had, was that better or worse than just... vanishing?

The aftermath, in particular, unsettled him. He'd known all the research at Facility 17 was classified, but the secrecy surrounding the incident went beyond that. Heath and Winslow had isolated him from his team. They'd treated him like a suspect. Maybe he should be treating this whole venture with more suspicion of his own. Strange things happened at the facility all the time. After a while, Emil and his team had simply accepted that sometimes doors opened on their own and things fell off tables with no explanation. They'd stopped asking Lange, who glared instead of answering, and Heath and Winslow, who smoothly changed the subject.

Beck had sworn he'd seen a bright light darting down the hallway once—but he'd been with Chávez, who hadn't seen a thing, and who had teased him about how all the drugs he did were going to interfere with their mission. Chávez herself probably had indulged back on Earth, since New York's laws weren't too strict on that point, and as long as she turned her master's thesis in, none of her anthropology professors were likely to care. But Beck was originally from Arkansas, and he'd only gotten out by joining the Orbit Guard, so Emil couldn't imagine him taking the risk.

Besides which, there was nowhere to get illicit drugs at Facility 17. Emil was in charge of the greenhouse and he wasn't about to get fired for unsanctioned plants. Still, they'd all laughed, because it was easier than taking it seriously. There was an understanding that these things had to be shrugged off. When you signed up for a secret mission that might take you to another reality, you accepted that some weird shit might go down.

Food disappeared from the fridge all the time, too. Lange had been obsessed with it for the past few weeks, accosting each of them and demanding to know exactly what they'd eaten. It had become a joke among them, Lange and his conspiracy theory about some food-stealing poltergeist. When it came to vanishing food, Emil suspected his team. There, at last, was a thought that made him smile. It had only been eight days since he'd seen them, but he missed them all the same. He'd get back to them and then together, they'd figure out what to do.

———

KIT SLEPT for twelve hours and woke up ravenous. He pulled on a pair of obscenely tight teal jeans and a grey tank top with a moving pink print on it and went down one floor. If you were going to do something out-of-control reckless, you might as well dress for it. It was nine at night and the lights from the freeway outside flooded his room. Whatever time it was, he wanted coffee. Barefoot, he padded down to Zin and Louann's kitchen. Emil was asleep on the couch in the living room, bent in a way that couldn't possibly be comfortable, with his hair mussed and his face slack. He seemed younger in sleep, and Kit realized that the entire time they'd known each other, Emil's expression had been tight with worry.

Well, maybe not the *entire* time.

Kit had to stop staring at this huge fucking stranger on Zin's couch. He shook his head, trying to clear it, and opened the fridge. He made himself a couple of sandwiches, inhaled both, and then started a pot of coffee. At some point, he turned around and Emil was looming in the doorway.

Not looming, exactly. Leaning up against the doorframe with his arms crossed over his chest, watching Kit with sleepy eyes. His feet were bare. They were proportionate to the rest of him—giant—and the same shade of warm brown and Kit didn't care about feet. But something about it made Emil seem vulnerable. Exposed. Kit felt like he was crossing some kind of line by noticing anything at all about Emil's body, and he escaped the intimacy of the moment by turning his attention to the coffee. He poured himself some, took a drink, and scalded his tongue.

While he coughed and put a hand to his mouth, Emil's eyes went wide with sympathy. "Do you need—can I—"

Kit waved him away. He gathered himself up and said, "Coffee?"

"No, thank you. Is there tea?"

Ugh. What was the point of tea? But Kit reached into a cabinet and pulled out a box of tea, then heated some water. "We can leave whenever you want," he said.

"About that," Emil said. "How precise are you? You know, when you... land?"

"How precise do you want me to be?" Kit was a goddamn professional who always hit his mark, provided some freak thing didn't push him into another reality.

Emil looked like he wanted to sigh. Instead he poured boiling water over the tea bag in his mug. "There are some people at the facility I'd rather not run into. Just a precaution. It would be nice if we could arrive in my quarters."

"Draw me a map."

Kit opened the junk drawer and rummaged through it until he found a notepad and a pen, which he handed to Emil. They could have used a display to draw it digitally, but paper felt safer. Unhackable. Emil picked up the pen and started drawing right away. As his pen moved, he said, "And Kit—I think—I think you should jump right back."

That was Kit's plan, but he resented Emil telling him what to do. How many more times would he have to say *I'm not a part of your team*? "I'm not some stupid kid you have to protect."

"I know. I just don't want you anymore mixed up in this than you already are," Emil said. "Which reminds me—I never thanked you. For saving my life."

"Saving your life? When?"

"Any number of times. When that thing attacked us in the Nowhere. When we were stranded in some unknown place that might not even have been in this reality. And you could have dumped me anywhere after that, but instead you brought me here."

Kit hadn't had any control over coming here. He'd panicked. "All I did was not leave you behind," Kit said. "Not a big deal."

"Still." Emil drank his tea and finished sketching a map of Facility 17. The asteroid was oblong. A hallway looped around the first floor in an elongated hexagon. "This is lab space here and here, and this is medical, and here's the gym, and the common room, and the kitchen, and the greenhouse, and here's where we sleep." With his pen, he tapped one of a series of identical rectangles on the right side of the map. "This one's my room."

"What's all that over there?" Kit asked. The map Emil had drawn took up a little over half of the asteroid he'd outlined.

There was a blank space beyond the labs and medical exam rooms at one end. "Rock?"

"And metal. Whatever's left of the asteroid. I guess Quint Services saved some space for possible future expansions." Emil looked up from the map and examined Kit. His gaze was intense and assessing. There might as well have been a cartoon light-bulb above his head. "So you can jump a long way. But could you jump, say, from here to the other end of the living room?"

"Sure. But why would I bother? It would take less energy to walk."

"A jump like that—it would be easier than what you did this morning, right?" Emil asked. "So you could do more of them in a day without wrecking yourself, right? Even if you were carrying something?"

Kit knew where this was going. "You want me to sneak you in somewhere. But ten seconds ago, you told me you didn't want me mixed up in this. Whatever 'this' is."

"No, I'm just... thinking," Emil said. "Never mind."

"You gonna tell me what's going on at Quint Services Facility 17?" Kit intoned the name and waggled his eyebrows.

"There was an accident in one of the labs." Emil described the incident in Solomon Lange's lab that had bruised him and caused him to get sent down to the surface for questioning. "I just don't like the way this thing was handled."

"Yeah," Kit said. He hadn't liked the sight of the Quint Services facility he'd seen, with Emil sedated and blindfolded in what amounted to a cinderblock cell underground. "And you didn't have doubts about your mission before?"

"Weird things happen at Facility 17, but they're mostly harmless. When you move into a secret facility in space to train for a mission to some other reality, you sign up for things getting weird. I wanted—and still want—to be a part of the exploration. I trust my team, and that's what matters."

"Huh," Kit said. *He* never would have signed up for that shit. He was fine down here on Earth, riding his bike and shopping for shoes and eating tacos and watching goofy scripted dramas on Zin and Louann's couch. What did it matter what else was out there in the universe? There was plenty to worry about already. Emil was brave. And stupid. Mostly stupid. "How come your whole team isn't runners? Wouldn't that make more sense than exploding a lab trying to make a door?"

Something passed over Emil's face so quickly that Kit almost didn't catch it. He looked down for a fraction of second, like he didn't want to talk about this. "We have one. Considering how rare runners are, one out of six is pretty good."

"Nobody in the Runner Corps wanted to sign up for this? I thought that was what they were into, serving their country, being government lab rats, whatever."

"No. And it's a private enterprise," Emil said. He didn't even bristle at the insult—he might not be in the Runner Corps, but Kit hadn't missed his half-interrupted reference to the Orbit Guard earlier. Emil was a former federal employee. And not just that, but a former member of a branch of the military that was decidedly antagonistic toward runners. The Orbit Guard provided space station security, and they didn't like it when people showed up unauthorized. Now Kit was sure he'd hit on a subject Emil didn't want to talk about.

Naturally, he said, "So. You were in the Orbit Guard."

"And?"

"You spend a lot of time trying to catch runners?" Kit emphasized *trying*. He knew they weren't any good at catching. They'd never even caught Travis, and Travis loved to stroll around up there, taunting them.

"I worked search and rescue. Saving people from vessels that had hit space debris or broken down. I don't have anything against runners, if that's what you're asking."

Kit pulled his mouth to the side. It was hard to get too mad about that. Still, it didn't change his feelings about the rest of the Orbit Guard.

"I understand why you might hold me in suspicion," Emil said, like they were about to have a heart-to-heart, and Kit rolled his eyes hard enough that Emil gave up and changed the subject. He put his empty mug down on the counter and pointed at his hand-drawn map. "You need anything other than this?"

"My shoes," Kit said dryly. He didn't need any other information. Sometimes when clients wanted him to go somewhere new, he asked them for descriptions of the place—any sights, sounds, smells, or even general feelings that might help him focus on it—but there was no way in hell he was asking Emil what his bedroom smelled like. Jesus. The thought gave him hives.

But far worse than not *wanting* to ask those questions was not *needing* to. Kit wouldn't have any trouble concentrating on Emil and directing them both to the place where he slept. No need to bring that up.

"Let's not put it off any longer, then," Emil said. "I'm ready."

————

HE WAS NOT FUCKING READY. Emil could never be ready for the Nowhere. He handled it worse than any other member of his team—they'd all benefitted from months of treatment. Beck could even run now. Emil hadn't been so lucky.

At least this trip was shorter than his last. That meant it only felt like a thousand years of head-squeezing, gut-churning misery, instead of ten thousand. How did Kit do it? What must it be like?

Like last time, Emil kept his eyes shut. He tried to retreat inside himself, to be as unaware as possible. And yet when Kit jerked them both to the side, he was conscious enough to know something was wrong.

Had that thing come back? Just at the moment Emil dared to squint into the Nowhere, there was a flash of blue light and then they were standing in a small, white, rectangular room. Emil breathed a sigh of relief, and then a familiar voice yelped, "What the *fuck*, Emil?"

Chávez's voice startled Kit, who jumped toward Emil instead of jumping away. He muttered "fuck," then his arms constricted around Emil and he actually hid his face in Emil's chest.

And then Emil glanced to the side and saw why.

His longtime friend and colleague Clara Chávez, a steadfast, loyal, ridiculously charming goofball of a woman who would flirt with a rock given the chance, was sitting in bed with her arms around a dark-haired woman Emil recognized as Dr. Jennifer Heath, Quint Services medical researcher. It took Emil a second to put the whole picture together—he wasn't accustomed to seeing Dr. Heath with her hair down and with no glasses on. Or with no pants on.

"Where the fuck have you been?" Chávez demanded. Heath gaped at her. For the first time in his life, Emil wished he was back in the Nowhere. "No, wait, don't tell me. Get out!"

"We were just going," Emil said calmly. His voice came from some other person. He took a step backward toward the door, hoping Kit would let go of him so they could speed up their escape.

It was too late. Dr. Heath was reaching for her glasses. "You were supposed to be back yesterday," she said, for all the world as if she wasn't in the middle of a make-out session *with one of her experimental subjects*. Whose idea had this been? She disentangled herself from Chávez and picked her pants up off the floor. She pulled them on while she talked. "What happened? Who's this?"

"I, um—" Emil's fake calm failed him. He wanted Kit to leave right now, but there was no way to tell him. He wished Kit had whisked the both of them out of here the minute they'd realized where they were, but that was foolish. Kit had just brought them a long way and he had to save his strength for the run back to Earth.

"Put some clothes on, Chávez," Dr. Heath snapped, mistaking the cause of Emil's discomfort. He'd seen Chávez in a t-shirt and underwear before—and less. They'd roomed together on Franklin for a few months and she'd been extremely cavalier about their shared space. Politely averting his eyes hadn't always worked.

This wasn't even the first time he'd walked in on Chávez making out with someone. That had never bothered him. She was a grown woman who could do as she pleased. It was Dr. Heath herself—and Kit, poor Kit—who were the problem.

Dr. Heath clipped her long, straight hair back and looked almost like her usual self, except for the circumstances. She stuck out her hand toward Kit as if this were a normal introduction. "I'm Dr. Jennifer Heath."

Emil quashed an urge to hug Kit tighter. They shouldn't still be touching each other. He dropped his arms to his sides, and slowly, Kit let go of him. His skin was just brown enough that the darkened flush in his cheeks wouldn't be obvious to most people, but Emil knew.

He shook Dr. Heath's hand. "Kit Jackson."

"Can you explain to me why you're a day late with this run, Mr. Jackson?"

"We encountered an unknown entity in the Nowhere," Kit said, cool and professional.

He did this for a living. Emil ought to give him more credit. Kit probably dealt with intimidating people on a regular basis.

Dr. Heath leaned in. "What sort of unknown entity?"

"You understand why it's difficult for me to answer that question," Kit said, with a hint of an insubordinate smile. He wasn't panicking like Emil was. *He can get out any time he wants*, Emil reminded himself.

"Can you describe it in more detail?" Dr. Heath asked. "Did it harm you or Mr. Singh?"

"Nothing major," Kit said.

"Would you mind if I examined you? If you made contact with it—"

"I mind," Kit said. And then he vanished.

———

EMIL WOULD HAVE BEEN RELIEVED, but Dr. Heath turned her attention to him. "I'd like to examine you as well."

"The rest of us have a few questions too," Chávez interjected. She'd put on pants in the few minutes since Emil had looked at her. God, but it was a relief to see Chávez. Even in the current circumstances, she was smiling. She nodded at Dr. Heath. "Don't worry, man, the bark is worse than the bite."

"As I recall, you enjoy both," Dr. Heath replied. Then she glanced between them and said, more seriously, "I'm just doing my job. If the two of you were doing yours, you would have stopped that kid from leaving."

Chávez laughed. "Stop a runner? I'm flattered that you think we ever had a chance, Jen."

Jen. How long had this been going on? They definitely weren't supposed to. Emil wouldn't mention it to anyone, but it troubled him. *Pot, kettle*, said a voice in his head. He shouldn't judge them. The small room, with its single bed and metal desk, felt cavernous since Kit's departure. Dr. Heath had pulled on a sweatshirt and was bending down to tie her shoes. Emil had to go with her. Not that it mattered if she examined him—it was in his contract that Quint Services oversaw all his medical needs. And he could tell her the truth, now that Kit was safe.

"You'd better bring Emil back quick," Chávez said. "We have catching up to do."

Dr. Heath shot him a look that Emil understood all too well —he knew what it felt like to get interrupted in the middle of... business. He said nothing. She walked out of the room and Emil took the instant that she wasn't watching to hug Chávez. He also shoved the plastic bag full of berries into her hand.

It was his job to share that material with Dr. Heath. Some impulse made him want to keep the secret. Heath and Winslow had dragged him out of that lab and hadn't told his team the truth about what happened. He could hold back a detail or two.

Chávez knew better than to react to Emil's unexpected gift. She tucked it away without a word.

"Just so you know, what you walked in on—it was her idea," Chávez said into his ear. "I wouldn't have instigated things. But she's persuasive."

"That's the problem," Emil said, letting go of her but keeping his voice low. "She has all the power."

"Are you defending my virtue? I'm touched."

"Clara," Emil said. "Are you really okay? This is what *you* want and not just a thing you can't say no to?"

"You know 'hot and mean' has always been my type. Besides, don't we have bigger problems?"

Emil frowned. He couldn't think of anything to say that didn't tread perilously close to hypocrisy. He had to let it go.

Heath was waiting for him in one of the medical examination rooms, so he went. She made him change into a gown and poked and prodded him all over.

"Your black eye is healing."

"Yes."

Heath adjusted her glasses and fixed him with a stare. Seated on the examination chair, he was still taller than her, but she had an air of authority. "Tell me what happened between last night and now, Singh."

"What Kit said. He took off and we were attacked by something in the Nowhere. I was sedated at the time, so I didn't see it. He said it looked like bluish light."

"You can't possibly have spent nearly 24 hours in the Nowhere. Where were you?"

"I don't know. I woke up in a desert. We were there for a few hours, waiting for Kit to regain enough strength to jump us back. He intended to come here, but we saw the thing again. Or rather, he saw it again and I saw it for the first time. Not that I'd trust my own observational skills in the Nowhere. He jumped back to his apartment and we spent some time recovering there. As soon as he was able, he brought me here."

"Not *here*. Clara's room."

"An accident."

"Where was he planning to land?"

"Definitely not where we landed. I am sorry about that."

She huffed, blowing her bangs off her forehead. "You've always struck me as discreet," she said. Then she narrowed her eyes. "Too discreet. There's something you're not telling me. You said *a desert*. Which desert? American Southwest? North African? Middle Eastern? Given a few hours, I know you'd have tried to ascertain what continent you were on."

"I did," he agreed. "We weren't on any continent I knew."

Behind her glasses, her green eyes went round. "*Jesus*. Emil."

"I know, I know, I should have told you earlier. Honestly, I'm still not even sure it happened. And I can't prove anything."

She opened a drawer, pulled out some plastic bags, and started bagging his clothes and his shoes right then. Relief that he'd stashed the best of the evidence with Chávez flooded him, but he tried not to let it show. Maybe Heath would prove herself trustworthy at some point, and then he'd tell her.

"That kid brought you to some other world and you just let him pop out of our lives!" she said, gesturing with one of his shoes in a plastic bag. "God damn it, Emil, you just ran our first mission by accident—unsanctioned—with some random kid, and now he's not even here to answer questions. The treatments haven't been working and the door was a pipe dream. We need that kid."

"What happened to all your objections to born runners?"

"Don't paint me with that brush. They weren't *my* objections," she said. "Just because the goal of my work is making more runners doesn't mean I hate the ones we already have."

"Then whose objections are they, exactly?" Emil had been told that his team couldn't have any born runners on it. He hadn't questioned it until he'd been in a conference room with Oswin Lewis Quint's face smiling down at him from one of the wall displays. Emil had been honored to meet him—live video was as close as he could hope to get to the real thing—until everyone's favorite billionaire had uttered the phrase *suspect loyalties* without hesitation. Quint had cast aspersions on a whole group of people based on an accident of birth. Thinking back on it, that moment was the first time Emil had ever worried about his work for Quint Services. It didn't sit right with him. He'd been on the receiving end of too much prejudice not to recognize it in other forms. But he'd comforted himself with the thought that he could do good from the inside. Besides, his team had all signed up and he couldn't abandon them. It had been too late to go back.

"It was Lange's theory that gave rise to it," Dr. Heath said.

Dr. Lange had called born runners *a people from Nowhere* and speculated that they might be at ease in the Nowhere because their origin lay somewhere on the other side of it. His speculation had stopped there, but the higher-ups at Quint Services had extrapolated. Perhaps born runners belonged to a different reality—a reality they might prefer, if they could ever return to it. Perhaps they really were *from Nowhere*, and if that were the case, how could they be trusted? For this reason, no born runners worked at Quint Services Facility 17. "But I think that was a kind of Darwin and Social Darwinism thing, you know? I don't think Lange meant for Quint or anyone else to take what he said in that direction. I can't see Lange giving a damn about patriotism or whatever you want to call it."

Emil tried to keep a neutral expression. But his hands, resting on the edge of the examination chair, clenched the vinyl beneath them. She hadn't answered his question. She'd excused herself and Dr. Lange from blame. But if they didn't believe that born runners weren't trustworthy, who did?

She shrugged. "It doesn't matter much now. That hypothesis benefitted my work. And you and your whole team. If Quint trusted born runners, do you think you'd be leading the team?"

"It's a disgusting idea," Emil said, ignoring her question. Kit hadn't even known other realities were possible. He'd spent his whole life in this one. To question whether he belonged here, whether he'd choose the world with all his friends and family and every person he'd ever known, over some abstract concept of a homeland, was absurd and xenophobic.

"I didn't see you shouting that at Quint when he said it. Instead you thanked him for the honor of participating in this mission."

Emil grimaced. He felt a frisson of shame. It was true that

he'd let that aspect of Quint's vision slide. This issue hadn't seemed so pressing until he'd met a runner he really liked.

"Don't beat yourself up about it. We're doing good work. And anyway, it makes no difference to me where that kid is from. We need him."

"The treatments are your life's work. And there have been some encouraging signs. You're not giving up on that, are you?"

"Of course not. Stop trying to distract me, Emil. How can we get that kid back here so I can examine him? I'm sure Vaughn will want a look, too."

It was strange to hear her refer to Dr. Winslow by his first name. Emil wasn't close enough to any of the researchers to talk to them like that, and he had a feeling they liked it that way. By the same token, it irritated him that she kept referring to Kit as *that kid*, but he didn't correct her. He didn't want Kit's name in her mouth. "Maybe we could recruit some born runners, you know, people we'd vetted. Kit doesn't even know how he did it. It was that thing that ran into us. He doesn't want any part of this, Jennifer." If she could use his first name, he could use hers.

"He wants *you*."

"What on Earth—"

"I saw it, Emil. For God's sake, the two of you held onto each other for ages after you arrived."

"The Nowhere is disorienting." And so was Chávez's room.

"For you, maybe," she said. "Not for him. You could convince him to work with us. Bat your eyelashes a few times."

"Dr. Heath." He was too horrified to say anything else. He wouldn't do that to Kit. And he didn't want to discuss sexual ethics with a researcher who was sleeping with one of her research subjects. Emil pushed himself down from the chair and planted his bare feet on the floor, looming over her. "This conversation is over."

"You have no authority to tell me that," she said. "If you

won't bring me that kid, you're my only test subject. I have to be thorough. Did you eat anything while you were there?"

He didn't want to answer that.

"For the good of the mission, Emil. For *science*. Come on. Cooperate."

"Yes," he said, deciding to share a portion of the truth. "Kit needed food before he could make the jump again. I found some fruit that seemed edible and non-toxic. A berry of some kind. I only ate a handful—I just wanted to make sure they wouldn't kill him. There wasn't time to test them in a safer way."

"I want a blood sample, in that case. Urine and stool, too. Did you shower after your return?"

Emil had been her patient—or test subject—for months now, and this was the first time he'd ever resented it. But it was part of his contract with Quint Services. "Yes, I showered."

"Damn. I wish you'd come back sooner. Everything's probably contaminated beyond use by now. Oh well." She waved a hand at him. "Go on."

She'd bagged up all his clothes. She was going to make him walk back to his quarters in this damn hospital gown. Before today, Emil wouldn't have suspected her of anything other than being too absorbed in her work to notice or care, but now it felt pointed. He'd embarrassed her and she was giving as good as she got.

"Jennifer," he said. She raised an eyebrow. He gestured at the gown. "We'll call it even after this, yeah?"

She shrugged. "That depends on you."

"I told you I wouldn't mention it to anyone," he said. "I meant it. As far as I'm concerned, I didn't see anything."

"Hmph," she said, and Emil didn't try to argue with that. He left the exam room, his gown flapping behind him.

[6]
SECRET PLAN

EMIL ALMOST MADE IT TO HIS ROOM WITHOUT INCIDENT.
He could see his door. Unfortunately, he could also see Miriam
Horowitz standing in front of him with her hands on her hips.
Her eyes were round with surprise. Other than that, she looked
like she always did, in dark jeans and boots and a jacket, with
her curly brown hair forced into submission, braided tightly,
and pinned into a bun on top of her head. Everything about
Miriam was severe, from the thick slashes of her eyebrows to the
set of her mouth. She might have been pretty in some other
context, but the impression Miriam preferred to make was
ferocious.

"Where have *you* been?"

She nailed that impression every time.

Emil took a breath. "Can we do this when I'm not wearing a
hospital gown in the middle of the hallway, Miriam?"

"You tell me, Emil. If I turn away for a second, are you
gonna up and vanish?" Her mouth was set into a hard line. She
crossed her arms over her chest.

It was complicated, choosing a team for a mission to parts
unknown. Who knew what they'd face? He'd had to select

people who'd be excited about the novelty and the danger, but who'd be cautious and who'd look out for their teammates. It was hard to say what skills would be useful, but Emil had been inclined to choose people with scientific or technical expertise. Dax had somehow acquired a doctorate in physics by the age of twenty-three. McCreery had served with Emil and he had training as a paramedic. Beck—Lenny, Emil really should think of him as Lenny by now—was an aerospace engineer and he'd never met a machine he didn't want to take apart and put back together, which was a pastime that Dax also loved. What mattered was that they all had a gift for solving previously unforeseen and unimaginable problems.

The only two who didn't have a background in the hard sciences were Chávez and Miriam. Chávez could fly anything you put in front of her, but more importantly, she was warm and friendly and she had a graduate degree in cultural anthropology. She had a deep interest in linguistics, but her real focus was conflict studies. If Emil had to defuse a bomb, he'd ask Lenny and Dax, but if he had to defuse an argument, he'd ask Chávez.

Chávez was there to make peace. Miriam was there to make war.

She was resourceful, loyal, tough, and her eyes lit up when she talked about space, but in terms of what she alone brought to the team—well, Miriam Horowitz was fearless. She had good reason to be, since Emil had never seen her miss a target, no matter what kind of weapon she was wielding. She was formidable with and without weapons. She could fuck up a man twice her size. Emil knew because he'd been that man on a couple of occasions in the gym.

The rest of them could fight, too, but Miriam was something else. When Emil had to choose who to take into the unknown with him, not knowing what threats he'd face, Miriam's name was the first one out of his mouth.

For all of those reasons, he wasn't thrilled to be the object of her glare now. "I swear I'm just going into my room to change. You can follow me in if it matters that much to you."

"You don't fucking leave us here, Emil," she said in a low voice. "You just don't."

But she stepped aside to let him pass. The door was programmed to respond to his touch, which was good since he didn't have a damn thing on. Miriam followed him inside, and as he was shutting the door behind them, she leapt into action.

Emil looked up and she was pressing Kit against the opposite wall, her upper arm across his throat. "Who the fuck are you and how did you get in here?"

"Stand down, Miriam," Emil said. His mind was racing. He'd told Kit to leave. Kit had said he would leave. He'd thought Kit had left. What was he doing here?

"You know this guy?" Miriam asked, indignant. She was already unhappy with him and now she felt like he was keeping secrets. Where was Chávez when Emil needed her?

"Yes. He's the runner who brought me back. His name is Kit. Please let go of him."

She backed off slowly and Emil watched the two of them stare each other down. Miriam was a little taller and a lot heavier than Kit. They were a study in contrasts. Kit was decked out in teal and hot pink. Emil would be surprised if Miriam own a single article of clothing that wasn't black, grey, or very dark green. Her underwear drawer was probably full of knives.

"Now, if the two of you will promise not to kill each other for a minute, I'm gonna put some clothes on."

It wasn't awkward to get dressed with Miriam in the room. Emil didn't know who she was interested in—if anyone—but he knew he wasn't in that category. Chávez and Lenny teased him all the time about working out, about whose attention he was trying to get, and one time when they'd been waxing ridiculous about *chiseled abs* or whatever, Miriam had interrupted with, "Would you two shut the fuck up? The only thing that matters about a man's abs is whether they're a comfortable surface for napping."

It had been so unexpected it had rendered them all speechless for a second. Terrifying Miriam Horowitz, a *cuddler*? By the time Chávez recovered enough to open her mouth, Miriam was glaring and blushing and stomping out the door.

Emil hadn't known she was capable of blushing until that moment. He knew she wasn't going to blush now. Miriam simply turned her head and waited. Kit, on the other hand, might not be looking, but Emil couldn't help but be aware that he was in the room. He pulled on boxers, jeans, and a t-shirt as fast as he could. A second too late, he noticed that the t-shirt had the Quint Services logo printed in black. So many of his clothes did. But it would be strange to take it off now, so he just left it. He turned around to face her, still unsure what he planned to say.

"I promise I'll explain, Miriam, but I'd rather just do it once. Do you think you could find Chávez, Lenny, Dax, and Jake and bring them here? As discreetly as possible?"

"Here?" Miriam looked around his room, which was identical to Chávez's in its furnishings. One single bed. One metal desk. One chair. One closet. The space already felt crowded with three of them. Seven people would be overwhelming. "Not the common room?"

"Not the common room," he confirmed, and her eyebrows went up and she nodded. Maybe it was a foolish precaution. It wasn't like his bedroom was secure. All it would take was one person putting their ear to the door. But Emil had to move fast and real secrecy would take time.

Given a moment alone with Kit, Emil said, "I thought you were leaving?"

"Couldn't," Kit said. He leaned against the wall and crossed his arms over his chest, a pose that might have been drawn from a magazine, nonchalant and sensual. An act, Emil suspected. He needed the support of the wall.

And then Chávez arrived from her room next door, ending their conversation. Her short brown hair, usually neatly asymmetrical, was still mussed from what she'd been doing with Dr. Heath not long ago. She was almost as tall as Emil, but of a completely different body type, one that Lenny had once described as "90% skeleton." She shuffled in more sheepishly than she normally would have. It wasn't being caught having sex so much as being caught having sex *with Dr. Heath* that had Chávez studying the floor tiles so carefully. The Quint Services research ethics committee would have a fit if they found out—or maybe they wouldn't. Maybe Quint Services wouldn't know ethical behavior if it bit them in the ass.

Lenny came into the room next, and his grin at seeing Emil was outsize even for him. "Hey, you're alive!" He banged his shoulder into Chávez's and she winced. Broad-shouldered and big-bellied, Lenny had been the star of his high school football team. He sometimes forgot his own strength. He was as friendly as Chávez, but far less focused. His glasses were always smudged or crooked or both, and he was always cajoling his mother and other family members to mail him fresh spices for new culinary experiments. "Told you he was alive."

"I never bet against that," Chávez said. "All I said was Winslow's story about a *family emergency* was bullshit."

That's what Dr. Winslow had told his team? The man didn't have a clue about them.

"Yeah," Lenny said. "Every time I make a mail run to Franklin, there's another package of those cashew things Mrs. Singh always sends up, and everybody loves them, *and* her, and I know

Emil would have told us if something had happened to our cashew-thing hookup."

"AKA his mom," Chávez said.

"Kaju katli," Emil said, supplying the name of the sweet. "And she goes by Professor Singh."

Chávez and Lenny smiled at that. Emil didn't correct their assumption that his mother sent the care packages, even though she was far too caught up in her writing to do any such thing. It didn't escape him that Kit was listening intently to all of this information about his family—and his team, who were almost one and the same. And Chávez and Lenny had kept up their buddy routine rather than ask any questions about Kit. He hoped it was a sign of trust: if Emil wasn't worried about this person, they wouldn't be, either. "And my mother is just fine, as of last week. So is the rest of my family."

"Well, that's a relief. What happened to the last box of those, anyway?" Chávez asked, a sly smile on her face.

"*You* ate them," Lenny said. "Right in front of me."

"Oh, that's right. I beat your ass in hockey soccer and won eternal glory and the sweet, sweet cashew spoils of victory."

Hockey soccer was sort of like soccer, but played by kicking a hockey puck across the basketball court, with the facility's artificial gravity lowered to make the puck slide more easily. Lenny and Chávez hated this comparison and any time Emil brought it up, they claimed he was being "disrespectfully reductive" and didn't understand the beauty of their masterpiece. The game had hundreds of obscure rules known only to its inventors. Emil broke new ones by accident every time he participated. Lenny and Chávez played hockey soccer religiously, always with a beer in hand and always for high stakes—like the sweets in Emil's care packages, which he himself didn't eat.

Lenny was black and straight and had grown up in a very white town in rural Arkansas. Chávez was a Puerto Rican lesbian from Inland New York. Either despite or because of these disparate experiences—Emil could never be sure—Lenny and Chávez were basically inseparable. Not coincidentally, they were the two warmest members of his team, the two who slapped backs and shook hands and gave out hugs and big grins the most easily.

Dax slipped into the room, closing the door quietly. Of average height and build, pale, freckled, and red-haired, fairly shy and highly unlikely to start a fight, Dax Strickland was the youngest and least physically imposing member of the team. But Emil had never met anyone more brilliant, and that included the prize-winning, highly paid elite researchers at Facility 17. Dax would eclipse them all some day.

Emil hadn't known Dax before hiring them, but even before the interview, Emil had been impressed. Twenty-three-year-old Dax had answered the receptionist's "Is that Mrs. or Mr. Strickland?" with a cool, unruffled "It's *Doctor* Strickland."

Dax was imperturbable, which helped them get along with a team full of weirdos subjecting themselves to experiments in space. Emil appreciated their intellect and their easygoing nature, but their most valuable quality was an ability to explain physics to non-physicists without condescension.

He'd once told Dax they were a goddamn genius, and they'd smiled and said, "Not thinking about sex or romance leaves me lots of brain space to solve problems."

Chávez had whooped, clapped them on the shoulder and said, "Dax, did you just accuse our fearless leader of thinking with his dick? That's amazing, I love you, never change."

"And his heart, figuratively." Dax was always soft-spoken and dry. "And not just him. You, too." A perfectly timed look at Chávez. "Especially you."

Miriam and Lenny had lost it at that, and even Jake had snorted with laughter. Chávez, impervious as she was to mockery, had cracked a grin and said, "You are not wrong, my friend, not wrong."

It was one of the best things in Emil's life, watching his team get along, knowing they could do great things together. He smiled at Dax as they came in and watched them look right at Kit and decide to say nothing. Miriam opened the door with Jake in tow a second later, and he looked even more solemn than usual. Emil gestured for everyone to sit down. Jake took his desk chair and the rest of the team crowded onto his bed. Kit remained standing.

"A week ago, Dr. Lange blew up his lab. I was over there to remind him to feed Niels Bohr. I heard this strange noise and started pounding on the door to get his attention when the whole thing blew off its hinges and threw me backward. I got hit in the head for my trouble and didn't manage to get him out. I'm sorry." Emil said. He glanced at Jake, the only one of them who might feel personal sorrow about this, since he'd had an inscrutable understanding of some kind with Lange. Jake looked down at the floor.

"I've been feeding the cat," Jake said. Emil nodded. Maybe he hadn't been friends with Lange after all. Maybe Emil had imagined those few times he'd seen them looking at each other. It would make so much more sense if Jake just liked the cat. That didn't account for the hesitant rasp in his deep voice, but Jake was pretty damn inscrutable himself. Emil liked him, of course. He was just more complicated than the rest of the team put together.

"Wait," Dax said. "Is Lange dead? And if so, what does that mean for the mission?"

"I honestly don't know," Emil said. "What did Heath and Winslow tell you?"

"You had a 'family emergency' and Lange had a 'minor acci- dent' in the lab that required him to shut down work for two weeks while Quint Services rebuilt. He decided to take those two weeks to return to Earth to visit his family. The transport that left the facility was carrying both of you."

That wasn't even *close* to believable. The broken lab windows made it clear the accident hadn't been minor. Emil had no idea who Dr. Lange knew back on Earth, but the idea that he would voluntarily take two weeks off from work to socialize was laughable. Heath and Winslow ought to have said he'd shut himself in his quarters to read papers for two weeks.

"I know he's reclusive, but he wouldn't just vanish," Jake said. "Not unless something bad happened to him. He would have asked us to take care of Niels Bohr."

Something in Jake's tone suggested that his affection wasn't only for the cat. Emil glanced at Chávez, who looked keen to learn more about their tightest-lipped teammate. Emil had served in the Orbit Guard with Jake and still hardly knew him. It was hard to imagine Jake becoming friends with the mysterious Dr. Lange.

"How'd you get to know him?" Chávez asked, casual.

Jake clammed up. Emil could see the tension rise in his shoulders. "Dunno. We talked. Once. Or twice. It was nothing."

"Okay," Emil cut in, rescuing Jake from further questions. "Let me keep going. After the ex-slash-implosion, Heath and Winslow came running into the lab. They dragged me out. I was pretty out of it then, and by the time I woke up, they'd transported me to Franklin Station and put me in a pod. They took me to a Quint Services facility on the surface, questioned me, and then had a runner bring me back. Everyone, this is Kit."

Kit frowned, dismayed by the attention, and said "Hi" to no one in particular.

"That's Dax, Lenny, Chávez, Miriam, and Jake," Emil said, hoping to elicit a warmer reaction. "They're my team."

"Nice to meet you," Chávez offered, smiling. "Again, I mean. With clothes on this time."

"I hesitate to ask how you met the first time," Dax said. "In fact, before you explain, let's forget I mentioned it."

"Right," Emil said, taking control of the conversation. "Kit was assigned to bring me back here last night. Instead, we were knocked off course and briefly stranded."

"Knocked off course by what?" Miriam asked.

"Stranded where?" Lenny said at the same time.

Emil glanced at Kit. This was his story to tell. Emil hadn't even been awake. Kit didn't look happy at having to address Emil's team, but he did it. "The thing that hit me was just... it looked like light. It felt solid when it hit me, though. I couldn't really say how big it was. Bigger than me. I've never seen anything like that in the Nowhere and nothing has ever pushed me out where I didn't want to be. That thing collided with us and knocked us into the ground somewhere we'd never been. A desert. Emil says it was another world. Maybe another reality."

His team erupted. He heard shouts of "holy shit" and "what the fuck" and "you went without us" among other wordless yelps and gasps. They quieted down, and Dax said, eyes alight, "What was it like?"

Emil and Kit looked at each other in silent agreement to leave out some parts of their story. "Strange," Emil finally said. "And not strange. It took me some time to put together that we weren't on Earth. There was life, but I didn't see evidence of sentience."

"Can we go back?" Miriam asked.

"I don't know," Emil said. "The trip was taxing for Kit, and we encountered that thing on our way back. We took a detour to Kit's apartment to avoid it. We were supposed to get here last night. But I think it's more pressing that we discuss why Heath and Winslow are covering up—however poorly—what happened to Dr. Lange. I don't like that they kept me from speaking with you until now, and I really don't like that they lied."

"Did they just lie to us or do you think they lied to the executives, too?" Lenny asked. "That might help us figure out what their goal is."

"They might be scrambling not to get shut down," Chávez pointed out. "With no Dr. Lange and no door, it's not clear how we'd go on the mission."

"Heath and Winslow's treatments?" Emil asked, mostly to get the conversation started. This was what he'd wanted all week, to brainstorm with this particular group of people. They'd get to the answers.

"You of all people should know they don't work," Miriam said.

"Not true," Dax said. "Lenny's trial was a success, and the rest of us—Emil excluded—have found it easier to *be* in the Nowhere, even if we can't get there by ourselves. That's a long way from failure. Given time and funding, Heath and Winslow could get the result Quint Services wants."

"There's been tension between the two projects since the beginning," Miriam observed.

"Hard not to have tension with Lange," Chávez said.

"I think, from what we know of Heath and Winslow's recent behavior and from what we know of them generally, that they're trying to avoid any trouble that might hinder their own work," Dax said.

"You think they want to sweep this under the rug?" Emil asked.

"Yes. I think they'd like us not to ask any further questions, and they're hoping to avoid any kind of investigation from corporate," Dax said. "Best outcome for them is all of Lange's funding gets funneled into their project."

"So they don't want us to be scared off, thinking Lange got killed—we're part of their research, after all—but they also don't want us poking around," Lenny said.

"Fuck that," Miriam said, and Emil heartily agreed.

Jake spoke up in the silence that followed. "So they're not going to look into what happened to Lange at all?"

"I'll look into it," Dax promised. They'd worked in Lange's lab, the single most thankless job at Facility 17.

"If we're going to find out what happened to Dr. Lange, that means running our own, unsanctioned investigation. In that case, we need to stay here," Emil said. He wasn't surprised that they all seemed to want to stay, but he'd been prepared to say goodbye if anyone didn't have the stomach for subterfuge. "And we need to be careful."

"What about you?" Lenny asked, looking at Kit. "Are you in on the secret plan?"

Kit looked amused and disdainful at this offer. "Hell no. I'm just here because I'm too hungry to go anywhere else."

Instead of being offended, Lenny laughed. "That, my friend, is a problem I can solve. Let's go to the kitchen."

"Wait," Emil said. "If anyone sees Kit, they'll wonder why there's an unauthorized new person wandering around Quint Services' ultra-secret asteroid facility. And if Heath or Winslow see Kit, they'll want to examine him."

"Well, he did lead our first mission, accident or not," Dax said.

"*You* might have consented to be science experiments, but I didn't," Kit said. Emil's whole team frowned at him. Their goodwill to strangers only extended so far, and everything about his posture and his tone conveyed scorn. "I'm out of here the minute I can be."

"That's fine," Emil said. Kit couldn't explain to Quint Services why he'd been so late with his delivery, not unless he wanted to become part of their investigation. And that meant Kit couldn't pick up the fee for this job. Emil had kept him from earning money for two days now, in addition to putting him in danger. "Let's disperse. We'll coordinate something later. Lenny, if you wouldn't mind meeting us in the kitchen in fifteen minutes?"

"Sure," Lenny said easily. "I wouldn't foist your cooking on anyone. That's got to be against some law."

"Cruel and unusual punishment," Chávez agreed. "We'll never know how Professor Singh, purveyor of cashew delights, raised such a culinary failure."

"Those come pre-packaged from the grocery," Emil said. His father did most of the cooking. And his sister, when she was around. His mother would never look up from her books and remember to eat if his father didn't remind her. The care packages had three names on the return address, but they were from Zora. It was absurd to send special-occasion sweets as often as she did, but she remembered him as a kid with a sweet tooth and she got a kick out of mailing things to space. Emil wished she could visit, as complicated as that would be. "And I'm not that bad."

Jake left the room during this conversation, and Miriam slipped out a few minutes later. Dax remained, watching Kit. They gave him a beseeching look. "I get that you don't want to be part of this, but would you at least talk to *me* about breaking through? It might give me insight into Lange's notes."

Kit sighed. "Fine. But I'm not talking until I get to eat something."

"Go with Lenny and meet us in the kitchen," Emil suggested to Dax. The two of them left together.

That left only Chávez in the room with them, who scratched the back of her head. "You're not gonna... tell the others, right?"

"No," Emil said. "It's your story to tell or not tell. But Heath might well be hiding something from all of us. The more I think about it, the more concerned I get. Please tell me if you need anything. If you want out, I'll help you however I can."

It surprised him when it was Kit, not Chávez, who spoke next. "Isn't the fact that she might be hiding things a reason to *keep* sleeping with her? If she doesn't trust Chávez yet, she might come around. Maybe she'll let something slip."

Emil had been horrified when Dr. Heath encouraged him to lure Kit into her grasp. Was it irony for Kit to suggest something so similar? And why didn't Emil feel as scandalized? He sighed and opted to gloss over Kit's comment. "Clara, this isn't an area where I can tell you what to do. Just... be careful."

Chávez nodded and walked out the door, leaving Kit and Emil alone.

"It's late, so there shouldn't be many people up," Emil said. "Follow me."

[7]

LOOK OUT FOR EACH OTHER

THIS WHOLE DAMN PLACE MADE HIM UNEASY. KIT COULD
have named a dozen reasons: the awkward arrival, the scientists
eager to examine him, the tight-knit group of strangers he'd
managed to offend, the attractive man who wouldn't even look
at him... but it was the Nowhere that troubled him. Not just
those things, whatever they were, but something about the void
itself. No matter where he was, Kit could feel the Nowhere, and
it felt the same everywhere—except here.

He had a stupid urge to tell Emil that something was wrong,
but he didn't think he could explain it.

So he kept quiet and followed Emil out the door.

Kit had a good memory for maps. He wasn't sure if it was a
cause or an effect of being a runner. Either way, he remembered
the hand-drawn map and he knew Emil's room was on the right
side of the first floor, near the end of the asteroid that Emil had
drawn at the top. The kitchen had been at the bottom of the
map. Because there was only one hallway that wrapped all the
way around, they could go left or right and still end up at the
kitchen, but going left would be shorter. They'd pass the gym,
the basketball court, and the common room on their way.

But when Emil peeked out the door, there were people to the left. So they went right, which took them past a lab space in the center of the facility. Kit didn't need a tour guide to know that it was the site of the accident. It had once had windows looking out into the hallway, but the glass had been replaced by brown paper.

And it felt *wrong*.

Kit hurried past the lab, around the end of the hexagonal loop of hallway. There was a storage room and more lab space on the right, followed by the massive greenhouse.

They heard voices coming from down the hall. It was the same group of people Emil had tried to avoid earlier. They must have cut through one of the central rooms and come out the other side.

Kit recognized one of the voices as Dr. Heath. The other belonged to an older man. The other scientist everyone kept mentioning?

It didn't matter. Emil grabbed him and pulled him into a closet before anyone could see.

Emil pulled him into the small space so quickly that they rattled one of the metal shelves. It was too dark to see, but Kit heard... ceramics? Oh, they were next to the greenhouse. This must be a supply closet full of gardening tools. He sniffed—that was definitely the scent of potting soil.

They stayed near the door, listening. Kit could feel space behind them, a corridor between shelves on either side, so he knew it wasn't necessary for them to be squeezed together. If he were feeling spiteful, he'd point that out. But he wasn't. He felt hungry, tired, confused, afraid, and tense, and having Emil next to him made him feel a little less of all that, which he liked. And if he said anything about it, it would end.

As a rule, Kit didn't like talking about these things. Especially not since his last talk with Emil had gone so badly. So for now, he was happy to pretend that circumstances had forced this closeness upon them and there was nothing to be done about it. So, apparently, was Emil. This moment of contact in the dark—his back to Emil's chest, where Emil's heart beat just a little faster than it should—was all they could have without talking about it. Was it wrong to enjoy it? Kit didn't care. He wasn't getting paid for this shit job, so he might as well get what he could.

It wasn't a crime to think about how their bodies fit together, or how big and warm and solid Emil felt behind him. It wasn't wrong to take pleasure in the way Emil had gripped him and pulled him in here like he weighed nothing, or in the way that, even now, Emil had one hand on Kit's hip and the other on his shoulder. Had Emil thought about where he'd put his hands? Had it been conscious? Or was it instinct? The touch was light, but ready. Ready for what, Kit didn't know. To pull or push him out of the way of danger, probably, or to hold him still and keep him quiet if someone came close to the door. Rationally, Kit knew that was what Emil was preparing for, but his brain suggested all sorts of other possibilities. Emil could pull him closer, lean down, and drag his teeth and tongue along the side of Kit's neck. He could let his hand wander down from Kit's hip...

They were both angled toward the door, listening, but Kit hadn't heard a word. Dr. Heath and that other scientist could be out there talking about how they wanted to vivisect him for all he knew. They were in danger. He really ought to pay attention.

Dr. Heath and her companion were still chatting out in the hallway. Kit heard a third voice in the mix. Another man. That one sounded vaguely familiar, but he couldn't place it. Not any of the people he'd met in Emil's room today. And he didn't know anyone else up here, so how could he recognize the voice? Hunger was making him hear things.

Dr. Heath and the older man were saying their goodbyes to this new person, wishing him a good night's sleep and telling him they'd see him tomorrow. He said a few pleasantries of his own, and then at last, Kit heard their footsteps moving down the hall back toward the quarters where everyone slept.

He waited for silence before reaching for the doorknob. Instead of silence, he heard scratching.

It sounded like there was an animal outside the door, dragging its claws down the metal until it shrieked. There was no room to back up, but Kit backed up anyway. His shoulders tensed hard. "Please tell me that's the cat you mentioned."

"That's the cat I mentioned," Emil said, totally unconvincing.

"You didn't even try." Kit spoke this complaint into the darkness, trying to pretend his pulse wasn't hammering from fear. It wasn't the cat. Was that blue light slipping in under the door?

He felt Emil shrug. "It's been happening the whole time I've lived here. It's kind of creepy, but no harm ever comes of it. It's mostly scratching noises, or things getting knocked off tables. We call it our poltergeist. Clara's been agitating to name it 'Quint.'"

"You've all lived here for months with some invisible *thing* that knocks objects off tables and drags its claws down walls, and you want to give it a *nickname*? Jesus fucking Christ."

"It would be different if anyone had ever gotten hurt."

"Oh, and us getting knocked off course into a different reality, that doesn't count?"

"You think it's the same thing?"

"I don't fucking know, Emil, and I don't want to find out! How can we get away from it?"

"Move to the right and walk between the two shelves. You'll

hit a door at the end of the closet that opens into the greenhouse. The lights should come on once we're in there, and we can walk back out into the hall."

Kit took a step in the darkness. He felt for the shelves on either side. The storage closet seemed remarkably neat—was it Emil who kept it that way?—and there was an easy, open path down the middle.

Had the scratching stopped or had Kit just stopped paying attention?

A blur of light appeared in front of his face, so bright and blue it made him squint. The stacked pots rattled. The blob of light shifted, and a stack went crashing to the floor. Emil grabbed him in both arms and pulled him back as the pots shattered. Shards slid everywhere. Kit felt one hit the side of his boot.

When he looked up again, the thing was gone.

"Are you alright?" Emil said, his voice a low hum in Kit's ear.

"Fine," Kit said, heart pounding and a droplet of cold fear-sweat running down his side. He was too startled to string together the sentence *it scared the everliving fuck out of me*, and besides, he didn't want to admit it. "You still want to give it a nickname?"

"Not really," Emil said. "Let's go."

He kept a hand at the small of Kit's back as they moved.

———

BY THE TIME they reached the kitchen a few minutes later, Kit was so adrenalized that he could almost ignore how hungry he was. It was fear carving into his gut. That fucking *thing* with its creepy scratching could move through the Nowhere. It could come *out*. There wasn't a safe place in the world—or out of it, since Earth was currently several million miles away.

Was it the same thing that had collided with him and Emil and knocked them into the desert? Or was there more than one? God, how was he supposed to live with the knowledge that the whole universe was full of scratching, glowing, hovering... ghosts?

We call it our poltergeist. Emil's whole team was fucking bonkers. Then again, they'd signed up to subject their bodies to a long-term science experiment and were planning a potentially lethal mission to unknown worlds. And none of them, not even the one who was a runner, seemed to be able to feel how eerie and wrong this place was. The Nowhere was all fucked up. Kit needed to get away from here.

But first he needed to eat.

Facility 17 was equipped with a gleaming industrial kitchen, spacious and brightly lit with a spotless, long metal table in the center of the room. It was the opposite of the cramped, dingy space where Zin prepped bar snacks every afternoon.

God, Zin. He had to get back before she freaked out about his absence.

Lenny and Dax were already in the kitchen. Dax was leaning against the counter while Lenny was pulling a casserole dish out of one of the ovens. He set it on the stove and lifted a metal spatula as though he were going to cut it apart into servings.

"You don't have to do that," Kit said. "You can just give it to me. The whole thing."

Lenny eyed him, then looked back at the dish. Kit could see now that it was mac and cheese. It could have been wilted spinach and his stomach still would have rumbled, but the sight made his mouth water.

"If you say so, kid. You know there's other food around. You could have a balanced meal."

"Not a kid," Kit said reflexively. He sat down at the table next to Emil. "And I don't care. Aren't you a runner? You should know."

Lenny picked up the dish and a fork and put both down in front of Kit before seating himself across from them. Dax sat down next to him. Kit dug in without waiting.

They all watched him in amazement for a few silent minutes, but Kit was long past caring. It felt so good not to be painfully hungry. He wanted so badly to be strong enough to run.

"I've only been a runner for a few months," Lenny said, shrugging one shoulder. "I don't really know what I'm doing. And I've always been hungry." He patted his belly and smiled.

"Lenny's an amazing cook," Emil offered. "He makes that mac and cheese from a recipe he invented."

"Tweaked," Lenny said. "You can't really invent a recipe for something people have been eating for hundreds of years."

"Take the compliment," Dax said.

They'd redirected the conversation away from the interesting subject while Kit was wolfing down food. The casserole was one-third gone by now. He was still too hungry to choose talking over eating, but Lenny brought the conversation back to runners anyway. He said, "I have so many questions for you. Do you know a lot of other runners? Is there like a club or something? Did you have to practice running or have you always been naturally good? And can you only get somewhere by thinking about coordinates or maps? Or can you jump in other ways—like jumping to a person without knowing where they are?"

Kit swallowed his bite. That was a lot of questions. "I know a few other runners. Or I did. There's no club." Kit thought of

Aidan Blackwood coming by every week, talking up his *union*, trying to get Kit to join as if Kit would ever sign up to be in a group of other people. Laila liked Aidan and his ideas, and every time she and Kit were out at Winfield's barbecue joint after a job, she'd tried to soften him up. *We have to look out for each other because no one else will,* she'd said. Then Laila had disappeared, just like Aidan, and Kit had known exactly who was looking out for him: no one.

"Running came naturally to me," Kit said. "But I have gotten better with practice. I've never tried to jump anywhere by thinking about a person." That was a little bit of a lie. He'd thought he could make it to Emil's bedroom on feeling alone. But he'd been wrong and he didn't want to discuss it. He ate a few more bites, then took a break to say, "How'd you become a runner?"

"The experiments."

"Well, I know that. I mean, why didn't the experiments work on anyone else?"

"I think if Heath and Winslow knew the answer to that, they'd have a team of six runners instead of one," Dax said. "Sometimes science is a lot more blundering around in the dark than people think. They tried a variety of approaches—"

"I always figured it was my great-grandmother," Lenny said softly, like he hadn't meant to interrupt Dax. He'd just taken his time putting that thought into words. "She was a witch."

Dax made a dismissive noise.

"You live on an asteroid circling the moon, you're trying to cross into some other reality, and there's a fucking poltergeist, but witches are a step too far?" Kit asked.

"The poltergeist thing is a joke," Dax said.

"I'm not laughing," Kit replied.

"We had an encounter on the way here," Emil said,

smoothing things over. "Some pots fell off a shelf in the green-house supply closet."

"See? Not so scary when you put it like that," Dax said.

"And what were you doing in the closet?" Lenny asked. From the way he waggled his eyebrows, it was meant to be funny.

Emil didn't catch it. "Avoiding Heath and Winslow," he said with a grimace. "They were with someone else. Is there a new person here?"

"Yeah, a nurse," Dax said. "Hopefully he's got better bedside manner than Heath."

Kit choked on a cough and went back to eating mac and cheese. He knew way more than he wanted to about Jennifer Heath's bedside manner. Emil shot him a warning look. He pretended not to see it, but he did want to change the subject. Still chewing, he pointed his fork at Dax and said, "And fuck you for acting like it wasn't scary. I'm a normal goddamn person, and when an incorporeal blue glowing thing menaces me, I react."

"Wait, what?" Dax said, eyes wide, just as Emil said, "You *saw* it? I didn't see anything."

"I fucking told y'all!" Lenny said. "I told y'all I saw some-thing and y'all made a joke out of it but now Kit's vindicating me!"

"Sorry," Dax said to Lenny. "It's not that we didn't believe you. Just that we couldn't really do anything about it. We still can't, I guess, but it seems like maybe runners can see this thing. These things?"

"Not sure if there's more than one," Kit said between bites. "It's hard to compare what happened in the Nowhere to what happened here, but I think the one in the Nowhere was bigger. This one was maybe this big." He held his hands just over shoulder width apart, then rotated them, keeping the dimension the same.

"Mine too," Lenny confirmed.

"The one in the Nowhere was bigger than me. So either there's one and it can change size, or there's more."

"Fascinating," Dax said.

Kit didn't agree. He looked at Lenny. "Can you tell how fucked up it feels here?" he demanded.

"Uh," Lenny said. "I don't know? Everything feels weird to me these past few months."

"Weird how?" Dax said. "Fucked up how?"

Kit shrugged. "Hard to explain. I feel the Nowhere everywhere. Like... currents in the air around me. Like a pulse. It moves all the time, but it's always... evenly distributed, I guess? There aren't any places where I can't feel it, just like there aren't any places where it feels especially strong. That's what makes it so perfect for traveling, I think—it touches everything. But that's not how it feels here."

Lenny was rapt. If he'd just become a runner and he'd been living here the whole time, he had no comparison for how strange it felt. Kit could see questions forming behind his eyes.

"It's not evenly distributed here, you mean." Dax was interested, too. They leaned across the table, focused.

"Right," Kit said. Emil hadn't said anything in a while, but he was listening intently. Maybe Kit should have tried to tell him earlier. "Think about a piece of fabric." He held his hands out in front of him, his fingers woven together. "The threads are like this. But if you pull one part of it really hard—"

"You could make a hole," Dax said. "And then the rest of it would be all bunched up and uneven."

Emil was nodding. "Dax, you think this is connected Lange's research."

"I do," Dax said. "We have to get into his lab."

Kit finished the last of the mac and cheese. He felt almost sated. "You mentioned other stuff to eat?" he asked. "Or drink? That might be better, actually. Juice, milk, coffee, literally anything with calories. And no, I'm not joking. I have a long run ahead of me, and there might be a fucking ghost trying to kill me."

Lenny nodded. "Sure."

Zin would fucking kill him for his manners. "And thank you," Kit added. "It was really good."

"Thanks. Just a slightly different version of what my grandma used to make."

"The witch?"

"That was my great-grandmother," Lenny said. He moved to stand up, but Emil got there first.

"I'll get it," Emil said. "You keep talking."

Emil went to the fridge. He pulled out a container of juice, crossed the room, and offered the whole thing to Kit. Their fingers brushed. On purpose? Kit wasn't thinking about that. He opened the bottle and took a drink.

"I didn't really know her," Lenny was saying. "She made it to the age of 93, but she passed when I was about three. I guess she was born in... 1977?"

"Fehim Terzi did Istanbul to New York in 2058," Dax said, referring to the first publicly acknowledged runner. "So your great-grandmother lived most of her life in a world where no one knew about runners."

"Except runners," Kit pointed out. Terzi was the first to make a spectacle of disappearing into the Nowhere and reappearing somewhere far away, but he was far from the first runner. Kit couldn't prove it, but he knew it in his bones. Runners had always been here. They'd just been quieter about it.

"I don't know for sure that she was a runner," Lenny said.

"Like I said, I didn't know her, and if she ever mentioned it to my grandma or my mom, they didn't pass it on. My aunts and uncles and cousins are always saying things like 'if you had a problem, Alice could always help' or 'she had a way about her.' Hard to say what it means. But I always wondered."

"You think it runs in families," Dax said. "Interesting."

Lenny shrugged. "I wouldn't claim to know. But when it happened that I was the only one of the six of us who took to it, I started wondering what was different about me, and every time, I came back to her. Alice Desjardins. She was born in Louisiana, and so was my grandmother, but they moved to Arkansas after a hurricane destroyed their house."

"But nobody else in your family is a runner," Emil said.

"I feel sure I would have been in a lot more trouble as a teenager if my mom could have sneaked up on me like that. So no, I don't think she is."

He looked at Kit, and as he opened his mouth to ask the question that Kit hated most in the world—*what about your parents?*—Kit said, "Don't." He'd never been able to answer that question. At this point, he didn't even want the answer. He just wanted people to stop asking.

Unexpectedly, Emil put a hand on Kit's shoulder. He didn't say anything or even look at Kit. The touch didn't feel illicit or thrilling and it didn't make Kit's insides light up and dance around. It was calming and comforting without being smothering. Kit relaxed a fraction. It almost made him feel like he could stay here.

Lenny didn't tangle himself in knots over Kit snapping at him, which Kit appreciated. Plus, he was a good cook. Kit should try harder not to be rude to him.

"So we've got a theory about why Lenny's trial was a success, a little bit more information about the poltergeist, and a lead on Dr. Lange's work," Dax said. "Not bad for a midnight meal."

"Is it a meal if I'm the only one who ate?"

"You ate enough for all of us," Lenny said, which was a line Kit had heard plenty of times, but he let it slide.

"I haven't even started asking questions," Dax said. "Tell me more about the other—"

They stopped abruptly at the sound of footsteps approaching the door. Better the sound of footsteps than the sound of scratching, but still, that was Kit's cue to leave. He let the Nowhere take him.

————

KIT WAS GOING to be trapped in this fucking facility for the rest of his life. He'd seen one of the ghosts again—not the one from the supply closet, but the first one, the one that had knocked him into the desert. Kit hadn't wanted a repeat, so he'd ducked back into the world without a thought for where he was going. And now he was blinking in the too-bright light of a room that was definitely somewhere in Facility 17. It had the same flooring, the same windowless white walls. There was a counter and a row of cabinets running along one wall, and on the other—

"Holy shit," Kit said.

There were two hospital beds in the room, separated by plastic sheeting hanging from the ceiling. He couldn't tell who was in the more distant bed, but he recognized the occupant of the closest one.

"Aidan Blackwood."

Aidan's eyes slitted open so that Kit could see green irises between the black fringes of his lashes. He was sedated, with an IV line in his arm. That was the only explanation for why he hadn't already come fully awake to chastise Kit about not joining the union.

No. Kit shouldn't be unkind. Something was very wrong here.

Aidan was even paler than usual, and his black hair was matted like he'd been lying in that bed for days. He'd always been wiry, but now he looked thin and sickly. The arm with the IV line in it was also handcuffed to the bed. Restraints couldn't hold runners. Sedation and starvation could. Aidan was a prisoner.

"Aidan," Kit hissed. "What's going on? What are they doing?"

"Get out before they come back," Aidan said.

"And leave you here?" Kit didn't enjoy Aidan's company, but he wasn't going to leave him in this hellish facility. "And whoever that is? No, I can't." Kit shook his head. He stepped toward the other bed and pulled back the plastic sheeting. He sucked in a breath.

Laila. Of fucking course it was Laila. She hadn't flaked on him. She never would have. A curious feeling of relief—Laila really *was* his friend—mixed with his horror at seeing her forcibly sedated in bed. Unlike Aidan, she hadn't come awake at all.

"She fights," Aidan said. "So they keep her under almost all the time. I fought them for the first few days—then I decided I could do more damage if I was awake at least some of the time."

Laila's hair, which she colored cotton-candy pink and kept styled in big, bouncy curls, was flattened and limp. None of her funky, asymmetrical makeup, which she wore every day to avoid facial recognition cameras, was on her face. That made Kit's eyes sting with tears. She'd hate that. She'd hate the stupid, pale blue hospital gown, too. God, how dare they. Kit hoped she'd screamed and kicked and scratched and bitten anyone who'd touched her.

He'd been angry at her. He'd thought she'd abandoned him. He was a fucking fool.

Laila had dark circles under her eyes. She wasn't as fat as Zin, but she wasn't wiry like Aidan—Kit usually thought of her as *soft*, a word that went well with her pink curls and her hugs, and not so well with her combat boots or the rage that lit her from the inside out. The world had hurt Laila and she was always ready to hurt it back. He wasn't surprised that she'd fought her jailers, or that the only way they could keep her from fighting was to knock her out completely. A few days of this treatment hadn't made Laila look as awful as Aidan did. But she still looked sick. Kit laid a hand on hers, which was cooler to the touch than it should have been.

"How do you feel about being in here with a criminal?" Kit asked Aidan. They didn't have time for this conversation, and yet he couldn't keep it inside. The urge to needle Aidan was too strong. And in his heart of hearts, Kit knew he could only save one of them at a time. When he picked Laila first, he wanted to be able to tell himself it was because Aidan was a dick.

"You know there are arrest warrants with my name on them. I care about justice, not laws," Aidan answered. "What does it mean to be a criminal when the law is unjust? And Laila needs a union more than any of us. She knows that, even if you don't."

Aidan was stubbornly refusing to be a dick. Him and his stupid idealism. "I'm just saying, she kinda ruins your whole 'runners aren't criminals' thing. Me too, I guess."

"Laila was a child when it happened."

"Fourteen," Kit argued. It was dumb that Aidan would say *when it happened* like the whole thing had been some accident, like fourteen-year-old Laila Njeim hadn't planned and executed a massive bank robbery all by herself. He was a little insulted on her behalf. She'd gotten caught and served time and hadn't kept a cent, of course. The two of them never brought up the subject now because she was embarrassed. But Kit still thought she was —and always would be—a fucking badass.

Laila's time in juvenile detention might have been something like this. They'd have had to keep her hungry and tired all the time in order to stop her from getting out. The thought made Kit clench his jaw—suddenly *fourteen* seemed a lot more like childhood. At what age did it become ethically acceptable to starve a person?

Aidan ignored Kit's argument. "And the laws that make you a criminal are equally unfair. We need a new legal framework that won't penalize runners for our abilities."

No new legal framework would put *emptying other people's safety deposit boxes* on the table, and Laila had proved that runners excelled at that. Kit didn't think border controls or customs agents would disappear from the world any time soon, either, which meant he'd be a smuggler for the rest of his career... if he ever got out of this damn facility.

Kit had to get Laila and Aidan out of here. But he hadn't meant to come here in the first place, he couldn't carry both of them at once, and those things were still waiting in the Nowhere.

"How long have you been here?" Kit asked Aidan.

"A week, I think. Hard to keep track. They brought Laila in after me."

"How did you get here?"

Aidan shook his head. "Don't know. Whatever it was knocked me out. But it had to be a runner. There's no way they'd risk using the elevator or anything more official for this."

"Another runner brought you here?" Kit's mouth fell open. Aidan was a dumb idealist and Kit had no time for comradeship, but still. He wouldn't betray other runners like that. *It's exactly what you did to Emil,* a little voice inside him whispered. *Would you have done it to Laila if Quint Services had offered you enough money?*

"The only question that remains is who. I'm sure it's someone both Laila and I know—that would have made us complacent. Unfortunately whatever they used to knock me out has left that whole day blurry."

"That's awful," Kit said. Quint Services had hired a runner that Aidan and Laila trusted and then paid that person to anesthetize them and bring them here to be experimented on. If Laila and Aidan both knew that person, chances were high that Kit knew them, too. Chances were higher, in fact, since Kit knew exactly who was in the business of not asking questions. And when he'd finally made it home from that other reality, Zin had said *your tall friend came by earlier this morning.*

Travis Alvey wasn't Kit's friend.

Especially not if he'd been the one to bring Laila and Aidan here. Kit didn't have proof, only suspicions. "Do you think the person might have messaged you beforehand? Is any of your tech in here?" Kit asked. "Maybe we could figure it out."

"They took it somewhere. I'm sure it's locked up far away from this room."

"Shit. I'm gonna get y'all out," Kit promised. "I just need to think."

"This place has fucked up the Nowhere somehow," Aidan said. "I didn't even know that was possible."

"I know. I feel it too. And there are these... ghosts. Or something. I keep getting knocked off course." Kit frowned. "But I feel okay now. I could try to get one of you out."

"If you only take one of us, they'll know something's up. They'll cover their tracks and move elsewhere," Aidan said. "Come back with someone else and take both of us at the same time. We can make it a few more days. We'll look out for each other."

That was what Laila had always said Aidan wanted to do with his union. Maybe Kit could stand to listen for once.

"Okay," Kit said. He tilted his head toward Aidan's IV. "You want me to take that out?"

Aidan shook his head. "They'll know if you do. And I'm fighting it."

"I'll be back as fast as I can."

[8]

EVERY PERSON FOR THEMSELVES

IT WOULD NEVER STOP FREAKING EMIL OUT, THE WAY runners could just vanish. He'd been cavalier with Kit about their encounter in the supply closet, and he didn't like to show fear in front of his team, but the truth was that the Nowhere scared him. He'd been worried, these past few months, that this secret cowardice was somehow preventing Heath and Winslow's trial from working on him. As if the Nowhere could sense his weakness, and it was rejecting him.

Worst of all, Emil was privately relieved by this rejection. He didn't want to spend any more time in the Nowhere.

And yet he was envious of Kit's ease with it, and Lenny's successful trial. It was a foolish kind of pride. He'd turned himself into an A student and a winning athlete. Why was he failing at such an important goal? Why couldn't he be the one who'd gained superpowers?

The footsteps that had caused Kit to run kept approaching, and eventually their owner came into sight. He was a young man Emil had never seen before, with wavy brown hair and blue eyes. He was strong-jawed and handsome in the way of classic movie stars, his face symmetrical and masculine, his shoulders square. He wasn't as tall or as big as Emil, but few people were. He would have looked at home in the Orbit Guard, but instead he was at Facility 17, presumably working for Quint Services.

"Hi," he said. "I'm Caleb Feldman. I just transferred here. I'm a nurse."

A stranger showing up meant it was time for Emil to be Team Leader. He'd been enjoying just sitting and listening to Kit—but Kit was gone. "I'm Emil. Please join us. Are you hungry?"

Caleb shook his head. "Just wired. Couldn't sleep and heard people talking. I hope I'm not interrupting?"

He was, but it wasn't his fault he'd landed in the middle of a mess. Emil opted for friendliness. "No, just a late-night chat among friends. This is Lenny and this is Dax."

"Where're you from, Caleb?" Lenny asked.

"Inland New York," Caleb said. "My grandparents hate it when I call it that and always complain that it's not 'the city' and it never will be. But it's also safe from the tide."

"Ha," Dax said. "So this'll feel pretty small, then."

Lenny laughed. "I'm from rural Arkansas and this place feels small."

"Even though you can look out the window and see the vastness of space?" Caleb asked. "Or the Moon up close?"

That was a good sign. Anyone who was romantic about space could probably get along with his team. And until they found evidence that they absolutely couldn't continue with the mission, Emil wanted harmony. "You're right," Emil said. "Can't beat the view. The people are alright, too. You wanna join us for hockey soccer tomorrow afternoon?"

"I'm sorry?" Caleb said, obviously fighting off a smile.

"Low-gravity asteroid hockey soccer," Lenny said, in his most serious voice. "Or as I like to call it, the beautiful game."

"Isn't that what people say about actual soccer?" Caleb asked.

"Shh," Dax said. "Don't tell him."

"Lenny is one of the originators," Emil said. "It can't really be explained, only experienced."

"It also can't be won," Dax warned. "So don't get your hopes up."

"We'll see about that," Caleb said. "So that's what you do for fun around here? Hockey soccer?"

"And science," Dax said.

"You get paid for the science," Lenny said.

"Still fun, though."

"Is it hard to be so far away from your friends and family?" Caleb asked. "What'd you say to them when you took this post?"

Emil was friends with his team. Sure, he had family on Earth, and a few old friends, but they were accustomed to him serving in the Orbit Guard. His parents and Zora knew they only got to see him occasionally, and that sometimes he couldn't tell them things. This was hardly a change at all.

Dax shrugged. "Most of the people I care about in the world are here."

Lenny nudged their shoulder, then fist-bumped them.

"We all signed up for an eventual mission to go even farther away," Emil said. "So we're not exactly a good sample. But I think it's natural to feel homesick. Are you missing someone in particular?"

Caleb lifted one shoulder. "Not really. I get along with my parents and my sister, but we're not that close. We'll be fine with some mail or a virtual visit every few weeks. When I told them I got this job, they congratulated me."

"'Sorry, Mom, I love space more than you,'" Dax joked.

"How long have you been working for Quint Services?" Emil asked.

"A few months," Caleb said. Emil was surprised by that, since Facility 17 was such a secret that only the highest ranks of Quint Services employees were aware of it. "I got a great evaluation and then pestered my supervisor about where the really exciting research was happening, and then just kept being so damn great at my job that finally they relented and sent me here." He flashed them a winning smile, and Dax and Lenny both returned it. "I'm so curious about Heath and Winslow's research. I did a lot of reading before I transferred up here, but it will be different to witness it in person. Are there any born runners up here to train you, in the event that the trials succeed?"

"No," Emil said as blandly as he possibly could. He hoped to God that Kit had made it out for real this time, for his own safety—even though that might mean never seeing him again. "Just us."

"That's a strange choice on Quint Services' part, don't you think?" Caleb pressed.

It was a touchy subject for a stranger to bring up in their first conversation. Dax and Lenny were reticent, waiting to follow Emil's lead. He was suspicious of this stranger, but he couldn't trust Quint Services, and honesty would keep things simple. Eventually, he said, "Yes. It is."

"Are you sure they didn't bring any runners in? As consultants or something?"

Caleb hadn't picked up on their reluctance to talk about this. Why was it so important to him? "Not to my knowledge," Emil said. "But I don't know everything."

"Wouldn't that be nice," Caleb said, gracing them with another easy smile. He was a good-looking man, and Emil wondered if he knew how charismatic he was. "Just wondering, you know. I had this friend, and back in the city—well, you know, Inland—they were always sending people around, trying to persuade him to join up. I thought they must be doing that all over. It's actually how I got interested in Quint Services in the first place. My friend didn't want anything to do with them, but after a while, the recruiter came around so much that I asked if they had any openings for medical personnel."

"Your friend was a runner?" Emil asked. The news that Quint Services was trying to recruit born runners was an interesting development, but he wasn't ready to let Caleb know just *how* interesting.

"Yeah," Caleb said. "Just a guy I know, really. We were roommates for a while. Aidan."

"Wait, Aidan *Blackwood*?" Dax asked. "That agent provocateur type? Quint Services tried to recruit *him*?"

Emil didn't miss the flicker of interest in Caleb's face. It was gone by the time he replied, nonchalantly, "Oh, you've heard of him."

"I think he came up in my research on runners," Lenny said. "Kind of an agitator, right?"

"You don't know him from the news?" Dax asked Lenny and Emil, disapproving. "Just because we're not on Earth doesn't give us license to ignore everything that's going on. Aidan Blackwood was in that photo that was circulating all over Elevate and other social media last month, the one of a young man getting knocked out by a cop. He jumped into Franklin Station wearing a t-shirt that said 'BORDERS DON'T EXIST' and started making an unauthorized speech in the commons."

"Yeah, that's Aidan." Caleb glanced at the three of them, suddenly uncomfortable. He must have realized that Emil and Lenny were former Orbit Guard personnel. It had never been his job to bust runners, or Lenny's, but Miriam had worked station security. She'd spent most of her time dealing with bomb threats made by Adamah—a religious extremist group that didn't believe humans should live in space—but she'd probably encountered her fair share of runners.

When Dax had described that photo of Aidan getting knocked out by "a cop," they'd meant Orbit Guard station security. Miriam wouldn't have done that to Aidan, if she'd been the one on duty. His memory flashed to her elbow pressing into Kit's throat, and he frowned. But she hadn't really hurt him, and she'd been trying to protect Emil from a perceived threat. Still, he gained some sympathy for Caleb's discomfort.

Emil had always found the anti-runner attitudes of others in the Orbit Guard distasteful, and he didn't like being lumped in with them. Would Kit feel the same way as Caleb or Aidan? Would he have reason to fear and distrust Emil?

"I think what he's doing is important," Emil said, and Dax and Lenny nodded their agreement.

Caleb still looked like he regretted bringing it up.

"It's late," Emil said, offering him an exit strategy from the conversation.

"Yeah," Caleb agreed. "I'll see you all tomorrow."

———

"HOCKEY SOCCER IS ALWAYS PLAYED with a beverage in hand," Chávez explained to Caleb while Lenny uncapped his beer and handed it to him with as much ceremony as possible. "An empty beverage is a penalty of negative one thousand points."

Caleb raised his eyebrows.

"Not drinking is also a penalty of negative one thousand points," Chávez continued.

"Hockey soccer is more of a drinking game than a sport," Emil said to Caleb.

"Disrespecting the game!" Chávez intoned. "Negative one thousand points."

"How is that disrespecting the game? It's just the truth," Emil said.

"Implying that hockey soccer is not a sport is disrespectful," Lenny said. "Implying that drinking games are somehow inferior to sports is also disrespectful."

"So that's negative two thousand points," Chávez said. She tsked. "You are not starting this game off well, Mr. Singh."

"Emil holds the all-time low score," Miriam said to Caleb. "I think it was negative forty-seven thousand."

"A low score like that is only possible in one-on-one. Hockey soccer is usually played in teams, but players are scored individually, and a team can vote to disavow players who damage their scores," Chávez said, adopting her most officious tone. "Three-on-three is traditional here at Facility 17."

Emil had offered to sit this game out to make the teams even, but apparently that didn't exempt him from receiving his usual punitively low score. Chávez and Lenny just liked to razz him because he was team leader—and because early on, he'd made the mistake of revealing how competitive he was, which meant they'd never, ever let him win. Since then, Emil had lost points for all of the following: drinking too slow, drinking too fast, spilling his beer, kicking the puck out of bounds, kicking the puck perfectly straight, sighing, having "beautiful, glossy, shampoo-ad-worthy ebony locks," laughing, not laughing, having "distractingly chiseled abs," and breathing. Lenny and Chávez had also once docked him points for "being too scrupulous a rule-follower, which is against the spirit of hockey soccer, and therefore *disrespecting the game*." But they'd also once awarded him one thousand points "for trying adorably hard" and five thousand "for being so fun to fuck with." So he still played. Besides, there was nothing else to do at Facility 17 on Sunday afternoons. And they were his team.

Today, the six people on the court had split themselves up into two groups. Chávez, Jake, and Miriam were on one team, while Lenny, Dax, and Caleb were on the other. Lenny finished distributing their beers and they arranged themselves on the court.

"It might start as three-on-three, but it always becomes one-on-one because there's a rush to betray each other at the end," Miriam warned Caleb.

"Disrespecting the game!" Lenny said. "The every-man-for-himself aspect of hockey soccer is a cherished part of our tradition."

Miriam, Chávez, and Dax shared a dark glance.

"Apologies. I meant to say the every-*person*-for-themselves aspect."

"Negative one thousand to Miriam Horowitz, disrespecting the game; negative one thousand to Lennox Malcolm Beck III, being kind of an asshole; five hundred to Lennox Malcolm Beck III, apologizing with grace and style," Chávez said.

"If 'being kind of an asshole' is against the rules, this game ought to be scored wildly differently," Miriam said.

"Negative one thousand to Miriam Horowitz, disrespecting the game!" Lenny boomed, pointing at her. She cocked her head and stared him down, unrepentant.

Emil walked between the two teams, placed the puck on the court, and said, "Start already." Then he got out of the way fast.

Chávez kicked it down the court before the other team could blink, but as she pushed past Lenny, Lenny grabbed her by one shoulder and leapfrogged over her head. This was Emil's favorite part of this absurd ritual—turning the artificial gravity down low to allow for inhumanly high jumps. Lenny came down in seeming slow-motion, cradling his beer to his chest. He caught the puck with the edge of his foot and turned its progress around by sliding it to Caleb.

Their new friend looked delighted to be included, but Jake got in his space and stole the puck before he could get far. Jake passed to Miriam, who sent it sailing down the court into the soccer goal at the end.

"Two thousand to Jacob McCreery for cat-burglary levels of stealth, three thousand to Miriam Horowitz for that beautiful shot, five hundred to Caleb whatever-your-last-name-is for bringing some fresh-faced optimism into this tragically jaded crowd, and ten thousand to Lennox Malcolm Beck III for leapfrogging me and not spilling a drop!"

"My last name is Feldman," Caleb said. "And how come only Lenny gets a middle name and a suffix like that?"

"Because he's three times cooler than the rest of us," Chávez said, retrieving the puck as the others rearranged themselves mid-court.

"If you're wondering if it's a conflict of interest for one of the players to officiate and announce the game like that," Dax said in an aside to Caleb, "it is."

"Disrespecting the game!" Chávez and Lenny said in unison. Chávez added, "Negative one thousand to Dax Strickland."

Dax took a drink, which was really the only thing to do in that situation, since shaking their head or rolling their eyes would likely have resulted in further penalties. They played another point, and Caleb, having caught on, managed to leapfrog Miriam and take possession of the puck. There were cheers all around. He passed to Dax, who scored a goal. That would have tied the match in any normal game, but Emil knew better than to point that out.

"Refill," Chávez called out and left the court. She sat at the table with Emil and took her time getting a second beer. "You alright?"

"Why wouldn't I be?"

"Dunno. Did something happen with that purple-haired runner? I haven't seen you look at anybody like that since I caught you being a maudlin drunk looking at photos of your exes. And I don't see him around today..." Chávez let this sentence hang in the air like a question.

He didn't sigh, even though he wished she'd never seen him looking at pictures of Lucas. Or had it been Rose? If he'd been drunk enough, it had probably been both.

"Maybe I'm not alright because our head researcher is missing or dead and the whole damn facility feels haunted," Emil said. It was a transparent attempt to change the subject. Chávez was trying to make him feel better, offering him a chance to talk about his feelings. But Emil didn't have feelings to talk about. Or he didn't *want* to have feelings, which wasn't exactly the same, but they'd go away if he ignored them. This was a wiser course of action than seeking advice from Chávez, who fell into bed so easily that she was sleeping with Dr. Heath.

"So you admit you're not alright," Chávez said.

It would be stupid to mope about Kit, a person he'd known for just over twenty-four hours. *A person you kissed*, his brain reminded him, but he shoved that thought away. Emil smiled, huffed, and shook his head. "I'm fine. Go play your game, Chávez."

"Ignoring a friendly attempt to check on your emotional wellbeing, negative one thousand," Chávez said, wagging a finger. But she left Emil alone.

There was more aerial play in the third point as Caleb got the hang of the low gravity. He scored "an elegant and worthy five-thousand point goal," but spilled his beer in the process, which carried a penalty of "negative five thousand points and shame heaped upon you from all sides," and he shot a look of sympathy at Emil as he began to understand how rigged the game was.

"Can I assign points for things?" Caleb asked.

"Of course," Chávez said. "Just follow the rules."

"Uh huh," Caleb said, skeptical.

Emil watched them play a few more points and completely lost track of the score. But it was a pleasant, if ridiculous, distraction, and he liked watching his friends enjoy themselves. After Chávez's little chat, the rest of them came over on their refill breaks, one by one, to speak with him about different things. This wasn't so different from other Sunday afternoons. Their regular match provided reason enough to be together— everyone, including Heath and Winslow and their six lab techs, had been invited to hockey soccer in the beginning, but its chaotic and arbitrary nature drove away all but the core mission team, who happened to be Chávez and Lenny's closest friends. Emil knew that was probably by design, and in his role as the team's grown-up, he ought to guard against the forming of cliques at the facility. It could lead to tension among the residents.

But there was tension among the residents now for other, far more urgent reasons, and if these people were a clique, they were *his* clique, and today it was convenient that nobody else wanted to be around them. The echoing basketball court covered up these private conversations, such as when Dax informed him that Lenny was going to jump the two of them into Lange's lab at four in the morning.

"Don't come," they said. "We'll be in and out as fast as we can. I'm just letting you know in case of emergency."

"I'd rather go with you," Emil said.

"Lenny can only jump one person at a time and a regular break-in will be harder to hide," Dax said. "I'm the one who can come closest to understanding Lange's notes and Lenny's the one who can get me in and out. It makes sense. Don't argue."

Emil frowned at them. "Fine."

"I'm hoping to find out more about the poltergeist," Dax added.

Jake, who'd just arrived at the table where they were sitting, shook his head. "I can't believe that name stuck." He filled his cup. Dax returned to the court, letting Jake have his turn, but Emil didn't expect him to take advantage of the opportunity. Jake usually just got another beer and gave Emil a friendly nod.

Today he had something to say, though. "They're not scary."

"Wait, 'they'? Why do you think there's more than one polt—"

Lenny walked up right at that moment, just in time to over-hear. He clapped Jake on the shoulder. "Uh huh. You're not scared of ghosts. Good for you, Jake. You're the manliest of all."

Jake grimaced and walked back onto the court without saying anything. Had he been on the verge of elaborating? Emil wondered what else he'd wanted to say.

"It's different when you can see them," Lenny said, defending himself to Emil.

"It's pretty creepy when you can't see them, too," Emil admitted. "All the weird noises, all the things falling over, I think I got used to telling myself it was no big deal. I learned to shrug it off. Then witnessing Kit's reaction reminded me how eerie it is."

"Yeah. I wish I'd gotten to ask him more questions." Lenny glanced at Caleb, currently being chased down the court by Jake and Miriam, and then back at Emil. "What do you think of him?"

Caleb's arrival in the kitchen last night had spurred Kit's departure, and all the worst parts of Emil resented him for it.

"He seems sweet. Maybe even naive. I'm not planning to reveal any secrets to him, but I don't think he'll harm us."

"He's a fucking star on the court," Lenny said, raising his voice so he could be heard across the room and lifting his beer toward his teammates.

"Stop talking and get your ass over here!" Dax demanded.

"Yeah," Caleb said. He beamed at Dax, then pointed at Lenny. "Abandoning your teammates to chat feels a lot like *disrespecting the game!*"

"Sustained! Negative one thousand points to Lennox Malcolm Beck III!" Chávez yelled. Lenny laughed and ducked his head and ran back to the court, where play resumed. Emil smiled, but he couldn't keep his focus on the court. He'd have to get up at four in the morning, just in case Dax and Lenny needed him. And he'd have to approach Jake privately and ask him what it was he'd wanted to say about the ghosts.

[9]

INTENTIONS

KIT STEPPED INTO THE NOWHERE, BUT HE WASN'T FAST enough to dodge the monster. The big one slammed into him and they popped right back into the world. Or Kit did, anyway. The monster didn't follow him out. Kit pushed himself upright and rubbed the back of his head. The white walls and floors looked the same as the rest of Facility 17, so he assumed he hadn't gone far. The room was a wreck. There were overturned tables and broken computers on the floor. One wall must have had a series of rectangular windows looking out into the hallway, but the glass had all been smashed, and now there was just brown paper taped over the empty spaces. There were signs on the metal door with warning symbols. *Keep closed at all times.* Across from Kit, the back half of the room was open, with no tables or chairs or debris. There were two large metal instruments, curved like parentheses, the opening one on the left and the closing one on the right of the room.

All the wrongness he'd sensed elsewhere in Facility 17 was concentrated there. The currents he could normally feel in the Nowhere slowed to a crawl and became irregular. He reached out with a hand—here, he could feel them, but six inches to the left, they were gone.

Or he thought it was six inches. His hand and his eyes disagreed. He saw his hand move six inches, but he felt it move way farther than that. The space inside the room was distributed all wrong, stretched in some places and squeezed in others.

This was Dr. Lange's lab.

It was as though the explosion that had rocked this room had fragmented the Nowhere. Now invisible shards of it hung all around him. Kit shuddered to think of what it might feel like on the other side of the large room, in between those menacing instruments. Luckily, the other side of the room might as well have been ten miles away.

Had the thing brought him here? Did it have intentions? Or was it just some glitch in the Nowhere resulting from whatever had gone wrong in this room? Kit didn't know and he didn't care to find out. He'd promised to get Aidan and Laila out of Facility 17, and the stomach-knotting wrongness of this room wasn't helping him toward that goal. This wasn't his problem.

He took a breath to settle himself, closed his eyes, and reopened them in the Nowhere—only to get tangled with the thing and forced back into the world, somewhere bright and loud and full of people. A terminal? A mall? Kit blinked, disoriented. Just as in the lab, he had a moment of wondering if the thing had been trying to follow him *out*. He had a strange sense-memory of... as if it had tried to grab him and hold on. But it had no hands. Or did it? Its shifting, ghostly form did seem to have appendages sometimes, and it felt solid enough when it attacked him.

No matter. It was nowhere to be seen. Kit left before anyone could ask if he needed help getting up from the floor.

The thing had to be waiting for him. It was on him in an

instant. Kit kicked and shoved, trying to get away and free himself, but only ended up twisting himself around and getting forced, face-first, back into the world somewhere. He flailed, grappling with a monster that was no longer there. There was sunlight and blue sky and air—and Kit would have been grateful that there was air, since getting popped out of the Nowhere and into the void of space seemed more and more likely, but there was *only* air.

No ground, no trees, no buildings, no nothing. He was falling. The wind ripped at his clothes. He risked a glance down and saw a city in miniature below, its tiny grid of roads and structures a blip in the surrounding green farmland.

Shit.

There was only one choice: back into the Nowhere. The strain of it dragged at every muscle and his brain groaned in protest, but it saved him from splattering on the ground.

It didn't save him from the thing, which attacked again. Kit wanted to scream, but he'd jumped into the Nowhere five times in a day. He didn't have the energy to run from the thing, let alone scream at it. They spent what felt like days hurtling through the void—sideways, forward, backward, up, down, Kit couldn't tell—until they plunged into a different kind of darkness, the icy water of some unknown ocean. Kit struggled, thinking the thing might have come with him into whatever world this was, but there was only the water and the darkness and the pressure, pushing into his lungs. He couldn't see anything, but reaching out with all his limbs only got him tangled in some ropy, slimy plant. It didn't get him any closer to air. Which way was the surface? *Was* there a surface? He needed air too much to think. He'd die if he didn't open his mouth, but there was only water.

When he blinked back into the Nowhere, he was alone. The sudden lack of pressure let his lungs expand, but he still couldn't seem to breathe or focus. Soaked, shivering, none of his senses or his limbs working, his brain a quivering mass of useless jelly, he let himself drop through the void.

———

KIT MATERIALIZED in mid-air in Emil's room and thudded to floor with a squelch. Emil dropped his book and jumped out of bed, crouching over Kit, who was freezing to the touch and wrapped in some kind of kelp. Seawater puddled beneath him.

"Kit!"

Kit coughed up water. Emil began chest compressions, firm and steady, clearing his brain of anything except the count. Twenty-eight, twenty-nine, thirty. He tilted Kit's head back, pinched his nose, covered his mouth and blew into it. Another round of compressions. Another breath. Then Kit's arms shot up and pushed at him, and he rolled to the side and coughed up more water on Emil's floor. He gasped for breath, his purple hair dripping into his face and his whole body trembling.

No time to consider it. Emil pulled off his waterlogged boots, peeled him out of his clothes, toweled his hair and the rest of him as best he could, and deposited him in bed. He stripped and crawled under the blanket, pressing himself against Kit, reassuring himself with the sound of his heartbeat and his breath. Where on Earth—or maybe that was the wrong expression. Where had he been? It had been a whole day since they'd last seen each other in the kitchen. Why had Kit jumped back here? What had brought him so close to drowning?

The thing. He must have run into it again. Emil lifted his head slightly and looked over Kit's shoulder to his room beyond. In the wet pile of Kit's things left on the floor, there was a long rope of some kind of dark green-brown seaweed. He'd have to examine it once he could be sure Kit wasn't hypothermic. Kit felt so small curled against him, freezing. He wasn't quivering anymore and instead was perfectly still. Emil wanted to rub his hands into Kit's cold skin, but he'd been trained not to. Kit had to warm himself up slowly. So Emil resisted his impulses and tried to feel secure in the knowledge that Kit was alive.

"You scared me," he murmured, unsure if Kit could hear him. Kit was certainly drowsy and out of it, if not fully asleep. "But I'm so glad you came back."

Kit had come here in a panic, fearing for his life. When they'd returned from the desert together, he'd brought them both to his own room, but tonight he'd come here. With no chance to plan or time to focus, his first thought of safety had been *Emil*. Even with Kit's chilled body pressed into him and leaching out his body heat, the thought made Emil warm. Kit had sidestepped Lenny's question about whether it was possible to jump to a person, but his arrival tonight was answer enough.

"I missed you," he told Kit. "I know you were only gone a day and we barely know each other, but... I missed you. Please be okay."

He could never have said that while looking Kit in the eye and worrying about how he'd respond. But lying in bed, under the soft light of his reading lamp, with Kit facing away from him, it was easy to speak the truth. In this suspended, anonymous moment, it was even possible to lean over and impulsively drop a kiss on Kit's temple.

When he settled back into bed behind Kit, his heart was hammering. He shouldn't have done that. *Why* had he done that?

Emil stayed quiet, listening to Kit's body in the silence of his room. Resuscitating Kit had terrified him and Emil was too worried and wired to fall asleep, but he could stay here with an arm slung over the dip of his waist and a hand against his heart.

Kit was asleep now, not about to vanish again, and Emil let his thoughts drift.

I haven't seen you look at anybody like that since... Chávez had said. It was funny to hear it, since Emil didn't feel like he'd looked at his previous partners any particular way. And Kit had nothing in common with either of them. He was so much younger, first of all, and instead of having a professional career, he made his living in a shadowy, cash-only criminal underworld. Rose and Lucas had both been Emil's age. Rose had been a graphic designer and Lucas had been a doctor. His parents had been delighted with both of them—proof that Emil was on the right track at last.

Rose and Lucas weren't the only people he'd ever had relationships with. There'd been two people in the five years since Lucas dumped him, but Chávez didn't know about Ella and Marco. They'd both been casual, no-strings arrangements in the year after the break-up, and Emil's nightmares had featured broken condoms and broken hearts during and after those liaisons. He wasn't cut out for casual.

He hadn't really been cut out for relationships, either, according to Lucas and Rose—no matter how good it had all looked on paper. He'd dated Rose for two years in his early twenties. She'd even moved to Franklin Station so she wouldn't have to take the elevator up whenever she wanted to see him. But he'd been working long hours, and she'd found someone else to occupy her time. She'd cried when she'd confessed, as if she were the victim. *I can't believe I did that to you*, she'd told Emil. *You're so perfect.*

Emil didn't like to remember that moment. Not because he'd been gutted, although it had hurt plenty. But even then, he'd known that if he'd spent more time with her, things might have gone differently. He'd made his choices and his career had won out. In a way, he'd left her a long time before she'd left him.

A perfect person wouldn't have done that. He'd failed. He wasn't perfect. Still, he hated how Rose had made *perfect* sound like an accusation. Like it was a reason to sleep with somebody else.

He'd taken up with Lucas for another two-year relationship —that was Emil's romantic expiration date, two years—soon after. There hadn't been any cheating in that one, but Lucas had essentially said *you're so perfect* and exited stage left.

"You checked off all these goals from your list—your education, your career—and now you want to check off 'relationship,'" Lucas had said. "And you're doing everything right! Almost. It's like somebody gave you a lecture on being a good boyfriend and you made yourself a to-do list. *Kiss Lucas when he comes home from work.* Check. *Make him dinner.* Check. *Have sex.* Check."

Emil hadn't understood what was wrong with his behavior then, and he still didn't.

"I have a terrible feeling that if I let you, you'd just stay with me forever out of some sense of duty. You do everything you're supposed to, and God, an awful little part of me wants to keep letting you do it, but I can't. Are you in love with me, Emil?"

"Of course." Lucas was good-looking and good in bed and they had a comfortable life together and Emil had no idea why he was making such a fuss.

Lucas had narrowed his eyes. "Are you saying that because it's what you're supposed to say?"

"I don't know what you mean!"

"Are you happy, Emil? Really think about it."

Emil hadn't been able to say anything. He didn't feel unhappy, exactly. But he supposed he didn't really feel happy, either. He'd never thought about it—no, that wasn't true. He specifically tried not to think about it. Because when the time came, he couldn't say yes.

"Right," Lucas had sighed, when the silence had grown overwhelming. "That's not really fair to either of us, then, is it?"

Emil hadn't argued. He'd been sad when both Rose and Lucas had left him. Looking back on it through the prism of what they'd said, he wondered now if it hadn't been a checklist kind of sadness—the expected follow-up to the loss of his dull, empty, checklist happiness. He hadn't cried. He hadn't thought of them longingly after the fact. He'd just numbly gone on with his life. Maybe that made him a soulless robot or an empty husk of a person, but he'd come to terms with that. Feelings were chaotic and terrifying and inconvenient. Advancing his career came more easily to him, and luckily, being single and childless had made him an excellent candidate for Quint Services' mission. Who wanted feelings when there were trips to undiscovered realities to be had?

Kit stirred against him.

Yeah. You'd be the most chaotic, terrifying, and inconvenient of all. Kit was all wrong for him. He couldn't bring a criminal home to meet Zora and his parents. And yet Emil had never felt anything like what he'd felt when Kit grabbed him and kissed him. His brain replayed that moment on a loop any time Kit was near him, as if thinking hard enough about it would make it happen again.

Kit felt warm against him. How long had they been lying here? Emil had lost track of time.

When Kit had vanished last night, all Emil could think about was how nothing like that kiss would ever happen again. It was a foolish thing to want—they were both caught in the middle of something incomprehensible and neither of them could afford distractions—and yet he wanted it anyway. That was the nature of want. It was the nature of all feelings to run wild, free from the constraints of logic and reason. Emil knew better than to want Kit. But not only could he not *stop* wanting, he also kept finding himself in situations that stretched the limits of his self-control. Situations where they had to touch each other. Sometimes without their clothes on. In bed.

And yet again, just like in the desert, Kit was vulnerable and not in control of all his faculties. Emil had to be the responsible one. It was his job to control himself. To behave morally.

Even if Kit stirred again and snuggled closer, even if he rubbed up against—

Emil couldn't finish that thought. He jerked his hips backward, putting space between them. Kit moved again, compressing the space between them to nothing. Emil bit his lip and closed his eyes and tried very hard not to be aware of his body, which was behaving decidedly against his wishes.

Kit murmured something. Was he sleep-talking?

"Pardon?" Emil said.

"I said, that's not where I wanted you to kiss me," Kit said.

Emil hadn't kissed—oh no. He had. He'd given in to a ridiculous impulse to kiss Kit's temple because he'd thought he was unconscious. But Kit was awake now and he'd been awake then and now Emil was caught.

"And don't tell me you didn't want to," Kit said, undeterred by Emil's long silence. He sounded entirely too pleased with himself. Emil had to work faster to compile a convincing list of reasons that they shouldn't, *couldn't* move forward with any of this. Kit continued, "I have a state-of-the-art lie detector."

And then he rubbed his ass against Emil's hard-on.

Emil experienced a second of perfect, thoughtless bliss—the softness of skin, the warmth, the pressure, the friction—before coming back to himself. "Kit, this isn't a good idea."

He tried to put on his most serious tone of voice, but it wavered a little. Kit had a fucking nice ass. And they were both so, so naked.

"That feels like a lie." Kit slid his body against Emil's, up and down and torturously slow. "A *big* lie."

"Please," Emil said, and he wasn't sure what he was asking for. He couldn't bring himself to say *please stop*, not when Kit was still writhing against him and telling him how big his dick was. God, but he was ridiculous.

Kit lost the wickedness in his tone, stilled, and said, "Emil, I almost died at least twice today, and my prospects for tomorrow aren't great. There is nothing you can say that will make me not want this. The only question now is whether you'll let yourself have it."

"Wait, what do you mean, your prospects for tomorrow aren't great?"

Kit sighed, impatient. "Almost every time I entered the Nowhere, that thing found me. It feels a lot like it's trying to kill me. Now, back to the topic at hand. You can take that as literally as you want, by the way."

Emil's hand was still positioned over Kit's heart. Kit laid his hand over Emil's and moved their hands suggestively downward.

"You must have been in and out of the Nowhere for hours, fighting with that thing. Aren't you tired?" It was a desperate, last-ditch evasive maneuver, and Kit wasn't fooled.

"Yes, I'm tired. And hungry. But as previously mentioned, I'm also not *dead*."

"Kit, we—"

"Do you not like me?" Kit demanded. "Because that's not what it feels like right now."

Emil was prepared to evade, but not to lie outright. Still, his voice didn't make it much above a mumble when he said, "I like you." The confession was so inadequate, it was absurd.

"You stopped us before and you're trying to stop us now. What are you so afraid of?"

This. Everything. You. "You were high the first time! And you were barely conscious when you showed up tonight! I can't take advantage of you, Kit."

"I'm awake and alert and I'll recite the alphabet backward if you want," Kit said. "Trust me, you're not taking advantage. I don't know how much more clearly I can express myself."

In the quiet that followed, Emil sifted through all of his panicked objections and settled on saying, "I don't usually do this."

"Yeah, well, me neither. I also don't usually get chased into the depths of the ocean and almost-drowned by a physics ghost," Kit said. "It's not a *usual* kind of day. The question is—do you want to?"

It was like the moment when Lucas had finally asked him if he was happy. A heart-pounding silence and then the truth. But it was nothing like that moment, because this time, Emil said, "Yes."

By some miracle, he managed not to say *what does this mean for us* or *promise you won't vanish afterward* or any of two dozen other inappropriate things. By a second, wildly undeserved miracle, Kit twisted around to face him, threaded his fingers into Emil's hair, and kissed him, quieting the racket in his brain. This, Emil could do. His partners had always been clear on that point. Pleasing people in bed was just one more skill that could be learned through practice and patience, and Emil was a good student.

The concrete immediacy of it was familiar and reassuring. They fit their lips together and Emil let his tongue slip against Kit's. As they kissed, he drew his hands down Kit's lithe body, around the dip of his waist and the curve of his ass. Even exhausted, Kit was adorably reactive, clenching his hands in Emil's hair and moaning into his mouth when Emil trailed one hand down his hipbone and into the crease of his thigh. He hadn't touched Kit's cock yet, but one glance down proved it was already straining and eager, wet at the tip.

The sight inspired Emil to break their kiss, although he couldn't resist kissing his way along the sharp edge of Kit's jawbone, or sucking a kiss into the tender skin just below his ear. Kit gasped at the graze of Emil's teeth, and he liked the sound of it. He bit the side of Kit's neck and was rewarded again. Tracking kisses over his collarbone and down his bare chest and belly made him squirm, and brushing his lips over the tip of Kit's cock elicited a throaty "*Fuck.*"

Emil couldn't even think about how hard he was. If Kit touched him—maybe even if Kit didn't touch him—this could all be over embarrassingly fast.

When Emil finally wrapped his hand around the base, Kit bucked his hips. Emil lowered his mouth over Kit's cock, sliding down until his lips met his hand. He moved his hand and his head in concert, slicking Kit down, then sliding up until he could run his tongue over the slit at the head. Kit's hands fisted tightly in his hair, not pushing or pulling but just hanging on for the ride.

Emil loved giving head. He loved tasting Kit, feeling the weight of his cock on his tongue, listening to him breathe and whimper. And he loved making himself wait, growing harder and harder with every tiny twitch of Kit's body.

With his free hand, he cupped Kit's balls. He reached under with his middle finger, rubbing the sensitive skin there, pressing against it. Kit thrust hard into his mouth when he did that, his hips snapping forward of their own accord, so Emil moved his finger down ever so slightly, until he was circling the rim of Kit's hole. Kit gripped his hair almost painfully hard at that touch. A little pressure and Kit was groaning and spilling into his mouth, hot and salty.

"Fuck, *fuck*," Kit said. "You are so fucking good at that."

Emil swallowed and kissed Kit's cock, flush with triumph. He laid his head on Kit's belly. All the blood in his body and all the thoughts in his head flowed down to his own erection, which was pointing straight up toward his navel, dripping and aching. One or two strokes and he'd go off. Even the thought of Kit's fingers brushing the length was almost too much.

Kit tugged at his shoulders, urging him to move back up the bed, and Emil went. When he arrived, Kit kissed him deeply, not caring about the taste in his mouth. He stopped for a moment, his hands in Emil's hair and his dark gaze fixed on Emil. "Wow, you're just... wow," he said, breathless and dazzled. "I don't even think you know how beautiful you are. I want to make you come."

He reached down between them and wrapped his slender, clever fingers around Emil's cock. He slicked it down in one stroke. Emil took a shuddering breath. "Slow," he pleaded. "I'm not going to last."

Kit slowed his hand. He slid up Emil's length at a glacial pace. "Yeah?" he asked. "You loved sucking me off that much?"

"Yes," Emil said, his eyes closed. Kit's hand felt so fucking good. It had been a damn long time since anyone else had touched him. Kit was slow and delicate and Emil was already wrecked, quivering in anticipation. He wanted the end but he never wanted this to end. He could hear his own breath catch.

"Beautiful," Kit murmured, tracing Emil's bottom lip with his thumb. He'd done the same thing when they'd been in the desert, and the memory came over Emil in a hot rush: how ready Kit had been, how pushy, how much he'd wanted Emil. Sober, Kit wasn't much different. He still stroked Emil's cock like it was his favorite thing he'd ever touched. "Will you come for me?" he asked, slipping his thumb into Emil's mouth so there was only one way to answer.

Emil's orgasm ran through him right then, a burst of plea-sure that left him shaking and spurting into Kit's hand.

"Fuck," Kit said appreciatively. He leaned over to drop a kiss on Emil's temple.

Then instead of settling back into bed, he let go of Emil and bolted upright. "Fuck," he said, in a completely different tone. It shook Emil out of his languor. "Something is really wrong."

[10]

A TREMOR

SOMETHING WAS WRONG WITH THE NOWHERE. OR something had been wrong, and now it was far, far worse. Kit had felt a shift. He was caught between a reckless urge to run toward it to find out what it was and a more sensible urge to run back to Earth—but he couldn't go into the Nowhere, not after the day he'd had. Even if he had the strength, that thing would find him.

At least he didn't have to die without knowing what Emil sounded like when he came. He'd never had sex like that in his life. It felt like the first time he'd ever had sex, period. He'd sucked off Travis Alvey plenty of times, but that felt like something they did to pass the time. It was always very clear what was between them: Kit put his mouth on Travis's dick in exchange for the same. It was a quick, easy way to an orgasm. Once, Kit had tried to kiss Travis—just for fun, not for any gooey feelings—and Travis had grimaced and pulled away. Sometimes he weaseled out of reciprocating the sex, too. But Emil had treated cocksucking like an art or an act of prayer, something he did for its own sake, something he took joy in. And he'd wanted to kiss Kit.

Kit touched his lips. He hadn't known it could be like that. The memory was almost good enough to distract Kit from the world falling apart around him.

Emil was already out of bed and pulling on sweatpants and a t-shirt. He tossed something at Kit. Kit didn't reach out in time and caught the fabric with his face instead of his hands. When he pulled it off his face, it became clear that it was a t-shirt. It was, in fact, the t-shirt Emil had been wearing on Saturday night when he'd introduced Kit to the team. It was white with the Quint Services logo printed on the front in black, and Kit was simultaneously enticed by putting on Emil's t-shirt and repelled by putting on *this* one. Aidan and Laila were still in that room, strapped into their hospital beds, slowly starving.

Does Emil know? The thought hit Kit hard. He'd assumed no, since Emil seemed so moral and upstanding. But Emil still worked for Quint Services, which was anything but.

There was no time for this. Emil said, "Tell me where we need to go."

"Lange's lab." It was the only possible answer.

"Shit," Emil said. "Dax and Lenny are breaking in there tonight—right now, actually."

Kit pulled on the t-shirt, which fit him like a tent, and then picked up the pair of gym shorts Emil had tossed onto the bed. They had a drawstring waist but were still comically large on him. He wouldn't be caught dead in this outfit normally, but today was a day for *not* getting caught dead. Emil tossed one more thing at him, and Kit dodged on impulse. It was an energy bar of some kind and it landed harmlessly on the bed.

"You need to eat, right?" Emil asked.

Kit nodded, grateful. How had Emil even remembered that, with so much else going on? He picked it up, unwrapped it, and bit into it as he hurried out of the room after Emil.

Emil had put on sneakers, but Kit hadn't forced his saltwater-encrusted boots back onto his feet, so he was barefoot. The lab was only a short way down the corridor. The thought of that room made him shudder, and yet he went anyway. Emil wasn't a runner. He couldn't know how wrong it was in there. He was stupid—and brave, but mostly stupid—and Kit had to go be not-stupid for him.

Emil proved this chain of thought remarkably on point by saying, "Listen, I've been thinking, and next time you encounter that thing, don't run from it."

"If you had time to think, I must not have done a very good job," Kit joked, but it came out sounding tired. He ached everywhere and this speed-walk down the hallway was making him regret not staying in bed. Fear alone was keeping him upright and mobile.

"I'm serious," Emil said. "If you keep running, you'll have to run forever. You have to grab it and find out more about it—or fight it, or even kill it, if you can—or you'll never solve the problem."

"Have we *met*? Do I look like I could fight off anything?" Kit asked. "Running away is my best and only skill. And why do *I* have to solve the problem? Maybe if I wait, it'll go away. Or someone else will solve it for me."

Emil scrunched up his face, puzzled by that attitude, but they rounded a corner and it gave Kit a moment to change the subject. "What if Heath and Winslow are at the lab? Maybe I'm not the only one who knows something is wrong."

"If they want to touch you, they'll have to go through me."

While flattering and a little bit thrilling, that didn't entirely settle Kit's stomach. There was too much uncertainty.

Kit recognized the papered-over windows of the lab from the outside. He could see shadows silhouetted against the paper and at least one of them was frantically waving its arms. He counted three people inside, having a conversation in urgent whispers. That was already bad—Emil had only mentioned Dax and Lenny. Who was the third person?

Emil knocked softly at the door and the whispers stopped.

Then he tried the door handle and the door swung open, unlocked. He walked inside and his team regarded him in silence. Their expressions changed when Kit entered, and they took in Kit's outfit—the too-wide collar of his t-shirt made it easy to see the marks on his neck—without a word.

The third person in the room was the big, quiet, blond guy. Jake? For some reason, he was holding a fat tuxedo cat. Its pupils were huge and its fur was standing on end, but it didn't meow.

"Why was the door unlocked?" Emil said in a low voice. "And what is Jake doing here?"

"We were asking the same thing!" Dax hissed.

"It doesn't matter," Kit cut in. "Y'all have to get out of here *now*."

"Why?" Dax asked. "I haven't had a chance to go through Dr. Lange's notes yet."

"Can you not see how fucked up this room is?" Kit asked. "Watch." Maybe they hadn't noticed yet. The room was contaminated by the Nowhere, but it was uneven. Some of the space behaved normally. But Kit had been here earlier and he could still feel those pockets of stretchy space.

The mess in the lab served him well, since he could just pluck a notebook from the floor. There was something obscene in the way it had been lying there with its pages fanned out, folded at odd angles, and Kit couldn't stop himself from smoothing them and closing the cover. But then he raised his arm and lobbed it into the air. There was a pocket of disturbed space in front of him, about seven feet off the ground, and the notebook hung there for ten seconds before falling back to the ground in a rustle of crumpled pages.

"Holy shit," Lenny said. "The Nowhere is leaking."

"This is like a fault line," Kit said, seeking an analogy. "And we ran over here because I felt a tremor. Probably when you jumped into the room."

"So let's get out of here," Emil said. "Jake can explain about the cat later."

Dax picked up the dropped notebook and then started opening drawers and pulling out others. "Lange didn't trust anyone," they said. "Everything unpublished is on paper and only paper."

Emil knelt next to them and picked up some of the stacks piling up on the floor, and Lenny followed his lead. Kit shifted. What part of *get out of here now* didn't they understand? He should run, and yet he stayed.

Out of the corner of his eye, he caught a flash of blue light. The cat in Jake's arms let out a loud meow. Kit whipped his head to stare at the back of the room, but there was nothing. When he turned back to check on Emil's team, Lenny was staring at him. "You saw that, right?"

"Yeah," Kit said.

"What is it?" Emil asked. "The poltergeist?"

"It was big," Lenny said quietly. It was almost drowned out by the cat's frantic meowing.

"Jake, get that fucking cat out of here!" Emil said. "I still don't understand why you brought it here in the first place!"

"More like the other way around," Jake muttered. "I'll go, but if Niels Bohr mauls my fucking face off on the way out, it's on you."

There was another flash of light, then a rip and a crash with no obvious origin point that left the walls vibrating, and an alarm began to blare. Niels Bohr the cat screeched, launched himself out of Jake's arms, and ran across the room. To the eye, it looked like the back wall was thirty feet from the wall nearest to them. The cat was dashing at full speed and still hadn't reached the halfway point. Jake had moved to follow it and Emil had bounced up and grabbed him to hold him back.

"It's just a cat, Jake. We have to go."

A flash. The door slammed shut. Another flash and one of the overturned tables flew across the room. Emil was herding Dax toward the door. They both had their arms full of notebooks. Lenny had his hands on the door handle and was yanking hard, but it was stuck. Jake was standing next to him, not helping, his eyes on something at the back of the room.

Kit saw it too: Niels Bohr jumped up, hovered for a second, and vanished.

He was rooted to the spot, the Nowhere reverberating all around him. The alarm blared. The door was still wedged shut. Could Kit jump? He wasn't even sure he could take a step.

"Lenny, get Dax out!" Emil ordered. "Jake and I will work on the door! If we're not out in five minutes, come looking."

Lenny grabbed Dax and all their papers in his huge arms and they disappeared. The room lit up again, and this time, Kit thought he saw a shape framed between the two metal parentheses of the instrument. It was the same damn thing that had been chasing him all day. Only here, in the world, it almost had a form.

It almost looked like a person.

The edges blurred and it was hard to keep the form in focus. It was like looking for a shape in the clouds, but Kit thought he could see a person: arms and legs spread wide, head tipped back, mouth open in a scream.

Kit stared in horror for such a long moment that he didn't hear Emil shouting his name or see the monitor sailing across the room until it was too late. Emil tackled him. The monitor hit Emil between the shoulders. It tumbled to the floor along with the pair of them, starburst cracks through its screen. Kit pushed

Emil off and shoved himself up. Emil groaned, still on the floor. There was a long cut down his back. Blood seeped into his t-shirt.

The thing appeared in flashes all around the room, closer and farther away, and everywhere it went, furniture flipped into the air or broke in two. Jake yelled, "Stop!" as if that could have any effect on the chaos.

For a moment, there was a lull. Jake used it to wrench the door wide with one hard pull. Then he ran back to Emil, lifted him over his shoulder like it was nothing, grabbed Kit by the hand, and they both ran out the door. The alarm blared behind them.

———

THERE WERE alarms all over the facility, but the halls were still empty as Jake strode out of the lab with Emil over his shoulder in a fireman carry and Kit hurried after him like some kind of stupid lost puppy. They'd shut the door behind them but he could still feel that room. Walls couldn't contain the problem. What if that... breach, or whatever it was, got bigger?

"Jake, I'm fine, I'm conscious, I can walk, please put me down," Emil was saying. Jake ignored him until they reached a medical exam room where he could deposit Emil in the examination chair. "Message Dax and Lenny that we're out."

It had been a short distance from the lab door to the exam room. Unfortunately, they didn't make it without being seen. Kit paused in the hallway. "Caleb?"

That was the voice he'd heard when he'd been trapped in the closet. He didn't really know Caleb, so it was hard to recognize him when he wasn't stuck to Aidan's side. He was brown-haired and blue-eyed, fit and handsome in a sort of inoffensive, interchangeable way, like someone in an advertisement.

"Kit? What are you doing here?"

Caleb was a lot bigger than him, but Kit grabbed him by the wrist, pulled him into the exam room, and shut the door behind them. Jake and Emil looked at both of them in surprise. "I could ask you the same thing," Kit said, stepping forward so that Caleb was backed against the door. "Did you betray Aidan?"

"What?" Caleb said. "What do you mean? Why would you ask me that?"

Kit narrowed his eyes.

"As I recall, you don't even *like* Aidan," Caleb said. "What do you know about him? Do you know what happened to him?"

"He's here," Kit said.

"I fucking knew it," Caleb said to himself. Then, louder, "Where? Is he okay?"

"I don't know where exactly. I jumped in and then jumped out." Kit glanced at Emil. "I think it's in that part of the map you told me was unused space. And no. He's not okay. But he's alive and we can find him."

"And what the hell is going on out here?" Caleb said to Emil. "Are you hurt? Let me see that."

Kit got out of his way. Now that he had some assurance that Caleb hadn't been the one to sell out Aidan, he sat down on the floor—collapsed like a puppet with its strings cut. He was so fucking hungry. And tired. He couldn't tell if he wanted food or sleep more. He let his head rest against the wall and watched Caleb work.

Emil turned around so Caleb could examine his back. He made a soft sound of protest as he lifted his arms up so Caleb could peel off his t-shirt. Jake turned aside, displaying a modesty that bordered on suspicious. A shirtless man was nothing he hadn't seen before. Then again, the shirtless man in question was quite a sight. There would be no point in Kit pretending disinterest in Emil, since he'd shown up at the lab wearing

Emil's clothes and his hickeys, so he looked as much as he wanted to. Emil's back was basically a work of art, broad shoulders and narrow waist and all that smooth skin in between.

There was a shallow laceration between his shoulders and to the side of his spine. Caleb put on gloves and began to clean the cut. Emil winced.

"Still waiting for an explanation," Caleb said as he worked.

"Me too, actually," Emil said. He was facing away from all of them. "Pretend I'm making serious, concerned eye contact with Jake."

"Niels Bohr wouldn't stop crying," Jake started.

Emil cut in. "Niels Bohr is a cat belonging to Dr. Lange, Caleb. Not a person, as you might have assumed without context."

"I fed him and tried to get him to play but he wouldn't settle down, and it was the middle of the night and he kept scratching at the door, so I let him out and I followed him to the lab. And he wouldn't stop scratching at that door, either. So we went in."

That was the most words Kit had heard Jake say at one time. Like most of Emil's team, he was intimidating at first glance. No amount of glances would ever make the woman who'd slammed Kit into the wall and pressed her arm against his windpipe less intimidating, but a second glance was all it took to see that Chávez, Lenny, and Dax were alright. Well, Dax was too smart for their own damn good, and Chávez was involved with that scientist, and Lenny believed some weird shit about runners, but Kit wasn't *afraid* of them. Jake, though, his softheartedness revealed itself more slowly. He'd liked the cranky scientist that everyone else hated, and he was still taking care of the guy's cat.

And he'd carried Emil over his shoulder despite Emil's protests, and Kit strongly suspected he'd done it just because it was funny, and that was a good sign.

"The lab was unlocked?" Emil asked.

Jake scratched the back of his head. "It was after I unlocked it."

"Dr. Lange gave you access to his lab? And you kept that to yourself this whole time?"

"I swear I didn't know! The door scanned me and just let me in. I'd never tried to go in there before, so I had no idea."

"I see," Emil said. "And you found Dax and Lenny already there."

"Yeah. Looking for Lange's notes, they said."

"They'd better find a way to fix whatever's wrong in there," Kit said. "It won't be long before something comes out."

Caleb looked suitably horrified by that prediction, at least. "What the fuck is this place?" he asked. "Talk to me about how we can get Aidan out."

"If I had another runner with me, we could both jump in and get Aidan and my friend Laila out—assuming the Nowhere is working," Kit said. "It wouldn't take any time at all. Except I can't seem to get anywhere lately, and there's no way I can make another run today without resting first, and also I'm gonna fucking collapse if I don't eat soon."

"So stoic," Caleb joked.

"Fuck off," Kit said with feeling.

"We'll get you taken care of," Emil promised. "And we'll get Aidan and Laila out, too. Maybe it's best to break in using more conventional methods, since the Nowhere has been so risky lately. Let's plan. How are they keeping Aidan and Laila in one place?"

"Starvation," Kit said. "And sedation. They were cuffed to their beds, too, but that shouldn't be an issue for a runner in good shape."

"Okay, so we'll bring them some food," Emil said. "Describe the room as best you can. How can we get in?"

Kit thought back to that room, its white walls and floors, the two hospital beds separated by a plastic curtain, the long counter with its cabinets full of medical supplies, a little partition off to the side where people could change into gowns. But there was something he hadn't noticed. "There's no door."

"What do you mean, no door?"

"I mean exactly that. There's a door to a bathroom, but no exit."

"That's not possible," Emil said. Then he grimaced. "Unless they excavated a whole different part of the asteroid. But how would anyone get in or out?"

"Quint Services has at least one runner working for them," Kit said, and then realized he'd failed to include himself in that count. "Well, they had two, but at this point there's no way they'll pay me. And I freelanced one thing—they must have someone on call." Kit had a sinking feeling he knew who it was. Travis Alvey had come looking for him at a strange time of day, and it just so happened to be the day Kit was late with a Quint Services delivery.

"They were always nosing around Aidan's business," Caleb said. "They hated the idea of the union, but they wanted his contact list. They were always trying to persuade him to come to their side. It's how I got my job, actually. I lied and said I'd put in a good word with him."

"So this runner... this person comes up here just to transport Heath or Winslow or whoever into that room?" Emil asked. "That's an expensive proposition."

That partitioned area wasn't meant to protect anyone's privacy while changing into a gown. It was to keep Aidan and Laila from seeing the runner who brought the researchers. "Quint Services built a secret facility in an asteroid to explore the possibility of entering other realities. Money's no trouble for them. You should see what they offered me to bring you back here."

Money he'd never see now. And it was Monday, so he was missing his regular appointment with Carl. There was no way he could jump back to Nashville, feeling the way he did. He couldn't jump into the hallway. He couldn't even stand. He was awake only by the grace of adrenaline, and he could feel that wearing off.

"So either we need sledgehammers or runners to get in," Emil said. "Runners are more discreet—provided the Nowhere doesn't spit them out somewhere deadly. In order to save Laila and Aidan, we need to solve our other problem. Next time you encounter that thing, you should fight it. Capture, subdue, or kill it."

"Kill it?" Jake said, and even in his solemn, deep voice, Kit detected alarm. He hadn't expected big, tough, built-like-a-wall Jake to be such a pacifist. That was probably his own prejudice —straight men made him nervous—and he regretted it. Jake was mysterious, but he was kind.

"You're assuming too much, Emil. Who says it can be killed? And even then, who says *I* can kill it?" Kit asked. He was glad that Jake was alarmed out loud. It meant he could be alarmed in private. Kit was afraid to speak aloud what he'd seen —a man, trapped and screaming—because it sounded so crazy. And yet this was his life: teleportation, asteroids, other realities. What was one more thing in the mix? Why not a tortured ghost?

"If Dax and Miriam put their heads together, the two of them can figure out how to kill anything," Emil said. The weight of his gaze was heavy on Kit. "And that thing has already tried to kill you, so I don't feel much sympathy for it at the moment. I'm not sure why you do."

It looks like a person, Kit almost said. *I think it's—they're in pain.* But he'd had his fill of creepy novelties for the day, and as Emil had pointed out, he didn't have much reason to feel charitable toward the thing in the Nowhere. So he kept his mouth shut.

Something changed, and it took Kit a moment to put together that the alarm had stopped blaring.

"That means Heath and Winslow are out there," Emil said. "We'll have to hide you from them."

Kit sighed. "I can put in one more run. It's just to the kitchen." That was all bravado, and nobody was convinced. Kit couldn't be sure he'd make it to the kitchen. If he was lucky, the Nowhere would swallow him and he wouldn't have to feel the gnawing in his stomach or the pounding in his head anymore. "I could take you with me, probably," he added, looking at Emil.

"Absolutely not," Emil said. So sharp. So stern. But Kit had seen the fear in his eyes. Emil cleared his throat. "Jake and Caleb, can you two go talk to Heath and Winslow while I get Kit to the kitchen? We can't go forward with any part of this plan until Kit's able to jump again—*safely*."

"And tell them what?" Caleb asked.

"Don't worry, I got this," Jake said. He took Caleb by the elbow and steered him into the hall.

Kit and Emil heard raised voices in the hall. "We didn't do anything, sir," Jake was calling. "I promise!"

"Why were you here in the first place?" That was an older man. Kit had heard him in the hallway when he'd been stuck in the closet with Emil. It was probably Winslow. Judging from his severe tone, he was very unhappy.

"We were walking the cat, sir," Jake said.

"Walking the cat," Winslow said, incredulous. "In a restricted laboratory that was recently the site of a dangerous accident?"

"I believe he sensed something, sir," Jake said. "He wouldn't stop crying. I opened the door for him—I didn't know I could do that, Dr. Lange must have given me access without informing me—and he ran right in. He jumped into the air and disappeared. Then things flew all around the lab and the alarm went off."

It was as close to the truth as possible. There was probably a digital log of who'd opened the door to the lab in the security system somewhere, so it made sense for Jake to tell Winslow that much.

"I thought I'd hit my head," Jake continued. "And so when I ran into Caleb, who'd been woken by the alarm and had come to see what was wrong, I asked him to examine me."

Winslow grunted. Then he launched into a lecture about protocol, and Emil gestured at Kit to slip into the hallway. Emil kept a hand at the small of his back, guiding him and keeping his exhausted stumbling to a minimum. They stole toward the kitchen in silence.

[11]
THE HAND THAT FEEDS YOU

EMIL PULLED A RANDOM ASSORTMENT OF FOOD AND DRINK
out of one of the fridges, and Kit peeled off the foil and dug his
fork in without even looking. Something sweet hit his tongue. It
was one million o'clock in the morning, he felt inside out and
unreal, a ghost had almost killed him, what did it matter if he ate
dessert first? He ate a key lime pie followed by half a chicken
casserole. By that time, he felt just human enough to succumb to
his own exhaustion, and he swayed on the bench. Emil caught
him by the shoulders before he went face-first into his food.

Emil was straddling the bench to Kit's right and he'd positioned himself *very* close. He held on so Kit was turned toward
him. "Do you need me to feed you?"

"Oh my God, no," Kit mumbled, looking down at his food.
Then, because fatigue had stranded him at the edge of intoxica-
tion and escaping death had made him reckless, he said, "I only
want that if it's a sex thing."

It was worth it to see Emil's eyes get that big. Kit's gaze
drifted lower, down to Emil's spread legs, wondering what else
might have gotten bigger. He would have to be dead not to think
about that. Even tired, they could make it work. They could curl

up in Emil's bed and Emil could kiss his neck again and reach down to wrap one of his big hands around the length of Kit's cock and it would feel so good. That was all he wanted, really. Well, and then they could fall asleep and wake up and do it again. He wanted that, too. A smile spread across his face.

"You are shameless," Emil told him.

Kit hadn't been shameless before. He'd barely ever messaged Travis about their arrangement, even though it was mutually understood that he could. It hadn't been shyness, although Travis had called it that. It was just that Kit knew some day Travis would say no to him, and he didn't want the feelings that would come along with that when it happened. Travis wasn't worth the risk.

Emil was.

Kit smiled at him with half-lidded eyes and poked him in the center of the chest. "Somebody has to be. You're hoarding all the shame."

"I'm not ashamed of you, Kit," Emil said, all too serious. "I don't want you to think that. And I'm not ashamed of being queer and I never have been. The whole team knows and so does my family. I just... feel funny. You're so much younger than me. And the circumstances have been... complicated. And I don't really do casual. And we don't know anything about each other!"

"Uh huh," Kit said. "Sounds a lot like you're ashamed of me." He ate a few more bites, because he was hungry, and because now he had a point to prove. "I already know everything I need to. What do you want to know? I love making money, buying clothes, eating, and sleeping, in that order—and, as it turns out, I love sleeping with you. What else you want? Address, date of birth, Social Security? Because you've seen my apartment and the other two don't apply."

Emil blinked. "They don't..."

Too late, Kit realized he'd drawn them into a conversational minefield. He had to do some damage control. "You know, the whole orphan foundling thing. It's a real tearjerker. More importantly, I'm cute and I owe you a blowjob. But if it makes you feel better, you can tell me about your childhood before I suck your cock."

"Kit."

Emil wasn't giving up on the subject. Kit had to turn things around. "I know about your parents from Chávez and Lenny's schtick. What about siblings?"

Emil hesitated. "Yes. An older sister."

There was a story in that hesitation, but Kit wasn't doing this to dig up stories. "Pets?"

Emil shook his head. "But maybe some day—"

"Whoa, we are not in the business of 'some day' here. Past and present only. Hobbies?"

"Wait, why are future hopes off-limits?"

"Because the aim of this conversation is to fulfill *my* immediate-future hope that I can convince you to have sex with me again. We're not getting married."

"That's kind of the problem, Kit. I don't just... have sex."

"You did. With me. It was great and we should do it again some time. If you don't remember, I'd be happy to remind you." Emil was ridiculous. *I don't just... have sex.* Well, Kit didn't have relationships.

"Kit."

"Emil, I am afraid of *actually dying an actual death* in the very near future. Shouldn't you, as a morally upstanding goody-two-shoes type, do all that is in your power to take my mind off it? I mean, when you think about it, taking me to bed is the only right choice."

Thank fuck, Emil laughed. It was a nice sound. But then he

put on his serious voice and said, "Kit. We'll figure out a way to keep you safe. I promise."

"A great way to keep me out of harm's way would be to take me to your bed and keep me there. Just saying."

"I don't sleep with people who don't want to talk about our hopes for the future," Emil said. "Including an immediate future that doesn't involve you getting forced out of the Nowhere and stranded in some inaccessible wilderness alone. Can we talk about that?"

"What do we have to say about it?" Kit asked. "Other than 'I'd prefer not to'?"

"I'd prefer you not to as well," Emil said. "Will you promise not to go into the Nowhere until we figure out a solution?"

"I can't," Kit said, thinking of Laila and Aidan. "But I will promise not to go anywhere until I'm in better shape. I could recover in, say... your bed."

Emil sighed.

"Fine, fine, we'll avoid the subject of your bed if it makes you unhappy," Kit said. It was a lie, of course, but Emil probably knew that. "But I'm exhausted and I'm not going to come up with any solutions right here and now, so there's no point in being serious. Let's go back to simpler things. I think you were about to tell me your hobbies."

Emil squeezed his shoulder, then dropped his hand before it lingered too long. "Alright. I can do that. Gardening. Plants. Or maybe that doesn't count as a hobby because they became my career, kind of. Um... working out, I guess? Oh, don't make that face, I get enough shit from Chávez and Lenny. It clears my mind. And I like hiking. It's been hard, living in this facility for months. I'm really looking forward to spending some time outside."

Kit wrinkled his nose. "For the record, this is not getting us any closer to sex. Do you like anything that *isn't* terrible?"

"I thought we weren't discussing sex," Emil said primly. "And for the record, I've never wanted to describe anyone as 'citified' until right now, and I'm from the suburbs of Chicago so I barely have a right to use that word. But you qualify. By the way, do I get to ask any questions?"

A dangerous proposition. Emil might go right back to the family Kit didn't have. "Answer mine first."

"Fine. I also like music. Zinnia Jackson especially."

"Ugh. I forgot how tragically dated and tasteless you were for a second," Kit said. They were probably back in safe conversational territory now, having moved away from Kit's past and his future. "How old are you, anyway?"

"I'm thirty."

Kit shrugged. "I'm twenty-one. Would you freak out about sleeping with a thirty-nine-year-old?"

"No. But that's different."

"Doesn't seem different."

"It does to me," Emil said.

"That's your argument-winning voice," Kit observed. "Your I'm-in-charge-listen-to-me voice. It's very sexy. And sometimes it works on me. But not now. You don't get to win the argument because of your voice."

Emil was studying something in a distant corner of the kitchen, avoiding Kit's gaze. His cheeks were flushed.

"*I* win the argument," Kit said. In triumph, he stabbed a bite of casserole with his fork and lifted it to his mouth. "You're all flustered now."

It probably would have been sexier to say that without chewing, but whatever.

"I don't even know what we're arguing about," Emil muttered.

"That's why you lost." Kit finished the casserole and pointed his fork at Emil. "Carry me to your bed."

It didn't have the intended effect. "Kit," Emil said softly and far more seriously than Kit wanted.

That was when Kit heard someone behind him clear their throat.

"Mr. Singh, you are aware that unauthorized persons are not permitted in this facility." Kit didn't have to turn around. He knew it was Winslow from the voice and the way Emil's expression went carefully, rigidly blank.

"Yes, sir," Emil said.

Kit swung one leg over the bench, spinning to face Winslow. "I was contracted by Quint Services," he said, and it came out cool and collected until he saw who Winslow was with. A tall, slender man with dark brown hair falling just so, framing his clever, green eyes. He was wearing a t-shirt in the same shade as his eyes under a fitted black blazer with the sleeves bunched up, and as always, Travis Alvey looked good.

"Kit," he said, struggling to hide the surprise in his voice. Then, slick as ever, he smiled. "Of course you found your way here—the money's the best around and nobody hustles like you. Well, except for me."

Did you come by Zin's to kidnap me like you kidnapped Laila and Aidan? Kit wanted to ask. *How much was I worth?* Instead he smiled back and said, "Travis."

"You two know each other," Winslow observed. It was five-thirty in the morning and he'd undoubtedly been woken by the blaring alarm in Lange's lab, but he looked well put-together in a blue button-down shirt. His wavy grey hair was all obediently combed into place.

"Yeah," Kit said, keeping his tone light. "Didn't realize we were both freelancing for Quint, though. We haven't talked much recently."

"I can see why," Travis said, giving Emil an appreciative once-over. Kit wished he could block Emil from sight with his body, but their size difference meant he had to settle for glaring.

Winslow didn't notice any of it. He zeroed in on Kit. "Mister…"

"Jackson," Kit said.

"You are the runner who was contracted to bring Mr. Singh back to this facility on Friday night, are you not? Come with me to the lab immediately."

Kit didn't move. Could he jump? Had he eaten enough? His poor, assaulted body balked at the thought of entering the Nowhere. But Winslow didn't know that, so Kit stared him down. "That wasn't in my contract."

"Neither was remaining in this facility," Winslow snapped. Then he softened. "If you consented to an examination by Dr. Heath, I would permit you to stay a short time. You could… conclude your business with Mr. Singh, and I would not consider it my duty to write him up."

It was disturbing to be offered a carrot by someone who was clearly accustomed to using a stick. It wasn't much of a carrot. Winslow had only bothered with this tactic because he thought Kit could vanish at any moment. He'd figure out soon enough that Kit was trapped.

From the way Travis was watching Kit, he already knew.

"Excuse me," Emil said. With his back to Emil, Kit couldn't see his face, but his tone was icy. "Kit has experienced a great deal of trauma this weekend, and Quint Services is to blame for all of it. He's only here now because he's in no shape to jump back to Earth without food or rest. We can't subject him to examinations or interrogations now."

Damn it, Emil.

"If Mr. Jackson will not agree to these terms, I must ask that he leave immediately," Winslow replied.

"I could take him," Travis said.

"The fuck you could," Kit said, standing up, the words exiting his mouth before his brain caught up. Travis had outmaneuvered Laila and Aidan, and presumably neither of them had been as exhausted as Kit was now. The effort of standing left him trembling. But it was too late to back down. "Don't touch me. I'll take myself when I'm good and ready." He turned his gaze on the prick scientist. "I'm just as authorized as *he* is."

"Mr. Jackson, you were authorized to make a delivery on Friday night. It is now Monday morning. Mr. Alvey's status has no relevance to your own."

"How about Laila Njeim and Aidan Blackwood? Are they authorized to be in this facility?"

"I don't recognize those names, Mr. Jackson."

"The fuck you don't," Kit said, because he'd committed to this attitude now and he had to wear *something* well. But his fork skittered off the metal table and clanged to the floor before he'd even finished. Kit's eyes darted to the tabletop, where a blur of blue light hovered.

"What the hell was that?" Travis asked.

"Nothing," Winslow said sourly. "Just a minor issue we've been having with our artificial gravity, since Mr. Singh's team likes to adjust it every week for their silly little game. We'll have it under control soon."

For some reason, when Emil stood up behind Kit, he muttered "disrespecting the game" under his breath. "I think we should go," he said, putting a hand on Kit's shoulder. Kit couldn't pay attention to anything but the thing—ghost, poltergeist, whatever—hovering over the table. The light ought to have been reflected in the metal, but there were no glints. It wasn't of this world, and yet it could interact. The chicken casserole dish went sliding down the table. It crashed to the floor and shattered.

Kit took some grim satisfaction in the way Winslow jumped.

Travis had paled, too, but he wasn't as startled. Unlike Winslow, he could see the ghost. It must be his first time seeing one, which was odd, since he must have been making runs for Quint Services for a long time. How unfair, that Travis the traitor could jump back and forth safely while Kit couldn't get away from the damn things. He'd thought they were just randomly violent and terrifying, but maybe they were trying to kill *him* specifically. That was so much worse.

"Mr. Alvey," Winslow said. "Please escort Mr. Jackson off the premises."

From the look that passed between Travis and Winslow, Kit didn't think for one second that Travis was meant to take him home. Winslow wanted him dumped in that cell with Aidan and Laila. They weren't going to let him leave.

Neither was the ghost—it had come after him almost every time he'd made a run. Maybe it was time to introduce it to Travis.

"Fine," Kit said, squaring his shoulders. He felt rather than heard Emil's tiny, stifled breath of protest. "Travis, let's go."

———

EMIL TRIED to keep his eyes off Kit's back as he walked out of the kitchen with the other runner, but it was futile. Winslow must have overheard something. He'd already have guessed that Emil and Kit were involved. Why couldn't it have been Heath who'd found them? At least with her, Emil had leverage.

"You have some explaining to do, Mr. Singh."

"So do you," Emil said sharply. What did he have to lose, really? His job? Why would he work for a place that would treat Kit and his friends—or any runner—with such disregard? "What happened to Dr. Lange, Winslow? Why did you lie to my team about the accident? And why does this facility have a room with no door where you're keeping two runners without their consent?"

Dr. Vaughn Winslow was the type of older white man who got described as "distinguished" because he put on a suit sometimes. He didn't look distinguished now, no matter what he was wearing. His face was a constellation of red blotches. His lips twisted in anger. "I ask the questions."

"I bet the media would really love a story about how Quint Services has a secret facility in space where they give highly experimental treatments to United States Orbit Guard veterans," Emil said. Once he'd stopped caring about his job, he'd found plenty of leverage. "And that part, you know I can prove."

"You consented," Winslow hissed.

"I did," Emil agreed. He heard voices in the hallway outside the kitchen and for a moment, it was hard to concentrate. Kit and Travis were still out there. They hadn't left. And they were arguing about something.

Emil had to fight his own battles. He pulled himself together and finished the thought: "Laila Njeim and Aidan Blackwood didn't."

It was a relief that he remembered their names correctly, and he could see in Winslow's face that he did. It helped that they were both runners of such reputation—Laila had been in every grocery store gossip rag at the time of the robbery, and Aidan's recent civil disobedience had made the news as well. "And I know you and Heath would love to get your hands on Kit, and he's made it quite clear how he feels about that."

"Do you know what it's like to go toe-to-toe with a corporation as powerful as Quint Services, Mr. Singh? Do you know what resources we possess? You can't even imagine all the ways in which we could make your life hell. I'd advise you to drop this line of thinking here and now. You can still answer my questions and return to your bunk with a job."

Winslow was threatening him. For now, it was only Emil, but how long until Winslow turned his eye toward the others? Emil had to stay here until he could be sure the team could get out safely. Kit was on his way already, he hoped. But Laila and Aidan were another question. And could Quint Services be trusted to handle whatever was happening in Lange's lab responsibly? Kit had called it a fault line. Lenny had said *the Nowhere is leaking*.

Either metaphor suggested the worst was yet to come.

Emil couldn't sigh. He had to endure whatever humiliation Winslow wanted to heap on him without reacting too much. This wasn't about his job. It was about his friends and Kit's friends. And Kit. And maybe more than that. For all those reasons, he had to please Winslow right now. Emil lifted his lips in a smile. It was more challenging than anything he'd ever done at the gym.

"Of course, sir. My apologies. I haven't slept much recently."

"What happened in Dr. Lange's lab at four o'clock this morning?"

"I don't know, sir. Something made the alarm go off."

"Were you there?"

"No, sir. I was here, helping Kit find something to eat. He materialized in my room in the wee hours, having been chased through the Nowhere by something we've been calling a ghost. You saw one earlier, when the casserole dish fell off the table." Emil gestured at its remains, still scattered on the floor.

"This is not a hotel, Mr. Singh. You are not permitted *guests*."

"The ghost hasn't permitted Kit to leave."

"How interesting," Winslow said, and for a moment, he wasn't a corporate lackey interrogating Emil but a scientist pondering the world. "Why is that, I wonder?"

Emil could only shrug and shake his head.

"It's not good to call it a 'ghost.' The name gives it an agency we can't be sure it truly possesses. You think there are multiple entities?"

"Yes, sir. Kit could see them—so could Lenny, and I think it's fair to say Travis could see the one in here. Kit said they were different sizes. One was larger than him and all the rest were smaller. They seem to be shapeless for the most part, but they have some substance in the Nowhere."

"And here, they're capable of knocking things off shelves," Winslow said. "That seems to be all they do, though."

"Except for the large one," Emil said. Winslow had been so genuinely interested that he almost slipped up and added *I think it was in the lab earlier.* "I'm sure Dr. Heath reported to you that Kit and I encountered it on our first run together, when it knocked us into what I suspect was another reality, or at least another planet."

"A subject on which I have many more questions," Winslow said. "But I suppose, for now, since the runner is gone and you've assured me you are awake only by coincidence and you were not in Lange's lab this morning, I can let you return to bed and we can discuss things at a more reasonable hour." Winslow was no fool, and his expression was skeptical as he spoke. Perhaps having him walk in during Kit's loopy, fatigue-inspired flirtations was a blessing in disguise. He thought Emil was being cagey because he was sleeping with Kit.

If only that were all there was to it. Emil merely nodded at Winslow and escaped the conversation as quickly as he could. As he stepped into the hall, he couldn't stop himself from looking around for Kit and the other runner, but they were nowhere to be seen.

———

Kɪᴛ's ᴘʟᴀɴ ʙᴀᴄᴋꜰɪʀᴇᴅ ɪᴍᴍᴇᴅɪᴀᴛᴇʟʏ. He'd expected Travis to step into the Nowhere, but instead he slung an arm around Kit's shoulders and manhandled him into the hallway. Travis pushed him against the wall. At least he kept his arm off Kit's windpipe. Still, he got way too close and practically spit in Kit's face with his question.

"How much did they offer you?"

"That's my line," Kit said. If Travis was asking, it meant he was worried. Maybe he didn't intend to dump Kit in that cell. "You afraid of the hand that feeds you, Travis?"

"As we both should be!" Travis hissed. "I can't believe you're *fucking* one of these scumbags. Do you know what they do to runners here? Do you know what they think of us?"

Emil wasn't a scumbag. Kit didn't want to talk about Emil with Travis. "You *work* for them."

"Yeah, because they fucking *own* me now, and if you stick around here, they're gonna own you. You have no idea what they did to me. You don't want to fuck with these people, Kit."

"If you're so scared of them, why didn't you ask for help? Maybe you didn't trust me, but you know Aidan would have taken up your cause. He lives for that shit. And Laila would have helped. You didn't have to turn on them."

"It was me or them, Kit. You'll see how it is soon enough."

"You'll see how it is when I get Laila and Aidan out," Kit said. "Go ahead and take me there. I'm not in great shape but between the four of us, we could work it out."

"Which part of 'don't fuck with Quint Services' did you not hear? They will *vivisect* me, Kit."

Travis always wore tailored jackets and sunglasses. His hair was devil-may-care. He rode a nicer bike than Kit's. He was too cool to say hi to Zin or Louann. He strode through the world, effortlessly edgy and not owing anyone a thing, but he was a caricature of a sexy bad boy. Travis Alvey was a goddamn coward.

"They fucked with me first," Kit said.

"They don't even think we're human!" Travis blurted. "Did you know that? Oswin Lewis Quint is part of some insane group that subscribes to this theory that runners are from some other reality, which is why we can get into the Nowhere, and therefore they can't trust us because we have *suspect loyalties.* To some other world! That's why they want to take us apart until they find out what makes us tick. They have no plans to put us back together." He took a ragged breath. "Think about it, Kit. Why are there no born runners working for Quint Services? How come they brought in this elite team of former Orbit Guard normals for a mission that specifically requires *our* skills? Why try to make more runners—or build a door—when there are already runners out there, and the whole point of us is that we don't need doors?"

Travis wasn't whispering anymore. His voice had risen in pitch and volume. If Emil and Winslow were quiet in the kitchen, they could probably hear him. The whole thing made Kit's heart pound, and he was too tired for that. Even the thudding of his heart sounded sluggish in his chest.

He didn't want it to make sense.

Does Emil know? he wondered again. Kit had concluded that Laila and Aidan's imprisonment was a surprise to Emil. And he'd seemed eager enough to get them free. But maybe he objected to the methods and not the idea. Had Emil known that Quint felt this way? Did *Emil* feel that Kit was some kind of untrustworthy alien?

No. Not possible. And yet... Emil hated and feared the Nowhere. It had been obvious in every trip they'd made. Did that fear extend to Kit himself? He didn't have the energy to consider it. "Are we going or not?" he demanded.

"I'm getting you out," Travis said, his voice low. "Winslow's look wasn't enough of an order. I'll pretend I misunderstood, okay? Don't come back once you're out. Steer clear."

"And what if they order you to come collect me?" Kit asked. "What then?"

"Then you won't be able to say I didn't warn you."

Travis tightened his grip on Kit's shoulders and jerked them into the Nowhere. He could have done it with more grace—or maybe he had, and Kit was so tired that nothing felt right to him. Would it have killed Travis to say "Here goes" or something? Kit would have loved even one more second to prepare his battered body for what he had to do.

He was lucky. Facility 17's poltergeist, one of the smaller ghostly entities, showed up right away. Kit squirmed out of Travis's hands and shoved him away. He dove for the ghost. He didn't have much of a plan, other than pushing the thing in Travis's direction and thinking *chase him not me* as hard as he could. Foolish, reckless, unlikely to work—it was the best Kit could do under the circumstances. If only he could catch the damn ghost.

It bounded away from him and he darted after it. His eyes on that blue light, he swam through the blackness until his limbs burned. It made turn after turn, streaking across his vision, and he found himself flipping over to chase it back in the opposite direction. Travis was no longer with him. Kit was dizzy. He had one turn left, maybe, before his concentration would be shot and he'd just have to let the Nowhere spit him out at will. He prayed the void would be kinder to him that the ghosts had been.

Just then, the little ghost flew back to him. It bumped gently against his chest, sending them tumbling through nothing. Kit wrapped his arms around it, still surprised by its solidity. *Gotcha. Let's go the fuck home.*

He ended up lying on his back in a bed identical to all the others in Facility 17. Not Emil's. Kit didn't care.

There was a large orange cat writhing in his hands.

What? He let go and it sat on his sternum and purred. The poltergeist, the little ghost, the thing he'd been scared of was... a cat?

Kit thought back over all the signs. The scratching on doors. The objects knocked off tables. *Goddammit.*

"Yeah, you think you're real funny," Kit said, narrowing his eyes at the animal, which, in addition to purring, was now kneading its paws into him. He didn't want to deal with this shit anymore. When he stretched his head back, there was a pillow beneath it, which felt like the best and most important thing in the world.

The stupid cat was still sitting, as heavily as it possibly could, right on his chest. Wanting to dislodge it, Kit rolled over onto his side. The cat, unfazed, curled up in the space between his bent knees and his chest.

EMIL DIDN'T ENTERTAIN ANY ILLUSIONS OF SLEEP, BUT HE did go back to his room. Or he intended to, but he was side-tracked by the meowing coming from behind the locked door to Solomon Lange's room. Hadn't Niels Bohr disappeared into the breach in Lange's lab? How could he be here?

He'd only been standing in front of the door for a moment before Jake came to his side. He didn't look like he'd slept since they'd last seen each other.

"I don't suppose you can unlock this one, too?" Emil asked, giving Jake a tired smile.

Jake recoiled. There was no other word for the way he backed away from Emil with his eyes wide. "Don't get the wrong idea about us. We had a few conversations, that's all."

Those *few conversations* had been enough for reclusive, permanently sour, notoriously secretive Solomon Lange to grant Jake access to his lab—but Jake hadn't known that until a few hours ago. What did Lange even think Jake would do in the lab? Jake wasn't a physicist.

"I'm sorry," Emil said. "That was inappropriate of me."

When they'd first met years ago, Emil had been hesitant to

come out to Jake. At first glance, he'd seemed exactly like the kind of macho straight guy who might be uncomfortable with queerness. He liked guns and engines and not talking about his feelings. Emil had misread him. Jake had never once been disrespectful or seemed ill at ease or hesitated to follow an order. And when Lucas had dumped Emil, Jake had been just as quick to offer a hug as anybody else.

No, Jake had never been uncomfortable with *Emil*. But the way he'd recoiled just now suggested he might be uncomfortable with himself.

On the other side of the door, the meowing continued. It was accompanied by occasional scratching.

"Heath and Winslow reprogrammed the lock anyway," Jake said. His only acknowledgement of Emil's apology was a single nod. "They had to get Niels Bohr out of Lange's room after the accident."

"So how did he get back in?"

"He didn't. Niels Bohr disappeared this morning, remember?"

"So there's another cat?" Emil said. Today was already weird, but that was a truly unexpected development. "Did Lange have a secret cat? Did someone else have a secret cat? Why have we never noticed?"

Jake shrugged. He tried the door. It didn't work.

A moment passed, during which Emil contemplated two wildly improbable ways to get into the room. Breaking down the door—nearly impossible. Crawling through the vents—impossible for him, although maybe he could persuade Chávez to do it. She was the worst choice, temperament-wise, but she did have the narrowest frame.

The third way into the room was asking Heath or Winslow to unlock the door. It would be successful, but unpleasant.

"Maybe we should just ignore it for now and go back to

bed," Emil joked. It made him smile to remember Kit saying *And why do I have to solve the problem? Maybe if I wait, it'll go away. Or someone else will solve it for me.*

Jake looked at Emil like he'd been replaced by an impostor. Fair enough. It wasn't usually Emil's nature to ignore a problem. Then Jake's expression changed completely and he dropped to his knees and pressed his ear against the door. Emil knelt down with him and listened.

The scratching had stopped. The meowing hadn't stopped, but it was only intermittent now. And in between the cat's cries, there was a voice murmuring sweetly, "Shh, I know you're hungry. The Nowhere makes me hungry, too. Shh, shh. There has to be food in here somewhere, and I'm gonna find it for you, because I need you to shut the fuck up so I can go back to sleep, okay?"

Kit. But what was he doing there? Where was the runner who'd been tasked with taking him away?

Emil could hear the click and rattle of desk and closet drawers being opened, and then the rustle and thud of a bag of cat food being set on the floor. "There we go," Kit was saying. "That's what you wanted. Now you'll shut up like we talked about, right? You know us runners have to stick together. The rest of them don't even think we're *human.*" A pause. Emil heard only the crunch of the cat eating kibble. "That was a joke. Sort of. Shit, I saved you and I'm feeding you and you won't even laugh at my jokes. Tough crowd."

At some point, Emil had closed his eyes. He didn't know when exactly, nor did he know when he'd started smiling like such a dope. But it was so sweet. And it was a rare, unguarded moment for Kit. With Emil, he was always offering with one hand and holding back with the other.

When he opened his eyes, Jake was staring at him incredulously. "Are you gonna knock, or..."

Oh, right. Emil knocked softly. "Kit. It's me. And Jake."

Enough time passed that Emil wondered if Kit had already fallen back asleep. He knocked again, and the door opened. For someone who'd demanded that Emil carry him to bed not forty-five minutes ago, Kit looked distinctly unhappy to see him. He crossed his arms defensively over his chest. Still, he stepped aside to let them in. Jake closed the door and all three of them stared at the orange cat happily eating from a mountain of food in its bowl.

"That," Jake said, "is Subrahmanyan Chandrasekhar."

"What?" Kit said.

"A famous twentieth-century physicist," Emil answered, "and, I'm guessing, one of Lange's cats. But I've never seen this one before."

He expected Kit to explain, but it was Jake who spoke.

"I know because he showed me pictures. Back on Earth, Lange had two cats. Subrahmanyan Chandrasekhar and Lise Meitner. During a particular breakthrough, he found himself in the lab all the time, obsessively tweaking his experiment. Every time he had to go home to feed his cats, it was an interruption. And he missed them. So all three of them moved in. Then there was another accident—the way he described it, it sounded just like the one that happened here. Lange survived, but the cats disappeared. For a while, he thought they were dead—that he'd killed them—and he couldn't go on with his work. Then things started moving around his apartment or his lab, getting knocked off tables, batted around. Sometimes he'd hear scratching. And he had the funny thought that maybe his cats weren't dead after all. So he kept working. He adopted Niels Bohr. And when Quint Services called, he accepted their offer. And his cats—all three of them—came with him."

"That's why you're not scared of the so-called poltergeist," Emil said. "Why didn't you tell us?"

"None of you seemed that scared, either." Jake shrugged. "I tried to tell you a couple of times. It just never worked out. The whole thing sounded like nonsense. Would you have believed me?"

"Yes."

"I wasn't even sure I believed it myself."

"I found the cat in the Nowhere," Kit said. While Emil had been listening to Jake, Kit had crawled into Lange's bed and was now lying on his side. He was still dressed in Emil's clothes and his hair was stiff with dried saltwater. It had been a hell of a night. "Or I guess he found me. I think he's the one who's been causing most of the trouble around here, but I guess maybe the other cat is still out there somewhere. I can look for her." He yawned. "Some other time."

"Our poltergeist has been a cat this whole time," Emil said. "Or two cats. That raises the question of the other ghost."

He didn't state it as a question. He had a feeling they'd all come to the same conclusion. Lange's cats had disappeared in a lab accident and been stuck in the Nowhere for months, manifesting only as bluish blurs of light. It didn't take a physics genius to guess that the same fate had befallen Lange himself.

"But why would he be trying to kill you?" Emil asked Kit in the silence that followed.

Kit had his eyes closed, as if the question didn't concern him at all. But he wasn't asleep yet, because he answered, "You said he was an asshole, right? Maybe that's been... amplified."

Jake shook his head, and Emil was inclined to believe him.

"I don't think he was that much of an asshole," Emil said.

"When I saw him, he looked like he was in pain," Kit said. "Maybe he doesn't know what he's doing."

"Maybe," Jake said. "But he pushes you out, right? And the cats never did."

"Yeah," Kit said. He'd opened his eyes for this part, but he didn't look or sound convinced.

"I don't mean to be too negative here, but are we sure the ghost is still... Lange? Can he think in there? I can't think in the Nowhere, and that's *without* any kind of sudden trauma. It's just being a normal person. Lange wasn't a runner before the accident, and now he's trapped in the Nowhere in some kind of in-between shape," Emil said. "Kit rescued the cat, and it seems to be alive and more or less normal, although with cats it's hard to tell. I'm not saying we shouldn't try. I'm trying to think all the way through things."

"I think he wants help," Jake said. "He's trying to get out and he doesn't know how. If he's in pain, he's probably not thinking clearly, right? He's latched onto you, Kit, because he thinks you can get him out. Maybe he recognized Emil the first time you two were together in the Nowhere, and that's why he came for you."

"Hmph," Kit said and closed his eyes again. Emil didn't blame him for skepticism. It was hard to feel charitable toward Solomon Lange even when you'd known him as a human being. When you'd only known him as a ghostly, would-be perpetrator of accidental manslaughter in the Nowhere, it was impossible.

"How'd you get the cat out?" Emil asked.

"Like you said. If you run, you have to run forever. You told me to grab it, so I grabbed it."

"Well, I guess we know what we have to do to get Lange out," Emil said, and Jake nodded. Kit said nothing, so either he was already asleep, or this was his way of dismissing them. Emil headed for his own bed with the impression that Kit was mad at him, but he had no idea what he'd done.

DIMENSIONAL PRIONS

THERE WAS WORK TO DO IN THE GARDEN, HE HAD AN appointment with Dr. Winslow later in the day that would likely turn into a debriefing, he really ought to take the seaweed that had been caught in Kit's clothes into a lab for examination, and normally he'd have been up and in the gym by now, but Emil was wrecked. He lay down in his bed, which still smelled of sex and seawater, and managed to catch three hours of sleep before someone knocked on his door. He got up right away and answered, hoping it was Kit.

It was Dax and Lenny. Dax's nest of red hair perfectly complemented their wild, delighted expression. "Lange's private journals were a goldmine," they said reverently.

"They've been pacing my room, alternately reading and talking nonsense for hours," Lenny said, pointing a thumb at Dax. "I told them it was time to share with somebody else."

"Might as well get Jake, Chávez, and Miriam in here," Dax said. "And Kit, if you want him."

"Let him sleep," Emil said. "If it's important, I'll catch him up later. I'll message the others. Let's meet in the greenhouse. I have work to do in there anyway, and the machinery makes a lot of ambient noise."

Emil slipped his shoes on and poked at his watch to contact the others.

"Ask them for coffee," Lenny said, and Emil did.

"What about that nurse Caleb?" Dax asked, their hand hesitating on the doorknob. "Do we trust him?"

"He patched me up this morning and helped Jake distract Winslow and Heath," Emil said. "But let's wait."

The greenhouse was Emil's favorite part of Facility 17, a vast, glassed-in space divided into subsections that he kept at different temperatures. There was a dazzling view of the cosmos above and rows and rows of his own personal space garden below and it was *magic*. Emil grew the usual kitchen garden herbs and vegetables—various greens, squashes, carrots, potatoes, tomatoes, onions, basil, and so on—and some things that most people didn't put in their backyards, like wheat and rice. It had been tricky, designing the bed for the rice, but Quint Services wanted to ship as little as possible to the facility, so they'd told him that cost was no object in laying out the greenhouse. He'd sectioned off part of the greenhouse into an orangery. It had probably been complicated, shipping all the fruit trees he'd requested up here, but he'd never asked. Maybe they'd used runners.

They'd certainly used runners to build other parts of the facility.

That thought dimmed the happiness he felt at entering the greenhouse. No matter how lush, it had been paid for by people who did terrible things.

Jake and Miriam were standing in the far corner of the main space between the end of one row of plants and a floor-to-ceiling window. They were staring out at the universe. Earth wasn't currently visible, but the facility orbited the moon fast enough that it would come around soon. Miriam, hardly turning away from the window, reached behind herself and plucked a handful of ripe berries from one of Emil's raspberry bushes. She offered her open palm to Jake, but he shook his head, so she ate them all herself.

There was a soft ding, indicating that the sprinklers were about to come on in this space, so Jake and Miriam opened the glass door that led into the orangery. Emil, Lenny, and Dax followed them in. Chávez arrived a few minutes later with a pot of coffee and some mugs jammed onto a tray. "You're a true friend, Clara Chávez," Lenny said, lifting a cup off the tray and pouring himself coffee. He shook his head at Jake and Miriam. "No thanks to either of you."

"I'm not your intern," Miriam said, glowering. "You're perfectly capable of getting your own coffee."

"As I was saying, Clara Chávez, you're a beautiful genius with the heart of a saint, absolutely irreplaceable, and you'll make some woman very lucky some day," Lenny said. He luxuriated in his first sip.

There were two benches and a low table in the center of the orangery. Chávez laid her tray on the table and began to pour coffee for the rest of them while they took their seats.

"Why limit myself to just one?" Chávez said, smiling beatifically and passing out mugs. "There are so many women out there who need to get lucky."

Jake was waiting patiently for this to end and Dax was rolling their eyes, so it was time for Emil to step in. Miriam, Jake, and Lenny had taken one bench. Emil joined Chávez and Dax on the other. He was glad not to host this meeting in his room, where Kit's discarded clothes and boots were still in a pile on the floor. "We have things to discuss."

"Yeah, I came here to talk about physics," Dax said.

Emil smiled at them, then said, "News first. Kit caught our

poltergeist—or one of them—and it turns out it was one of Dr. Lange's cats. It had been involved in an accident, similar to the one that happened here. We now have reason to believe that Dr. Lange himself is trapped in the Nowhere, and that it might be possible to get him out."

"Great," Dax said, tapping the piles of notebooks in their lap. "Then he can explain this to me."

Emil told all of them everything he could—the breach in Lange's lab, Laila and Aidan being held in an inaccessible cell on the asteroid, that other runner Travis showing up with Winslow and attempting to take Kit away—and shock and dismay crossed their expressions.

"Shit," Chávez said.

"I always knew Quint Services was a little shady, but I thought it was, you know, tax evasion, regular billionaire stuff. I didn't think they were kidnapping people," Lenny said. "You think Heath and Winslow signed off on that? And we've been making small talk with them this whole time?"

Chávez's face turned green. She'd been doing a lot more than small talk.

"That's a lot of problems for us to solve," Miriam said, stepping past emotional concerns and heading right for the practical. "What do you suggest we tackle first?"

"If we have two runners in good shape, it shouldn't be hard to get Laila and Aidan free," Emil said. "The Nowhere has been risky lately, but I think this is worth the risk."

"I'm game," Lenny said. "Kit can help me get there and back."

"Can't we fix the Nowhere? That's on our to-do list anyway, right?" Miriam asked.

"It's on the list," Dax agreed. "Saving Dr. Lange will make it far less dangerous, but what we really need to do is repair the breach. I'm not sure how to do that yet. Laila and Aidan are suffering now, so we have to get them out first."

"That room has plumbing and wiring and ventilation," Chávez said. "Even if there's no door, it's connected to the rest of the facility somehow. You sure we can't break in any other way?"

"It's not a question of taking a sledgehammer to some drywall," Lenny said. "It might be solid ore between here and there."

"Quint Services must have excavated another part of the asteroid to make that space," Miriam said. "We could suit up and examine the outside."

"Speaking of the room," Emil said, "we can't just get the prisoners out. We also have to make sure that Quint Services can't replace them with new prisoners."

"Destroy the room," Miriam suggested.

"Threaten to go public," Lenny said.

"Knock Heath and Winslow's fucking heads together," Chávez said, her jaw clenched in anger.

Emil raised his eyebrows at her. "All good ideas. Miriam and Dax, you work on concocting something that'll destroy that room—without, say, blowing the rest of us into space. Jake and Clara, pull together something that can go to the press if we need to. Photos, video testimony, text, whatever. Lenny, you're on call to jump in there. Be ready in a few hours. When Kit wakes up, we're doing this."

"And what will you be doing?" Chávez asked.

"Distracting Heath and Winslow somehow," Emil said.

"Let me help you. With Heath."

"Are you sure—okay," he said, stopping mid-question once he saw her face. "I could use the help, in that case."

Chávez offered him a crooked smile. "You know me. A real femme fatale."

"Nope, sorry, that role is taken. If anyone around here is a femme fatale, it's Miriam," Lenny assured her. "In the most literal sense of 'fatal.'"

"I don't know if that was a compliment, but I choose to accept it as one," Miriam said.

"Oh, it most definitely was," Lenny said cheerfully. And then a small miracle occurred: Miriam smiled at him. Seated between them on the bench, Jake furrowed his brow in puzzlement.

"Right," Emil said. "So that's the plan for now. Dax, tell us what you found."

"If I hadn't spent three months being Lange's beleaguered assistant, I'm not sure I could read these notes at all. He writes for himself and only himself. No real sentences and huge logical leaps. But here's what I got," Dax started. "We start with a relatively common premise, although one that's not accepted by everyone. The Nowhere is unfolded space."

"In addition to being a membrane between realities?" Emil asked.

Dax nodded. "Think of it this way. There are more dimensions than we can perceive—ten, according to some. We perceive three spatial dimensions, plus time, but the others are all folded up. All matter in our reality, let's call it Reality A, is folded in a particular way. But in another reality, let's go wild and call it Reality B, everything is folded differently. In between these two realities is the central hub of unfolded space that we call the Nowhere.

"Folded matter likes to remain folded. It's more stable. That's why, if you're a normal human being, having a runner drag you into the Nowhere is miserable. Being unfolded is not fucking fun. But runners can handle unfolded space just fine. The question has always been *why*."

"Isn't that more of a question for people in biology, like Heath and Winslow?" Chávez asked.

"Everything is physics," Dax said airily. "What I found in Lange's notes can't really be called a hypothesis, but it's speculation. As we know, Lange thinks it's ancestry. In his notes, he specifies that he thinks runners are created when one parent crosses over from another reality and has sex with a local. Remember how I said that Reality A and Reality B have different foldings? The resulting child has both in their body. One foot in each reality. It gives them access to the unfolded space of the Nowhere."

"So runners can pass into the Nowhere because they have something in their bodies that's similar?" Emil said.

"Yes," Dax said. "They can withstand being unfolded and refolded better than the rest of us."

"And why is it possible to turn some of us into runners, but not others?"

"Ancestry again. Born runners most likely have parents from different realities. But you can imagine a born runner who settles down in Reality A and starts a family with somebody from Reality A, so their children have less of Reality B's particular folding in their bodies. And if those children stay local, their children have even less of it," Dax said. "The heredity of it isn't perfectly regular and predictable. But according to Lange, through his help, Heath and Winslow have stumbled on a way to increase the amount of differently folded matter in someone's body, if there's any to begin with. That is to say, if someone had a runner ancestor."

"So it *was* my great-grandma!" Lenny said, beaming at Dax. "Glad to know I'm on the same page as one of the most brilliant people alive. Oh, and Lange, too."

It was easy to make Dax blush.

Chávez raised her mug. "And here's to Ms. Alice Desjardins and her mysterious ways."

"So that means she—or rather, one of my great-great-grandparents was... really not from around here," Lenny said.

Dax nodded. "And every born runner we know has a parent from some other reality. Lange theorized that some people fall through—those are his words. That sometimes there's a weak spot in the membrane between realities and someone crosses over by accident. He actually thought accidental crossings were common, but survival was rare. Anyway, if the accidental-crossing survivor has a child with a local, that child can cross over on purpose."

What would Kit think of that? He hated being asked about his absent biological family. Emil would be hesitant to bring it up, even though it might interest him.

"I think," Dax continued, "and I'm not reciting Lange's notes anymore, these are my own thoughts—that what went wrong for Lange was this. He only had the example of runners to go on, and they make it look easy. He thought all he needed was access to the Nowhere. A door. But crossing the Nowhere has two steps. First, you get unfolded. Second, you get refolded. Lange managed the first step with his door, but not the second."

"So what happened to Lange and the cats, getting stuck in the Nowhere, that could happen to any of us who walk through the door," Emil said. "Except the runners."

"Yes. We can all walk through the door into the Nowhere. Crossing the threshold back into the world—any world—is the hard part."

"Kit saved the cat just by grabbing it and holding on," Emil said. "Maybe the solution will be that simple for Lange, too."

"I'm guessing there's nothing in there that will help us close the door, or else you'd have said so by now," Lenny said.

Dax nodded. "We'll have to think on that."

"What does this mean for Heath and Winslow's experiments on us? If they haven't worked already, they won't?"

"Oh, Lange had a lot to say about that," Dax said. "Once he had the idea that what makes a runner is a combination of matter from Reality A and Reality B, Lange got interested in Heath and Winslow's work. And by interested, I mean 'judgmental.' But anyway, according to him, you put enough Reality B matter in a Reality A resident and you should end up with a runner. Ideally, the matter will be something like bone marrow. It makes blood cells. It's generative."

"Being paranoid and kind of a jerk, I'm guessing Lange didn't share ideas with either of them," Emil said. "Because we all love getting months and months of regular injections and mystery pills."

"And x-rays and every other kind of scan," Lenny said.

"Don't forget all the peeing in cups," Chávez joked. "That's my favorite."

"As far as I can tell, he didn't share the idea," Dax said. "But bone marrow transplants aren't exactly pleasant. And since I just pointed out that marrow is ideal because it's generative, you're all invited to think for a second on which kinds of cells are *most* generative."

"Eggs," Jake said. "And sperm."

Everyone grimaced, but it only lasted a second before the comments and questions started.

"Well, they've never asked me for that kind of sample, at least," Lenny said.

"If a woman is pregnant with a runner, does she get runner abilities for the period of gestation?" Chávez asked.

"Should we assume Quint Services is doing fucked-up things to embryos in some part of this facility?" Miriam asked.

"Back on topic," Emil said. "Lange might not have shared this idea of putting matter from born runners into normal people to give them abilities, but it didn't stop Heath and Winslow from kidnapping born runners. We can assume they came to their own conclusions."

"I wasn't quite finished," Dax said, a note of apology in their tone. "For now, there's just one more thing I have to tell you. Do you know what a prion is?"

"A misfolded protein," Jake said. "When they come into contact with other proteins, they cause those proteins to misfold as well. It's the cause of Mad Cow Disease."

"Yes," Dax said. "Lange wrote about something he calls *dimensional prions*. Like misfolded proteins, except they contain folded space. If they come into contact with matter that is folded differently, they alter its folding to match their own."

"Are these theoretical?" Emil asked.

Dax took a breath. "No. Lange made some in his lab."

"I sense an 'and,'" Emil said.

"He thinks Heath and Winslow stole them."

"They're using them on us," Lenny guessed. "Somehow, that's what made me a runner."

"A bone marrow transplant would be a lot more straightforward," Jake said.

"The dimensional prions work faster than that, in theory. And there's no hospitalization required, just an injection," Dax said.

"Isn't there a problem with prions, though? The Mad Cow problem where they change the folding of *everything*?" Jake asked. "So eventually, a person with dimensional prions from Reality B isn't a runner anymore. They're just a regular Reality B person."

Emil was seated on the bench across from Lenny, so he had a good view of his disconcerted expression, his brown eyes wide behind his glasses.

"Well, you're right about one thing," Dax said. "Lenny

might only be a runner temporarily—it's too soon to tell. But the dimensional prion isn't folded like Reality B matter. It's something slightly different—call it B1. It acts on Reality B matter, folding it into a different configuration. So Lenny has three foldings in him right now: A, B, and B1. Before the experiments, he was only, say, 12.5% Reality B matter—not enough to be a runner. But the more different foldings you have, the easier it is to access the Nowhere, or so Lange claims. So Lenny can be a runner with 87.5% Reality A matter as long as his remaining 12.5% is two different foldings."

"But eventually the dimensional prions refold all that B matter into B1 matter, and he'll be back to two foldings," Emil said. "And we don't know how long 'eventually' is."

"I'll keep that in mind," Lenny said. "Doesn't inspire a lot of confidence. Guess I'd better stick to short runs."

"So the experiments aren't going to work on the rest of us?" Miriam asked.

"I don't have access to Heath and Winslow's notes, so I don't know exactly what they've injected us with," Dax said. "Going off Lange's notes, I can imagine some experiments that might be successful, at least temporarily. I'll have to think about it after we've solved our other problems."

"Thank you, Dax," Emil said. "I think we should go our separate ways for now. But stay in touch, and let's all keep an eye out."

———

EMIL HAD PROBABLY BEEN KNOCKING SOFTLY at the door for a long time before Kit woke up. Kit lay in bed and let him knock a few more times. He wanted to go back to sleep and not deal with any of this.

But Subrahmanyan Chandrasekhar meowed and pawed at

the door, stretching his long orange self all the way up to the doorknob.

"Don't get your hopes up," Kit told the cat as he got out of bed. "He's not your person."

His muscles complained as he walked the short distance to the door, his body aching in ways he didn't know were possible. He rubbed his eyes and scrubbed a hand through his hair and it came away gritty with salt. What would he give for a shower? His own shower, not whatever high-tech nonsense was in this facility. The drains would probably be set up to harvest his DNA.

Kit opened the door. Emil looked wrecked, dark circles under his tired eyes, and Kit had been through worse, so he could only imagine what kind of sight he made. Starved and exhausted and dirty, swimming in Emil's too-large t-shirt.

"Hey," Emil said. He gave Kit a soft little smile.

God, he was pretty. Kit didn't want to be mad at him.

"You feeling any better?"

"No," Kit said. "But I'm alive."

"Want some air?" Emil said. "Well, technically it's the same recirculated air as we're breathing now, but I was thinking I could show you my garden before... well, you know."

Kit didn't want to walk anywhere—his body nearly collapsed in protest at the thought—but for some reason, with his eyes still half-closed from sleep, he said, "Sure. Whatever."

It was like giving a dying person their last request, he told himself. One last nice thing before the end. He padded out the door after Emil, who paused to wait for him in the hall. Kit must have looked pathetic. Emil put a hand on the small of his back and slowed down until they were keeping pace.

Kit didn't care about plants, but he had to admit, the garden was impressive. It was far larger than he'd expected, a greenhouse with multiple rooms, each one full to bursting with green.

The whole ceiling was glass, and beyond that, there were stars on stars on stars.

And Emil beamed at him, giving him the biggest, brightest, dorkiest smile.

"Yeah," Kit said, dazzled. When Emil smiled at him, it made him stupid. He wanted to say *wow* and *it's beautiful* and *you really take care of all this?* and also *is there anything in here to eat?* but then he remembered what Travis had told him, and he tamped all that bullshit down. "Good job or whatever. Is there a place to sit around here or should I fall on the floor?"

"Right, right, I'm so sorry," Emil said, steering him toward a bench. It faced one of the windows. Kit slumped down into it, grateful not to have to stand any longer. "Are you sure you'll be okay to do this?"

"No," Kit said. "But I've already waited too long."

Emil hovered over him for a moment, not sitting down. Then he walked away and reappeared with an apple in his hand. He gave it to Kit.

Goddammit. Stop being kind. Kit took the apple and bit into it without saying thank you. It was sweet, juicy, perfectly crisp. He wanted to close his eyes and draw out this moment, to think of nothing but the taste on his tongue, but Laila and Aidan were waiting.

As Kit was eating, Emil outlined the plan he'd told his team earlier.

"I'm bringing Caleb in," Kit said when Emil was finished and he'd devoured the apple. "Laila and Aidan might need immediate medical attention. I don't trust him myself, but he's close to Aidan, so I think he'll cooperate."

"But that adds a trip on the way out," Emil said. "You can't take two people at the same time."

"Caleb might be able to get them into shape to make a

short run," Kit said. "They didn't go into that room of their own power, but if they can, I want them to get out on their own."

"That's... very thoughtful of you," Emil said. "But we have to design this rescue to be effective above all else."

"And that means bringing Caleb," Kit said. "The more functional runners we have, the better off we'll be. Who knows what's going to happen in there?"

"Point taken," Emil said.

"And I don't need your approval. You're not my fucking boss," Kit said, seizing on his momentary irritation. He had to rip the bandage off. It was time to ask questions. "Did you know? About Laila and Aidan. About any of it."

Emil had such serious, dark eyes. When he turned to Kit, he seemed to have understood already where this conversation was headed. The knowledge haunted his expression. "I didn't know about Laila and Aidan."

That answer was an obvious dodge. "And Oswin Lewis Quint's view of runners as some kind of untrustworthy aliens? Did you know about that?"

Emil was silent. It was answer enough.

"Fuck you," Kit said. It wasn't the brilliant, cutting remark of his dreams, but it was how he felt. "How could you? And don't tell me that *you* didn't feel that way—not you personally, oh no, never that—just the massively influential billionaire you work for. So different. Completely forgivable. I should let it go that you knowingly signed up to work for some ultra-powerful asshole with a shiny smile who thinks I'm not human. No big deal."

"Kit—"

Kit forced himself to stand. Emil was still sitting, so for an instant, he could loom over him. "Don't. When this is over, we're done. Don't look for me."

Emil raised his hands, palms up, a gesture of surrender. "Okay. If that's what you want."

"I just fucking said it's what I want," Kit said, and if he sounded even angrier, it was because his eyes were burning. Tiredness, he told himself. That's all it was.

"Can I ask you for one thing?" Emil said. "It's small, I promise."

Kit said nothing. He couldn't afford to give anything away. This would all be so much simpler if he were just angry with Emil, instead of... whatever it was he felt. He *was* angry. So why was it so hard to do this? Travis had pissed him off and he hadn't needed a whole goddamn whirlwind of feelings to deal with it. It had been sharp, clean anger—solidified by the knowledge that he and Travis were done forever.

This was different, and Kit didn't want it to be different. Emil was just like Travis—a hot guy he'd had sex with. A hot guy who meant nothing to him. Nothing ever lasted and Kit knew that. He'd always known that. He should have been prepared for this moment. He shouldn't have let Emil bring him to this fucking greenhouse, the one beautiful corner of this otherwise soulless prison carved into a space rock, and he shouldn't have let Emil touch him with what felt like concern and affection, and he shouldn't have let Emil give him an apple.

He shouldn't have let Emil kiss him.

All of that had confused the only issue that mattered, which was that Emil worked for a piece of shit bigot who thought Kit and everyone like him were untrustworthy and uncontrollable. Born con artists and criminals. Traitors in waiting. Emil had signed up for that.

Kit had been silent for a long time, so Emil spoke again, "All I want is for you to check in after the rescue. One message. You don't even have to message me. Just somebody up here. Let us know you made it out."

That wasn't so much. And yet it was. Emil wanted to know he was alive. Emil would be... what? Reassured? Comforted? Emil's request dug into Kit's insides like a fish hook, the barbed end of some line connecting them. It hurt, and Kit wanted to sever that line. But he knew better. Line or no line, that hook would still be buried in him. "Fine," he said. "But that's it. Now I'm going to find Lenny and Caleb so I can get this over with."

[14]
ADRENALINE

KIT COULD SEE THE HUNCH IN EMIL'S SHOULDERS AS HE left the greenhouse, but he ignored it. It wasn't his fault. Emil was the one who'd done something wrong. He deserved whatever he was feeling. And there were more important things to focus on.

Lenny and Caleb found him not long after that, both somber. What had Emil told them? *Kit's pissed off—don't make it worse.* No, even in his most spiteful imaginings, Kit couldn't picture Emil revealing any of their earlier conversation. Probably Lenny and Caleb had just seen his tragic, hangdog expression and picked up on it.

Caleb was wearing a black backpack loaded down with something. When he saw Kit's glance, he explained, "I thought I'd bring a few medical supplies, and Lenny suggested we pack some food, and uh..."

"Miriam and Dax prepared explosive charges," Lenny said. "That's the heaviest part."

"Good," Kit said. He grabbed Caleb around the waist with no preamble, making him blink and draw back in surprise. Caleb was bigger than him, and fit, but he didn't feel anything like Emil—and Kit didn't want to think about that. This was all business. You wanted to take someone through the Nowhere, you had to hold onto them. It didn't mean anything. Kit looked at Lenny. "You know how to follow me through?"

Lenny nodded.

Kit jumped. The Nowhere made him twitchy now since he'd been knocked around so much, but this was a short enough run that by the time he caught a hint of blue light in his peripheral vision, they were done. They stepped into the walled-off room where Aidan and Laila were still lying in their beds, worn down, angry, and cuffed.

Unlike last time, Laila was awake. It was a relief to see her face, those wide-set brown eyes and that big smile. "Kit!"

She had the sweetest, lightest voice—and she knew it and used it to great effect when she swore. "Laila," he said, smiling. Laila was on the very short list of people who hadn't let him down, right after Zin and Louann. He'd thought he might have to cross her name off that list, but he'd been wrong. It felt good to see her, and despite his fatigue, he'd crossed the room to touch her hand before he even knew it. She squeezed his hand. "We're gonna get you out."

"So Aidan's been telling me," she said, the sweetness in her voice turning sharp. "I wasn't sure I believed him. He said you came here by *accident*. That you didn't even know I was in here. That you weren't looking for me."

Kit tilted his head and let his mouth draw to the side. He'd messaged her a few times and gone to her apartment, but he couldn't fault her assessment. He should have realized something was wrong. But still. "Well, if I'd *known* you were kidnapped—" he started.

"Oh, right. Next time I'll leave a note that says 'Dear Kit, I've been kidnapped. Love, Laila.' I was missing for days! We were supposed to work together and I missed it. You must have looked for me at least a little, right?"

Caleb handed Kit a pick for Laila's handcuffs just in time. He fiddled with the lock until he got them to pop open. "I just thought you'd left," he said, freeing her hands. "People do that."

"Not me," she said. Caleb had examined the intravenous lines and removed them, studiously ignoring this conversation. Laila rubbed her uncuffed wrist, then held her hand out so that Kit could help her sit up straight. "You could have at least dropped by Detroit and asked my roommates, Kit, come on."

"I did! They told me you'd gone out. I thought they meant to the grocery or something. They didn't seem freaked out. I thought they were trying to get me to leave. And I'm rescuing you," he protested. "Is now really the time for a lecture?"

Caleb had moved on to helping Aidan out of bed. Lenny was setting charges around the perimeter of the room. Laila was leaning on Kit and she felt far too light. He reached into the backpack they'd set on the floor and offered her a pouch of some kind of pureed fruit. Kit was dimly aware that Aidan and Caleb were talking, and their conversation must be less awkward, because Lenny had opted to talk to them.

"Don't placate me with food," she said, opening it and sucking half of it down as fast as she could. Caleb had said something about how it might be easier for them to digest. She continued, "You really thought I'd stand you up. We've worked together for years, you're my best friend, practically my brother, and that whole time, you thought I was just waiting for the right moment to abandon you."

"I—" Laila thought they were best friends? Kit had never thought of it that way. Maybe he'd never let himself.

"Kit," she said and held up a finger as she swallowed the remainder of what she was eating. "I feel like someone ran me over,

I love you and I've never been happier to see you in my life, and I'm so fucking mad at you I could scream. And how is that I was abducted and imprisoned for days and somehow *I* feel the need to hug *you*?" And then she was clinging to him, still soft but with sharper edges than before, and that made his throat close up with guilt. Then Laila was crying, her face pressed into his shoulder, and suddenly he was crying, too. "I was so scared," she whispered.

"Me too," Kit said. He sniffled. He didn't *want* to be crying, but if Laila was going to hug him and cry, what could he do? In a way, it was a relief to let something out. It had been a tough few days, and it wasn't over. "Still am, actually."

"I hate to interrupt," Caleb said. "But we should go. I just gave Aidan a shot of adrenaline and he's going to try to get me out of here. Laila, I'd like to give you one, too."

"Kit can take me," she said. She'd angled herself to face Caleb but her arms were still firmly around Kit. "I'm not done scolding him."

"I will," Kit promised. "But take the shot anyway. The Nowhere's all fucked up here and I keep getting attacked by this thing. Trust me, you want to be able to run."

"Alright," she said. "I can barely feel it anymore. Who knows what they've been doing to me." She stepped away from Kit and let Caleb give her the injection.

"How much time do we have with the charges, Lenny?" Kit asked.

"I figure I'll detonate them right as we jump," Lenny said.

"Okay," Kit said, unsure why he'd bothered to ask. Lenny seemed to know what he was doing, and it wasn't like Kit had the authority to instruct him otherwise. But he didn't know what else to do with himself, standing there waiting for the moment they could leave this awful room behind forever. He watched Laila take a deep breath and close her eyes, testing to see if she had the energy to make a run. Aidan was tapping his fingers against his thighs as he stood watching Caleb pack up his syringe.

"Well."

Kit jerked his head up. Travis had materialized behind the partition screen. Kit hadn't heard a thing until he'd spoken. He'd stepped smoothly into view, hands behind his back, and was making eye contact with Kit. "For the record, I didn't want to do this," he said.

The sight of Travis made white-hot rage streak through Kit, burning away his fatigue. "The record doesn't give a shit."

"I'm here to offer you a deal," Travis said. "You stay, Laila and Aidan go free."

Kit laughed. "What puts you in a position to make offers? We're on our way out."

"I thought you might say that." Travis unclasped his hands and brought them forward. He was holding a gun. No, not holding—aiming. At Kit. "This is the other side of the offer. You and everyone else in this room die."

Kit risked a glance at his companions and took stock of their expressions. Aidan and Laila: defiant. Caleb: scared. Lenny: unimpressed. Among the four of them, they had three quasi-functional runners, one of whom was a veteran who happened to be holding a detonator for a bunch of charges placed all around the room. Kit was standing directly across from Travis and the gun was aimed at him. Caleb was within Aidan's reach. He trusted that Laila could get herself out. They had no reason to bow to Travis or Quint Services or anyone.

"I know what you're thinking," Travis said. "You're thinking you could jump before I shot you. And maybe you could. But I know you've had a bad few days, and we both know the Nowhere isn't what it used to be, especially for you. And you know I can follow you and bring you back here."

Kit said nothing.

"None of the rest of them matter," Travis said, casually swinging his gun to point at Caleb's head. "Stay or go, live or die, it's all the same to me. You're the one I need."

Kit didn't even have to tell Aidan to go. He already had his hands on Caleb. One second they were in the room, the next they weren't. Travis swiveled in Kit's direction, aiming the gun at his head. "Come on, Kit. It's not that bad. A few samples, some tests. If you're cooperative, they'll treat you fine. They'll even let you see the big handsome one you like so much."

"Laila, get out," Kit murmured. "Lenny, you too."

Lenny had the detonator. He could blow up the whole room. He knew it, Kit knew it, and Laila knew it. Travis didn't. But Kit wasn't going to leave Travis in here to die, no matter how wrong things had gone between them. Kit might be a career criminal, but he wasn't a murderer. If they were going to leave this room, Travis was going to come with them. That meant disarming him. Kit glanced at Lenny, wishing he could transfer his thoughts without speaking them aloud. Of the three of them, Lenny had the best chance of wresting that gun from Travis's hands.

"Don't fucking tell me what to do," Laila said.

The distraction was perfectly timed: Travis's gaze slid to her for just a second, but it was long enough for Lenny to tackle him. Kit heard a blast and didn't wait to find out how wildly off Travis's aim was. There was a bullet coming. He jumped.

[15]
NOT A THING

LAILA WOULD HAVE HIS LIVER FOR LEAVING HER AFTER he'd promised not to. He hoped she would, anyway—every recent trip into the Nowhere had felt like his last.

At least this time when the ghost showed up, he expected it. *Lange*, he reminded himself. *Not a thing, not a monster, not a ghost.*

Lange hadn't gotten that memo and he slammed into Kit with as much force as always. Kit tried to calm the panic that choked him. Lange wasn't malicious. He wasn't trying to kill Kit. Emil and Jake had agreed on that.

That was cold fucking comfort as they went tumbling through the void together. Kit struggled, trying to get a grip on Lange. He'd pulled that cat out of the Nowhere and it had instantly been a cat again—shouldn't the same be possible with Lange? But Lange pushed and pulled against him wildly, fighting him and making it impossible to direct them anywhere.

Kit had chased the cat for ages, and he'd only caught it when it had chosen to come to him. It hadn't been hard to pull the cat out of the Nowhere because the cat had *let* him do it. Lange wasn't letting him do anything. Every time Kit thought he had a hold, Lange shifted and Kit was grabbing nothing. There was no logic to his actions, not that Kit could perceive. He was driven by fear. He didn't want to submit to Kit's hold on him, but he didn't want to be alone in the Nowhere, either. He beat against Kit with everything he had. Maybe Emil and Jake had been wrong. Maybe he *was* trying to kill Kit. How long had it been? How far had they fallen? If Kit stepped back into the world, where would he be?

Too tired to fight any longer, Kit let Lange send them sailing through the Nowhere. When he dropped back into the world, he landed on his back in something cold and wet.

[16]
COMPLICATED

EMIL SPENT HIS AFTERNOON IN A MEDICAL EXAM ROOM with Winslow, answering every question in meticulous detail and at great length, letting Winslow prod him and take all the samples he wanted. He tried not to think of how Chávez might be distracting Heath, and he especially tried not to think of what Heath and Winslow needed distracting from. Was Kit okay? Had the rescue been successful? Would he hear the explosion when it happened?

"What's this cut between your shoulders?" Winslow asked, parting the back of his hospital gown and peeling back the tape and gauze with no gentleness. "It looks newer than your black eye."

"I hurt myself in the gym," Emil said. He twisted around to face Winslow. He could have answered most of the man's questions in a conference room, with both of them fully dressed, but Winslow had wanted him here, vulnerable. Powerless. He'd put himself in a position of authority. And so far, Emil had let him do it. He'd undressed and sat calmly and answered all the questions and breathed in and out when he was told to.

Winslow's watery blue stare said he didn't believe a word of what Emil had just said, but he didn't press Emil for more information.

"Mr. Singh," he said, at length. "I realize there has been some tension in the air since the incident, and I'd like your opinion on how we could resolve it. There are ten weeks remaining in the experiment, and assuming all goes well, your team is supposed to run a mission after that. I don't want to live under a dark cloud of suspicion for ten weeks, and I assume you and your team don't either. What can we do?"

Stop kidnapping and torturing runners.

"I think the team would like more transparency," Emil said. He'd spoken many similar, suitably professional and polite sentences on behalf of his team in the past. The words had never tasted so much like dirt. But he hadn't heard anything like an explosion yet, and that meant the mission wasn't over. "They were unhappy not to be told about the incident, and I can't say I was happy to be kept from communicating with them in the aftermath."

"That was for your safety. You had a concussion."

"Surely some accommodation could have been made," Emil said.

"Perhaps you're right."

"And I think it's clear to all of us that Dr. Lange didn't return to Earth for personal time," Emil said. "How can there be trust without honesty?"

"An excellent question," Winslow said. "Perhaps you'd like to be a bit more honest about how you've spent the past two days."

"First, I think I'm owed an explanation of why you lied to my team about what happened to Lange," Emil said. He was still perfectly calm. He might be half undressed and seated in the exam chair while Winslow stared him down, but when it came down to it, they were two men alone in a room, and one of them was sixty-something and never went to the gym. Emil could have his power back whenever he wanted it.

"Ah," Winslow said, as if he'd just come to the same conclusion. "The situation is delicate, you understand. We didn't want to alarm anyone."

"My team signed up to travel to other realities. They're not easily alarmed."

Winslow turned away and began to open drawers and rifle through them. The gesture betrayed nervousness. If he'd given up on appearing collected, he must be looking for something he could use against Emil, a drug or a weapon of some kind. As casually as he could, Emil stood up. He was ready for anything Winslow could do to him.

Neither of them was ready for the sound of the explosion.

It was muffled by the wall of rock between them and the secret room. On Earth, they might have mistaken it for thunder. But they were not on Earth. Emil could see Winslow's face in profile going from fear to shock to outrage. However the rescue mission had gone, this moment signaled the end of Emil's career. Before Winslow could turn, Emil grabbed his arms and twisted them behind his back.

"You're coming with me."

———

THE GREENHOUSE SUPPLY closet wasn't an ideal place to hold prisoners, but his team had blown up the only ideal place to hold prisoners on the asteroid, and Emil was grateful for it. He brought Winslow to the closet, where Chávez was waiting with Heath. Heath was furious. Chávez looked bored. She tossed Emil a pair of handcuffs, and he cuffed one of Winslow's wrists, threaded the cuffs around part of the heavy metal shelves, then cuffed the other.

"This is mutiny," Winslow was saying. He'd been spouting some version of this the whole time Emil had marched him down the hall. "You'll all be fired. You'll be *ruined*."

"Yeah, yeah," Chávez said. She'd cuffed Heath to the other end of the shelves. Emil wondered what kind of distraction she'd provided, and then hated himself for wondering. Chávez had volunteered to provide a distraction, and she'd done it, and that was enough. When she looked at him, her usual smile was gone. "I'll stay with them. Go find the others."

They were in Lange's room. Dax had hacked the lock on his door earlier so they could feed Subrahmanyan Chandrasekhar after Kit left, and then it had seemed useful to have an empty room. Emil felt his pulse pick up as he walked. He'd get to see Kit again. He wasn't supposed to be excited about that. Kit was upset with him. But if they could just see each other again, if Kit would just look at him, maybe they could—but no. Emil quashed that train of thought. He and his team were rescuing prisoners and attempting mutiny. He was too busy to worry about what one prickly, irritating, and bizarrely alluring twenty-one-year-old criminal might think about him.

And yet his heart kept beating faster.

The team wasn't in Lange's room. It was Dax, Miriam, and on the bed, that runner who'd tried to take Kit away. He was unconscious. Dax had their arms crossed and Miriam had her hands on her hips. "We should tie him up. It can't hurt."

"It won't do any good," Dax was saying. "Sedation is the only way to keep a runner in one place."

"Hi," Emil said. "What's going on?"

"Things went a little bit sideways in there," Dax said.

"Caleb is treating Lenny and the other two runners in one of the exam rooms," Miriam said. "Jake is with them. But anyway, this piece of shit tried to kill them, so Lenny tackled him, hit his head, and took his gun. But they didn't want to leave him in the room to die."

Miriam clearly disapproved of that last decision.

"Caleb injected him with a shot of something and said he should be out for a while," Dax added.

"Chávez and I, uh, subdued Heath and Winslow and left them in the greenhouse supply closet," Emil said. He wanted to ask where Kit was. Why hadn't either of them mentioned him? Miriam had said *the other two runners* but Emil couldn't tell which ones she meant. "She had handcuffs from somewhere."

"Aidan filched them from the secret room," Miriam said. "He's a smart one."

"When they got back from the secret room, we all stumbled on Chávez and Heath having one hell of an argument," Dax said. The tips of their ears were red. "It was... personal."

"You could have heard it from Mars. Didn't seem staged, either," Miriam observed. The two of them exchanged a glance, then looked at Emil, and he put on what he hoped was a convincingly bewildered who-could-possibly-have-guessed expression. "Anyway, Aidan gave Chávez the handcuffs then."

"So we're watching this runner for the moment," Dax said.

"It'll be challenging to keep him hostage," Miriam said.

"Ethically challenging, too," Dax said.

"He shot Lenny!" Miriam shouted, throwing her hands up.

"Whoa, I think you two might have buried the lede," Emil said. "Lenny got shot?"

"He'll be fine," Dax said. "Caleb is taking care of him. Lenny even said he thought the gun went off by accident when he tackled Travis."

"Bullshit," Miriam said. "This asshole jumped in there and pulled a gun on them. It's not an accident that he threatened their lives. And Lenny only said that so I wouldn't murder this piece of shit on the spot."

Dax and Emil exchanged a glance.

"And it... worked?" Emil asked. In mission simulations, Miriam followed orders as well as the rest of his team, but orders came from him, and he made them as unambiguous as possible. Lenny saying *it was an accident* wasn't an order, not by a long shot. Emil had never known Miriam to be sensitive to other people's requests.

Miriam gestured sharply at Travis, unconscious but alive in Lange's bed. That hadn't been the point of Emil's question—he'd been far more curious about why Miriam perceived Lenny saying *it was an accident* as *please don't murder him*, and why she'd listen if she didn't believe the accident part—but he decided to let it go.

"Well, this whole thing is a challenge," Emil said. He'd made a plan for the rescue, but had failed to think through the consequences of staging a mutiny and occupation of the facility. He didn't say that out loud, though. They needed him to be in charge, and he'd already expressed too much doubt. "If you're keeping an eye on him, then I'll go check in with the others."

Emil was only in the hallway for a few minutes, but it was enough time for his foolish heart to start hoping again. Maybe Kit was one of *the other two runners* that Miriam had mentioned. Maybe one of the others had simply gone home. But when he stepped into the exam room, Kit wasn't among its occupants. Instead he saw Caleb bandaging a wound on Lenny's arm, Jake trying to stand off to the side as unobtrusively as a man of his size could, and two young people sitting on the ground, slumped against the wall and each other, sharing a blanket. They were both wearing hospital gowns, and until this moment, Emil had forgotten that so was he. Chávez, Miriam, and Dax hadn't mentioned it.

Emil recognized one of the people as Caleb's friend, the agitator Aidan Blackwood, although he didn't look much like the notorious photo of his altercation with station security. In the photo, he was wiry and wild-haired—not quite handsome but memorably sharp-featured. A victim, but one who might fight back. The young man on the floor was too thin and too pale. Even his black hair looked dull, as if they'd starved him of color as well as calories. His eyes were closed.

The young woman with her head on his shoulder looked similarly beaten down by her experience, although she wasn't dangerously underweight like Aidan. She had light brown skin and, judging from her roots, underneath all that pink dye, her hair was black. Aidan's head was resting on hers. Unlike him, she was awake, her brown eyes trained on Emil. She was sucking something out of a little plastic pouch and she didn't stop to introduce herself.

This must be Kit's friend Laila. In normal circumstances, she must be stunning. Was that why she looked familiar? Had she been an actor or a model at some point? Emil couldn't place her, but he knew he'd seen her before.

He'd already spent too much time staring. He turned his attention to Lenny. "Miriam and Dax told me you got shot. It sounded fairly heroic, actually."

"Y'all would've done the same," Lenny said.

"It was heroic," Caleb confirmed. "And we're very lucky you don't need surgery."

Lenny grimaced at the word *lucky*, or maybe it was Caleb's touch. But he didn't comment. He focused on Emil and said, "I don't know where Kit is. Sorry."

As Emil was working out how to respond, Laila finally spoke up. "That little shit promised to stay with me and then he just fucking vanished."

"He *was* getting shot at," Caleb said mildly, not looking at her.

196 / FELICIA DAVIN

"Whatever," Laila said. "He'd better come back soon. If he's dead, I'll kill him."

It was something about her sour, flippant "whatever" that made the gears turn in Emil's brain. Laila looked familiar because she was notorious, just like Aidan. He'd seen her picture in the media years ago, when she was the fourteen-year-old Franklin Station Bank robber.

Emil tried to keep this realization off his face. He focused instead on Laila saying *he'd better come back soon*. That was good news. Kit and Laila were friends. Kit didn't want to see Emil again, but he would come back for Laila.

"Are there more of these?" Laila asked, waving the pouch in the air. "Or real food?"

"Take it slow," Caleb advised her. "But yes, there should be more in the pack."

"Aidan and I ate them all." Laila nudged the empty backpack with her foot.

So much for taking it slow. Emil smiled, thinking of Kit informing Lenny that yes, he could eat all of that. "I'll take you to the kitchen," Emil offered. "And I'm sure we can find you some clothes and a place to rest."

Aidan opened his eyes halfway. "I just want to sleep."

"You can take him to my room," Caleb said, keeping his focus on Lenny and not turning to face Aidan. "I won't be there for a while."

Caleb had taken the last empty room on the first floor, at the far end of the facility from Emil's. Heath and Winslow had rooms on the second floor, as did their six lab techs. Those people represented another problem, although Emil hoped that once presented with evidence of wrongdoing, they'd come around to his point of view.

"I'll take him," Jake said. He'd been so quiet that Emil had almost forgotten he was in the room, as tiny as it was. "I don't think anyone'll give us any trouble."

Emil nodded. "Good. And then go give Chávez a break from guard duty in the supply closet."

Emil helped Laila to the kitchen, sat her down at the table, and rummaged through the fridge. No wonder food had been disappearing faster than normal for all those months. Heath and Winslow had been feeding Travis Alvey. And then these past few days, he'd been trying to keep Kit alive. He put a carton of orange juice on the table. "It's looking a little ransacked in here. I'm not much of a cook, but I can handle scrambled eggs, if that sounds okay?"

"Literally any food sounds okay to me. You could offer me a whole pig and I would eat it," she said and then drank straight from the carton. After a long gulp, she put it down and sighed. "That adrenaline wore off fast. I'm not gonna be able to run for *days*."

"Aren't you allowed to eat non-halal stuff if you'd starve otherwise?" He was guessing her reference to pork was about religion, and coming from the infamous Franklin Station Bank robber, that was a surprise. But he tried not to show it. People were multifaceted, and they could change. He started cracking eggs into a bowl and didn't stop until the carton was empty. Eggs and meat were the hardest things to get up here, and it gave him some pleasure to give such a precious resource to Laila.

"Are you Muslim?" she asked, surprised. "And I was joking. Kit's probably told you, we eat barbecue whenever I'm in Nashville."

"Kit doesn't share that kind of thing with me. And I'm not Muslim, but a lot of people in my neighborhood were, and as a kid, I asked too many questions," Emil said, rueful. "My grandparents were Hindu. My parents are atheists. Unless you want to count academia as some kind of religion. I don't know what I believe. The more I know about the universe, the harder it is to figure out."

"I didn't grow up religious, but after I got out"—Emil assumed she meant *out of juvenile detention*—"some people took good care of me, and *they* were religious. So it's... I don't know about the institutions, and I certainly don't know about the divine, but I know those people. And they're good people. I don't follow their rules or live like they live, but sometimes I wish I did."

Laila worked with Kit sometimes, which meant she was a smuggler. Sometimes smuggled goods were innocuous—just a result of people trying to get around state laws and tariffs. More often, smuggled goods were guns and drugs. Emil didn't say anything about that. "I'm sorry about what Quint Services did to you. If you need to stay here to recover for a few days, we'll take care of you."

"I'm worried about Kit. You don't know that kid. He gets in trouble, like, well, this." Laila gestured broadly at Emil and the Facility 17 kitchen with her left hand, keeping the juice carton to her mouth with her right.

"I'm worried about him, too," Emil said, smiling privately about how much Kit would hate Laila referring to him as *that kid*.

"Oh, so you've met." A pause. "How did you meet, anyway?"

Laila might as well have said *is this your fault?* and Emil couldn't tell her it wasn't. "Quint Services hired him to bring me back here. I had to go down to the surface for questioning. We got knocked into another reality on our way back. Maybe you've seen the thing in the Nowhere?"

She shook her head. "Kit told us about it, but I didn't see it when we jumped. That's what makes me worried—he jumped first, so maybe it followed him."

Emil's heart sank. It was a good guess.

"Anyway," he said, whisking milk into the eggs. "I guess you know most of the story by now. Things got complicated."

He poured the eggs into the skillet and began to scramble them. They were almost finished by the time he realized how quiet Laila had been.

"Emil," she said. "That's your name, right?"

"Yes."

"Emil." A pause. "Is 'things got complicated' a euphemism for 'I had sex with Kit'?"

"*What*," he blurted, whipping around to look at her. How could she possibly have guessed? "I—"

"It's okay," she said, laughing. She waved a hand at the skillet. "Don't let those burn, I really need them." He turned around and focused on finishing. Laila kept talking. "Don't worry, nobody on your team said a word. But I've known Kit a long time. And Lenny seemed very concerned about how to tell you he wasn't with us. Also, you said 'things got complicated' in this kind of forlorn way and then turned around to brood into the eggs. You're not that hard to read."

Emil served Laila a giant plate of scrambled eggs and sat down across from her. "When you say you've known him a long time..."

"I don't mean that he would have fallen into bed with anybody who looked at him right," Laila said. "You've met him. You could've guessed that. He's guarded. As far as I know, it's only ever been Travis, and they don't actually... well, they've both tried hard to keep it from becoming a relationship. I guess that turned out to be for the best."

Emil made a noncommittal sound. Nothing involving Travis was *for the best*.

"I meant that Kit wouldn't have stuck around with you unless he wanted to," Laila said.

"He didn't," Emil said softly, "want to."

"Uh huh," Laila said. She didn't seem to believe him, which was absurd because Emil had heard Kit say the words *don't look for me*. Laila hadn't been there. And Emil couldn't tell her why Kit was so angry with him, because she'd be angry, too—and she had every right to be.

Chávez came into the kitchen and dropped into the seat next to Emil. The tired slump of her shoulders matched the downward cast of her eyes.

"Did you want something to eat?" he asked her.

"What? Oh, no. I came in here to check on you."

"I'm okay," he lied. "Are you?"

Chávez ignored him in favor of saying "hi" to Laila, who mumbled a greeting in between bites.

"I'm Chávez."

"I know," Laila said. "I heard that doctor screaming at you."

"Oh."

"She was very businesslike when she examined me," Laila continued. "I'm glad to know she can scream. My name is Laila."

"I know," Chávez said, almost smiling. That uplifted corner of her mouth made Emil realize he'd rarely seen Chávez go so long without smiling. He felt a pang of sorrow. It had been a hard day for her, too. At least Laila's ruthless, satisfied *I'm glad to know she can scream* remark seemed to have cheered her up a little. Or maybe it was Laila's face.

"I get that a lot," Laila said. She eyed Chávez's narrow frame. "I guess you don't have any clothes that would fit me. I'd be better off asking him."

"We'll find you something," Emil said. Miriam's clothes might fit, since she was shorter and thicker than Chávez, although not nearly as curvy as Laila. But this conversation was uncomfortable enough without him interjecting commentary on the bodies of the women he worked with, so he kept his mouth shut.

"And a bed," Laila said.

"We can find one of those, too," Chávez said.

If she were feeling more herself, Chávez would have said that flirtatiously. Offered up her own with a wink. It would have been inappropriate, but Emil had no doubt the Franklin Station Bank robber could handle herself. Instead, the exchange was flat, a testament to the fatigue and uncertainty that gripped all of them.

"I'll clean up here," Emil said. "Go get some rest."

"You wouldn't think I'd need it," Laila said. "I've been in bed for days. And yet somehow I'm tired." She gave Emil a curious, interested look. "Not too tired to talk more about you and Kit, though."

"*I'm* too tired for that," Emil said firmly.

"He's a lost cause," Chávez told Laila on their way out. "But good for you for trying."

Emil cleaned up the kitchen and then planned how to clean up the mess they'd made. He wanted to talk to his team, but they were all recovering or occupied by something important. Should he get in contact with someone higher up at Quint Services? Should he call station security at Franklin? They wouldn't be able to hold Travis Alvey any better than his team did. They wouldn't know how to save Lange or fix the breach in the Nowhere.

And none of them would know where Kit was.

He found all six lab techs and had a talk with each of them. The news he delivered distressed them, but they believed him, at least. He pulled together a schedule so that someone was always watching Heath and Winslow and someone else was always watching Travis. He left boxes of packaged food and some extra folded clothes outside the rooms where Laila and Aidan were staying. They'd have to feed Heath and Winslow at some point, too, but having seen their captives, Emil wasn't feeling too charitable about that.

He went into the greenhouse to think. Usually, the feel of earth in his hands soothed him and made it easier to come to the right conclusions. But Emil worked for hours and nothing came to him. And when he finally went back to his room to shower and change for bed, he admitted to himself that he hadn't really been thinking. He'd been waiting for Kit.

Evening light streamed through the forest, painting the snow gold and peach and striping it with the long purple shadows of the trees. Kit was fucking freezing.

He hugged himself, Emil's t-shirt soaked from where he'd fallen into the snow, and tried to stop his teeth from chattering. He took one more wet, bare step into the snow, the cold of it stinging. He had no idea where he was, if it was Earth or some other world, if there were people around, but he knew he was going to die. He didn't have the energy to make another run, and even if he had, Lange would be waiting in the Nowhere. He'd freeze to death before he found enough food to win his energy back. Maybe he should just lay down in the snow right now and let it happen.

He trudged through the snow instead. Maybe there was a drier, less snowy place to die. Kit knew that didn't really make sense, but he was miserable and exhausted and he couldn't hold himself to that kind of standard anymore. Making sense was for people who hadn't been shoved into other worlds. People with shoes, even.

His whole life, he'd believed that no one was looking out for him. Now it was true.

Zin and Louann weren't runners. They couldn't look for him. Laila and Aidan couldn't possibly come for him in time. Travis wouldn't. It looked like Lenny had been shot just before Kit had jumped. Those were all the runners who knew he'd left. And Kit had told the one non-runner who might have the dedication to find him *don't look for me*. He was well and truly fucked, and it was his own doing.

He wished he'd said goodbye to Zin and Louann. It had been days and he hadn't even messaged them.

It had been years and he'd never once told them how he really felt. He insisted on paying rent. They needed the money, but it was more than that. It was to keep up one last barrier—if he paid rent, he could tell himself he was their tenant, not their kid. He was nobody's kid. Never had been. His biological parents had fucked off to who knows where, the Home hadn't ever lived up to its name, and his foster family had been a joke. Every time he'd wanted to trust someone, to make himself comfortable, he'd been burned. With Zin and Louann, it had been years, and he was still scared that some day they'd lose interest. They'd want his apartment back. They'd ask him to leave and they wouldn't miss him.

Barefoot in the snow, with his body temperature dropping, he realized he'd been scared of the wrong thing. Zin and Louann were his family. They were home. Here, some unknowable, unbridgeable distance from them, with no way to get back and his death looming, he knew he should have told them so. There was a thing to be scared of: they were never going to know.

He didn't know how long he'd been walking. It felt like years. The forest all looked the same to him. Pines and more pines. Emil probably could have looked at the trees and learned something from them, like whether this was Earth, but Emil wasn't here. Kit knew fuck-all about trees.

The forest ran in front of him and behind him as far as he could see, but mountains rose to the left and the right. As the altitude climbed, the trees thinned and the snow thickened. There were a few bald patches, cliff faces too steep to hold snow. Kit looked to either side, searching for anywhere that looked dry and sheltered. A dark spot in the ridge to his right might be a shadow from overhanging rock. It might be a cave.

He turned toward it, hoping he'd have enough energy to get there. More snow had begun to fall while he was walking. It was melting in his hair and trickling down the back of his neck.

Unlike Emil, Kit wasn't *usually more prepared for survival situations.* There'd been a backpack full of packaged food and medical supplies on the floor of the secret room and he hadn't had the presence of mind to grab it before jumping. He should've known Lange would be waiting for him. How many times had it happened? Why hadn't he thought of carrying something with him until he'd seen Caleb and Lenny show up with preparations? Why had he rushed headlong into rescuing Laila and Aidan, not even bothering to put on shoes?

He'd been in such a hurry to get away from Emil. It seemed stupid now. Not his anger—that was justified. But he shouldn't have let it push him into danger. He should have taken the time to think through the possible consequences.

Kit wasn't accustomed to living like that. He wasn't a goddamn soldier. Life was exciting, but rarely dangerous. Until a few days ago, he'd never had any trouble jumping to exactly where he wanted to be. He made money, not plans. Consequences were for other people.

He wanted to silence the voice in his head that reminded him that if he hadn't pushed Emil away right before jumping, some of this could have been prevented. *I had a right to be angry*. But Emil would have respected Kit's anger while still offering calm, distant, professional advice on how to survive, if Kit had let him. He was infuriatingly mature like that, even when he was wrong.

Emil would have apologized, if Kit had let him. He would have done everything in his power to make it right.

Isn't that exactly what he was doing when he helped you rescue Aidan and Laila?

It didn't matter. Kit was never going to see Emil again. He stumbled, hardly able to feel his feet. Now that he was closer, he could see the dark spot he'd thought might be a shadow was definitely an opening in the cliff face. Kit walked up to it, feeling the burn in his calves at the slight incline, and then had to get down on hands and knees to see inside. It was a cave. The mouth was smaller than the interior, which was mercifully dry. It was a few degrees warmer inside, out of the wind and the snow, as good a place to die as he was going to find. Kit crawled inside and collapsed.

When he awoke, he wasn't sure how much time had passed. It took him a moment to recall his circumstances. His body ached and he didn't fully understand how he was still alive. The cave was impenetrably dark to his right, but to his left, light streamed through the entrance at a different angle. Had he slept all night? Had he woken because it was morning? No. Something else had changed. The scrabbling of animal claws against the loose sediment floor of the cave echoed in the darkness.

Kit wasn't alone.

[18]

TEA

EMIL WAITED TWENTY-FOUR HOURS FOR KIT TO COME back. He did other things in that span of time, but they were never in the front of his mind. He checked on Lenny, who was cheerful despite having a bandaged wound on his arm, and Aidan and Laila, both still weak but improving. He saved Laila for last, since she was the one most likely to know if Kit had come back.

He hadn't.

If Emil was honest with himself, he'd scheduled himself as Travis's guard this afternoon on purpose. But since he'd just stolen a syringe and a dose of adrenaline from Caleb's stockpile before going to the room where Travis was being held unconscious, he wasn't feeling particularly honest.

Emil didn't like to intimidate people. He didn't feel intimidating on the inside, since most of what he wanted in life these days was to tend his garden or go for a walk in the woods. He remembered a time when the world had responded to him differently, when he'd been a chubby little kid that people wanted to pat on the head. Now when he passed among people he didn't know, they were more likely to surreptitiously straighten their posture. Over the years since he'd become so physically imposing, he'd adjusted his behavior accordingly, and now he spent a lot of time smiling, being polite, making himself non-threatening.

When he walked into the room with Travis Alvey, he shed every last one of those mannerisms.

He woke Travis up roughly, dragged him upright, and kept a grip on his arm.

It was easy, even satisfying, to loom over Travis. He was taller that Kit, but he wasn't a large man. Fashionably slender, he didn't look like he spent much time in the weight room. Emil invaded his space and forced him to back up into the wall.

"You feel good about yourself? Feel big and strong?" Travis said. He was probably aiming for defiant, but his voice quavered at the end. He was, as Emil had suspected, not in shape to make a run. Not without help.

Emil smiled, glad Travis had gotten the point. "You're going to help me."

"Why would I do that?"

"Pick a reason," Emil said. "You threatened some people I care about, you're powerless and I've got a hold on you, anyone who might have been your ally in this facility is chained up in a closet, and I think maybe, just maybe, you care if Kit lives or dies."

"I pointed a gun at him," Travis said. "So I don't know why you'd think that."

"You didn't kill him." Emil tried hard not to make it a question.

"Of course not. He jumped. It's hard to shoot a runner." Travis didn't say that defensively so much as offensively, like he was daring Emil to try.

"If I wanted to kill you, you'd be dead," Emil said, channeling Miriam. As angry as he was with Travis, he didn't actually want to kill anyone.

Travis scoffed. "You wanted to feel scary a second ago, but you don't have the guts to kill me. You'd make your little attack dog do it."

Emil shrugged. "Or I could hand you over to the two people whose imprisonment and starvation you facilitated. It'll take them a while to get back on their feet, but once Laila and Aidan can access the Nowhere again, it'll be pretty hard for you to get away from them. I'm sure they have a few things to express."

Travis had done a valiant job of keeping a disdainful expression on his face, but his eyes got a touch bigger at that. It almost made Emil wonder if he felt guilty. Then he plastered on his smugness again and it was like it had never happened. "Fine. What do you want?"

"Kit hasn't come back here," Emil said. "Not even for Laila. If he had any control over where he was, he'd be here or at Zinnia Jackson's. I need to know if he's alive. You can get me there."

"What's in it for me?"

"You get me there and back, I'll forget to sedate you, and then you'll be free," Emil said. It was distasteful, letting Travis go unpunished after he'd shot Lenny, but it also solved the problem of holding him prisoner. Emil couldn't plan a rescue mission and a mutiny based on Heath and Winslow's unconscionable mistreatment of Laila and Aidan and then turn around and starve his own captive.

He didn't know Travis well, but given that he was in Kit's circle of acquaintances, he probably lived on the fringes of society, taking payments in cash for being a supernatural courier. Work for Quint Services, steady and high-paying, had probably seemed like a dream to him. And if he'd developed some objections along the way, it would have been too late. Heath and

Winslow would have threatened him and anyone he cared about.

Travis let out a humorless bark of laughter. "I'll never be free. You don't understand what they did to me. Heath and Winslow made me their little captive pet."

"But you're a runner."

"Not anymore I'm not. They poisoned me. Now I can only get into the Nowhere if they give me their antidote, which they dole out in tiny doses so I can follow their orders. Wouldn't be surprised if they'd done the same to Aidan and Laila."

Travis was Heath and Winslow's first experimental subject. *Shit.* Emil's grip loosened.

"I don't know where they keep it, of course," Travis said. "But I know it's around here. I can't run unless you get me some. Of course, once you give me that shot, you won't have any control over where I take you." He obviously took pleasure in the thought. "I could leave you in the Nowhere."

Emil didn't let his revulsion show. That wasn't possible. Emil was enough of a coward to know. When the experiment had started, he'd asked every scientifically minded person he knew, a number of whom were world-class experts on the Nowhere. If a runner lost hold of you, the Nowhere just spit you back out—usually, but not always, right where you'd started. That little bit of uncertainty was enough to keep most runners holding on tight, but it was just the randomness of the exit point that was a concern. You couldn't get stuck in the Nowhere.

At least, that's what Lange had said before he'd gotten trapped there.

"You're right," Emil said. "That's a risk I'll have to take."

"Let go of me. I'm not going anywhere until you bring me the antidote."

"The shot of adrenaline worked on Aidan and Laila," Emil

said. With reluctance, he dropped his grip on Travis. "If they went through the same treatment as you..."

"Sure, maybe it'll work one time. But that's not enough. You find me Heath and Winslow's stash, you bring me all of it, or we're not going anywhere."

"What does it look like? Can you give me any other useful information?"

"It's a clear liquid. Heath is always the one who gives me the injection."

Emil stalked off. He convinced one of Heath's lab techs, a young woman named Mei, to unlock the lab and every cabinet in it. She couldn't or wouldn't answer any of his questions about this alleged antidote. Emil couldn't tell if Heath had really been so secretive, or if Mei was afraid of crossing her.

Emil decided to trust her when she huffed, tried to pull her hair into a ponytail, and then gave up halfway through, carding her fingers through it and knocking her glasses askew. "Of course I'm afraid! But she also kept secrets. This whole place is creepy as fuck. Look. I don't want to believe anything you've told me about what Dr. Heath was up to, but something's telling me it's all true. I came here with you, right? I unlocked the door. I'll do what I can. We'll go through the lab together. If I know what it is, I'll tell you."

Mei could identify every clear liquid they found except one labelled DPR8. There wasn't much of it, only a few syringes' worth, but Travis would just have to deal. "Thank you, Mei."

"I want out," she said. "I don't know what's going to happen here, but I just want to get out and work in a normal lab. No more cutting-edge science for me. No more being caught between you and Quint Services. And no more ghosts!"

"Do the other lab techs want out too?"

"Can you imagine them wanting to stay?" Mei asked, which was a good point.

"I'll see what I can arrange," Emil said. He couldn't make any promises since Travis might drop him in the ocean in the next thirty minutes, and he had no real negotiating power with Quint Services anyway, but he would try. "Lie low, okay?"

"As if I'd do anything else."

Emil left Mei and brought the liquid to Travis. He complained, as predicted, about the small quantity, and he would have backed out of their deal if he'd known that Emil was holding back on him, but Emil administered that lie and the injection into Travis's arm with calm authority.

"They'll find me," Travis said. "If I can't run."

"If you need a shot every time you jump, this leaves you with two jumps after you bring me back here. You'll just have to choose wisely." Emil almost added *I know that's not something you're good at* but he decided against further antagonizing Travis before they jumped.

Travis eyed him. "You should be more afraid of Quint Services than you are. But whatever. I'll take you to the shitty bar where Kit's weird old lesbian friends live."

They're his family, Emil wanted to say. But what did he know? He'd met Zin once. And Kit had told Emil not to look for him, and here Emil was, teaming up with the man who'd pointed a gun at Kit and started this whole mess.

"Not like it's hard for me," Travis continued, looking extra smug and suggestive. "I've been there enough times."

"Take me to the front door," Emil said sharply. "Not Kit's bedroom."

And that was how he ended up in front of Zinnia Jackson's bar with Kit's ex-fuck-buddy. He knocked and she called out "We're closed!" in an irritated voice.

"It's Emil," he said, knocking again. "We met... Saturday morning." The days were running together. "I was with Kit."

The door swung open. Zin held a broom menacingly. Her

red curls were flattened underneath a bandana and she'd been crying. Her expression went from stormy to surprised and back again as she took stock of the two men at her door. "If you're gonna tell me Kit's dead, do it now and get out of my bar."

They weren't technically in her bar, but Emil knew better than to point that out. "So you haven't seen him?" he asked, his heart falling.

"Not for days," Zin snapped.

"He disappeared yesterday afternoon," Emil said. He tried to put on his reassuring-figure-of-authority voice and it didn't work. He sounded faint. "He was... with me, more or less, before that. I was hoping I'd find him here."

Zin's whole demeanor changed. "Oh, baby," she said, and passed the broom to Travis so she could hug Emil. "I know."

She wrapped her arms around him and pressed him into the soft bulk of her body. Emil didn't deserve this comfort. Kit had told him not to come here. He took it anyway, letting Zin squeeze him and murmur "you'll find him, I know you'll find him" in his ear.

She let go eventually. Travis shoved the broom back at her, furious about the whole exchange, and she accepted it without really looking at him. "Do you want to come in for some coffee? Tea?"

Emil had all the information he needed. Kit wasn't here. He needed to go plan another rescue, one he had no idea how to carry out.

But Zinnia Jackson had hugged him and invited him in and for the first time since he'd arrived, there was the faintest ray of hope in her eyes. "You can go through his things if you need to," she said. "For clues."

Emil didn't think there would be any clues. This wasn't a normal missing persons case. "Yes. Tea would be lovely."

He could almost feel Travis roll his eyes.

"You too," Zin said, addressing Travis for the first time. "I know you've never liked me, but you meant something to Kit, and you're helping Emil, so you might as well come in."

Travis didn't protest any part of that assessment, but he did follow Emil into the bar. Zin was already in the tiny kitchen in the back, pulling things out of cabinets. "Go ahead upstairs," she called. "You know the way."

It was awkward, going into Kit's bedroom while Travis hovered in the doorway. Travis had spent a lot more time here than Emil, but he leaned against the doorjamb in silence while Emil knelt on Kit's mattress and sorted methodically through piles of clothes. His wardrobe was a rainbow of color and texture arrayed around Emil. There were a few items that Emil didn't fully understand, and it made him wish he'd known Kit longer and seen more of his style. But there was nothing to indicate where he might be, or if he was even alive. It was beautiful and utterly useless.

Emil folded things and began to put them back as neatly as he could. He paused with a sweater in his hands. It was red with a wild, zigzagging black pattern, it looked far too big for Kit, and Emil suspected the slashes in it were purposeful. There was nothing at all practical about it, and yet Emil held onto it. Kit might be anywhere, in any climate, and if he was found—when he was found—he'd need clothes. He'd worn Emil's t-shirt and shorts into the secret room. As far as Emil could remember, he'd been barefoot when he'd made the run. His boots were still on Emil's floor, tangled in seaweed.

Emil selected an assortment of clothes for every type of weather he could imagine and he plucked another pair of boots from Kit's floor. Then he got up.

Travis raised his eyebrows at Emil holding an armful of Kit's clothes. "Thieving? Didn't think you were the type."

Emil had done plenty of shoplifting in his misspent youth,

but Travis was correct. "I'm going to find him," he said, pushing past Travis and heading downstairs. "Now come on. Award-winning vocal legend and pop icon Zinnia Jackson invited us to tea."

Tea would have been lovely if Travis hadn't sat there glowering the whole time. Zin smiled when she saw the pile of clothes in Emil's arms. "You know," she said, leaning on the bar across from him. "The first time I ever took him shopping, that was when I knew."

"When you knew?" Emil asked.

"Oh, I liked him before that," Zin said. "Even loved him. He'd been with us for a few weeks by then—we found him in the back alley, looking at Louann's bike. No idea where he'd come from. But he looked hungry, and we had food, so we invited him in. We spent a long time searching for any family members, or foster family, any kind of caretaker, but he didn't want to talk about it and nobody seemed to be missing him. It broke my heart and I thought, well, *I* want to keep him safe, even if nobody else does. So we let him stay. But when I set that boy loose in a store and told him I'd buy him whatever he wanted to wear, he came back with an absolute mess of textures and colors—you would not believe what he'd managed to find— that was when I knew he was my child."

"Ah," Emil said, thinking back on Zinnia Jackson's pop career, filled with feathers and sequins and leather and mesh. She'd never shied away from any color or pattern. "A family resemblance."

"He didn't know it then," Zin said. "Maybe he still doesn't. But I knew. And I saw the look on Louann's face in that store. She's a hard woman to read, unless you're me and you've been crazy in love with her for decades. She just kinda smiled and said 'Guess he's staying.' And I knew that was Louann speak for 'every time I look at either of you I want to explode with love, I am so wild about both of you I can hardly contain it,' and some-times I like to prove to her that I can speak her language, so all I said was, 'Guess he is.'"

Emil smiled at that story. "Kit seems a little bit like her, too."

"Oh, no, not really," Zin said. "Louann's quiet and under-stated by nature, but she expresses herself all the time. You just have to know how to listen. It's different with Kit. He's afraid."

Their conversation suddenly felt even more intrusive than going through Kit's things. And Emil had no doubt that wher-ever Kit had ended up, he *was* afraid. "I should go," Emil said. "If we're going to look for him, there's no time to waste."

[19]

NOBODY'S AREA OF EXPERTISE

TRAVIS DEPOSITED EMIL IN HIS ROOM AT FACILITY 17, eager to get away from Zin's bar. "You're not gonna reneg, right? I'm free to go?"

"Yeah," Emil said, tired. He had more important things to do than keep Travis Alvey locked up, and he was puzzled when Travis kept staring at him instead of simply vanishing, like Emil wanted him to.

"You know I can't make another jump today—not without a little help."

"Mm." Emil had forced him to jump to and from Earth, not long after he'd jumped out of the secret room. He had to concede the point. "What do you want?"

"Your bed—without you in it, don't get any ideas," Travis said. "And something to eat. I'll be gone tomorrow."

"Fine."

"No 'but where am I supposed to sleep tonight?' protests?" Travis asked with a lascivious smile. "You're closer to your team than I thought."

Emil didn't dignify that with a response. He wasn't going to be here tonight, if things went to plan—although calling what he had a *plan* was a gross overstatement. "I need you to leave the door unlocked while I'm here. You've been stealing from the kitchen for months, so you can feed yourself," he said and then turned and left.

His shift with Travis would be over in two hours, which meant he had two hours before someone discovered that Travis wasn't sedated in Lange's bed and started asking questions. It made Emil ache to deceive his team, but it would hurt more to invite them on an unplanned mission that had a high probability of killing him.

Miriam was in the supply closet watching Heath and Winslow. That was good. She'd do what he asked, even if she questioned his motives in private. When Emil walked in, she straightened her already straight spine and looked him in the eye.

"I'd like to talk to Heath alone," he said. "Travis is unsupervised for the moment, but he's unconscious. I'll take Heath back to Lange's room with me so we can have our conversation there."

Miriam handed him the key to the handcuffs without a word. He uncuffed one of Heath's hands so the cuffs were no longer wrapped around the metal shelves, then he led her out into the hallway and shut the door behind him. When he turned to enter her lab, Heath raised her eyebrows. She waited until they were inside with the door closed to say, "You're lying to your team."

"I'm protecting my team," he said. Mei had closed all the cabinets so their earlier ransacking wasn't so obvious. Emil was grateful she'd covered their tracks and gotten herself out of sight. "You wouldn't understand."

"What did you bring me here for?"

"Your work with the dimensional prions," Emil said. "I need to get through the Nowhere and back out again. I think you're repulsively amoral, but you're the person I know who's best qualified to do this. Make me a runner."

"Assuming that's even possible—three months of experiments haven't had much success—why would I do that? You've been keeping me in a closet."

"You help me, I lie to Quint Services and put the blame for everything on Winslow," Emil said. "Your reputation will survive intact and you can get another job somewhere else."

"Uh huh." Jennifer Heath hadn't gotten this far in life by being a fool, and she looked suitably skeptical. It was a crazy plan, after all. "This is insane and it's not going to work. And I can't believe I'm even bothering to point this out, but if you think I'm repulsively amoral, why would you let me inject you with something you barely understand?"

"Oh, that," Emil said. "Because you're going to inject yourself first."

Rage chased shock across her features. "This isn't going to work," she repeated, her voice low and her jaw tight.

"The way I see it, we know how to get someone into the Nowhere—the door in Lange's lab," Emil said. "That'll unfold me—and you, since you'll be testing this on yourself—just fine. The problem is refolding. So it's only half the work you had to do before, when you thought you needed to make your test subjects unfold *and* refold."

"Why me and not Winslow?" Heath asked. "Couldn't you just as easily have made him the same deal? Did you think I'd be easier because I'm a girl?"

"I thought you'd be easier because Chávez saw something in you worth getting to know," Emil said. It was the truth. That and he'd been through her whole lab with Mei, so he had a reasonable idea of its contents. "And I know you wanted me to persuade Kit to stay in this facility. My methods are a little different from what you suggested, that's all. But think, Jen—

he's the first runner we know of to cross into other realities. Multiple times now. You don't want him to be lost to science forever, do you?"

"If it means I have to walk into the back of Lange's lab, sure I do," Heath said. "If you wanted pure scientific fervor, you picked the wrong co-author."

"Sorry. I think you misunderstood. This isn't a negotiation. We're walking into the breach together regardless, so either you inject us with something that gives us a fighting chance of ever getting out, or we both end up like Lange." He had to convince her. There was no time to let doubt creep into his tone or his expression.

"Emil. This isn't you. You don't want to do this to me. You care about following the rules and doing the right thing."

"But you don't."

"Jesus, you are not who I thought you were," she muttered.

"You confined and tortured two innocent people," Emil snapped. And she and Winslow had poisoned Travis, though Emil was less willing to think of him as innocent. "I've been making small talk and eating breakfast across the table from you for months. Don't talk to me about *you are not who I thought you were.*"

Heath gave him a stony stare. Neither she nor Winslow had expressed anything resembling regret or apology since their unofficial arrest. Maybe they intended to deny their involvement. Could they slip away unpunished? The thought turned his stomach.

He didn't actually intend to drag Jennifer Heath into the breach. He didn't want to lead his life in that eye-for-an-eye, torture-for-torture way. But she had to believe she was going with him. He couldn't trust her otherwise.

The door opened.

Fuck. Emil could have sworn he'd locked it.

Dax slipped into the room. The door clicked shut softly behind them. "This is a stupid plan."

Emil supposed now wasn't the time to quibble about saying hello or how are you. "It's the only plan," he said. He should probably ask how Dax figured it out, and if they'd told anyone else.

"Really? *Her*?" Dax asked, eyeing Heath. "You're gonna let her inject you with something risky before you go bounding off to the un-making of all your matter?"

"It's what we've been doing for months," Emil said. "Just a little more rushed and a little less official."

"We didn't know she was *evil* beforehand, Emil," Dax said, as though they were exercising great patience. "You sure you don't know anybody else brilliant and crazy enough to work with you on this? Someone who, say, doesn't have a history of imprisoning people and starving them?" They waggled their eyebrows, raising them so high they disappeared into fluffy red hair.

"I didn't think you'd let me go alone," Emil said quietly. And then with more force, "And I can't let anyone go with me. It's too risky."

"Yeah," Dax said. "I know. Just imagine we had this conversation already. I played the whole thing out in my head on the walk over here. I can't stop you from going and you won't let any of us come with you, but for fuck's sake, at least let me be the one who doses you."

That was unexpected. Still, Emil hesitated. "It's not really your area of expertise."

"Emil, it's nobody's area of expertise. No one has ever done this before. Lange walked into that breach and he hasn't walked back out yet," Dax said.

"Neither of you listened to me," Heath interjected. "It's not going to work. The prion only acts on matter that is folded in a certain way—a different way from the matter in our reality. If Emil had any such matter in him, the prion would already have worked."

"That just means we need to find some way to get other matter into him," Dax said.

"Sure," Heath shot back. "Because there's so much material from other realities just lying around."

"Actually," Emil said, thinking of the plastic bag he'd taken from Zin's kitchen and the seaweed on the floor of his room. "There is. Do you think it would be enough to ingest it?"

Dax said yes at the same time that Heath said no, then they stared at each other. "Bone marrow or blood would be better," Heath said.

"Yeah, we know you're a vampire," Dax said. "None of our runners are in good enough shape to give you blood right now, and we definitely don't have time for a bone marrow transplant. Eating something from another reality is our best bet."

"It's a fucking bad bet," Heath said.

"You just need to know that you can make it *out* of the Nowhere one time," Dax continued, ignoring Heath. "Hopefully you'll make it to wherever Kit is and then he can bring you back. If you don't make it to where Kit is..."

"It's a one-way trip," Emil finished. He'd miss the team and Zora and his parents, but he couldn't live with himself if he didn't try. "I know. I thought about it. I'm still going."

"I know," Dax said. "I had this whole conversation in my head already, remember? But if anything bears repeating, it's that."

"So what else am I going to say?" Emil asked, smiling.

"It's all going to be very noble and determined," Dax said, taking his question seriously. "And if I try to argue with you that the life of a person you met a few days ago isn't worth your own, you won't listen."

"I wouldn't leave any of—"

"Us, I know," Dax said. "But he's not one of us. Not to me, not yet. But he means something to you, so I'm here, doing what I can to keep you alive."

"Thank you," Emil said.

"Put her back where you found her," Dax said with a tilt of their head toward Heath, who looked disgruntled. "And stop trying to hide things from us. We're smart. That's why you picked us in the first place."

"Right," Emil said. He took Heath back to the supply closet. Miriam frowned at him in a way that promised future arguments, but she knew better than to start anything in front of their prisoners.

When he returned to Heath and Winslow's lab, Dax was preparing a syringe. The liquid inside it was unremarkable, colorless, odorless, and clear.

"It looks so unassuming," Emil said. Normal prions weren't something any sane person wanted in their body. Something called a dimensional prion ought to inspire a similar reaction. But as Heath and Dax had already pointed out, Emil's plan wasn't anywhere near rational.

"It can be any kind of matter," Dax reminded him. "Its most important property is something we can't perceive."

Emil had received so many injections over the course of the last few months that getting one more shot didn't feel momentous. He exposed his arm.

"Let's wait," Dax said. "I didn't want to ask in front of Heath, but what do you have from another reality that you're planning to eat?"

"Two different plants," Emil said. "Some berries that I happened to bring back after the first trip Kit and I made. And some seaweed that Kit got tangled in when Lange pushed him into deep ocean water. The berries are... well, I won't say *safe*, but they won't kill me. Not sure about the seaweed."

"Apparently I missed a lot. Also, gross." Dax made a face. "How are you planning to eat it?"

"Uh, with my mouth?"

"No, I mean... are you going to eat it raw? Put it in a blender?" Dax asked. "Assuming we test it and it's non-lethal."

"Oh." Emil hadn't considered any of that. Lenny was the best cook among them, but he'd just been shot. Maybe Jake would have an idea. Emil vaguely remembered a story about Jake working in a diner as teenager. Then again, Emil didn't care what it tasted like. He just needed enough of it in his body to get him out the other side of the Nowhere.

The next few hours were a blur. He documented as much as he could about the mysterious seaweed—and now that Dax had asked him how he planned to eat it, the dried, salt-encrusted ropes of it did look distinctly unappetizing—and the berries he'd brought back from the desert. At least he knew they didn't taste bad, although their side effects were likely to be embarrassing. He'd handle it.

When he returned to the lab, Laila was sitting in a rolling chair with her feet up on the desk in front of her, chatting with Dax while Dax did something he couldn't see at one of the lab benches. Emil almost didn't recognize Laila—she'd curled her hair and put on a startling amount of makeup in asymmetrical, mismatched black blocks around her eyes. Where had she found makeup or a curler? Emil would guess that the grey t-shirt and sweatpants she was wearing had once belonged to Miriam, but they hadn't fit Miriam like that.

"Hey," Laila said. "I heard you're going to get Kit."

Emil braced for an argument. "Yeah."

"I gave Dax some of my blood," she said. "For you. They say we're compatible."

"You didn't have to do that! You're recovering—"

"I should be going to get him," Laila interrupted. "If there was any way I could, I'd be gone already. But I had to stop to breathe on my walk over here and every time I stand up, I black out for a second. So the best I can do is help you. Let me."

"Can you really afford to give blood right now?"

"I'm alive. I'll make more," Laila said. "Besides, Dax says you need to stuff yourself full of as many different *foldings* as possible. I'm a fucking pretzel. Have at it." She gestured grandly at Dax, and now that Dax had turned, Emil could see they were handling a bag of blood.

"Thank you, Laila."

"Find Kit," she said.

Emil's life was just a series of people demanding to help him. As he was accepting Laila's blood transfusion, Miriam and Jake showed up. Jake was carrying a huge pack specifically for backpacking. Miriam had brought him an assortment of weapons, including a handgun, knives of varying sizes, and a very large can of pepper spray.

"Come back so I can yell at you about how stupid this was," she said.

"Sounds great," Emil said.

"I forbade Lenny from coming over here since he just got shot," Miriam continued, impervious. "But he says he loves you." She shifted her weight from one foot to the other, supremely uncomfortable at having been burdened with this message.

"And he had very specific instructions about which flavors of protein bar to pack," Jake added solemnly. "Chocolate Peanut Butter Power Blast, in case you were wondering."

"Thank you," Emil said, and it wasn't nearly enough.

In the end, after determining that the seaweed was non-lethal, he put it in a blender. The resulting smoothie was both grassy and salty, and Miriam and Jake regarded him with silent horror as he downed it.

"You must really, really like him," Dax said, awed.

"I'd do the same for any of you," Emil said. He'd saved the berries for last, knowing the effect they were going to have, but once he'd eaten them, there was nothing left but to stuff Kit's clothes into his pack and go to Lange's lab.

———

EMIL FELT FUNNY, to say the least. He couldn't tell if it was the strange cocktail of medicine and food or if he really did have some new sense of what was wrong in Lange's lab. Jake let him in, since no one had reprogrammed the lock yet, then waited in the hall. They'd agreed that he had the best chance of getting Lange's attention, so he'd remain in the lab while Emil was traveling to give him a chance to cross without interference.

Emil stood near the door for a moment, staring down the other side of the room. It was just a white wall framed by those two large, curved pieces of metal. It shouldn't have been threatening.

But his brain alternated between perceiving it as thirty feet away and perceiving it as some impossibly long distance from where he stood. It was disorienting, as though everything kept shifting in and out of focus.

Someone touched his hand and it felt so good he almost melted.

"Whoa, they gave you the good stuff," Chávez said. She wrapped her arms around his neck and Emil wanted to cling to her forever. "Don't die."

"I accidentally got Kit high when we met," Emil confessed. He could feel it now, uncurling from nothing. Warmth coursed through him. He wanted her to touch him some more. She could make his brain light up. They could just stay here, hugging, and be happy forever.

"The same stuff you're on now?"

He nodded. It was funny, now that he thought about it, that despite the drug, he wasn't feeling particularly... lustful. Maybe it was just that he didn't have sexual feelings about Chávez. Not that she wasn't attractive, in a lanky, athletic kind of way. But he knew she'd never want him, and that had no appeal. Kit, on the other hand, had wanted him from the start. He wished Kit were here right now.

"That's a hell of an introduction," she said. She let go of him and he very much wished she hadn't. As soon as she'd left, he could feel the room creeping up on him again. It was too big. "Is that why things went south between you two?"

He shook his head. He must look funny because Chávez was trying hard not to smile at him. "Quint's a bigot," Emil said. "Against runners. I knew and I worked for him anyway."

"Ah," Chávez said.

She hadn't known Quint was a bigot. Emil had tried to put it out of his mind. He hadn't told anyone. Was she angry? She should be. "Kit was upset. As he has every right to be."

"Are you risking your life because you feel guilty, Emil?"

"No." It came out with more force than he intended. "I can't let him die."

"Okay," Chávez said, and she chewed her bottom lip like she was considering something. "Look, I don't really know him, but... isn't he basically a smuggler? Doesn't he work for bad people all the time?"

"Yeah, but *I* shouldn't've."

"Sure, of course. Forget it. Find him, save his life if you need to, apologize again. That should be enough." She patted him on the shoulder.

He wanted another hug. He didn't want to walk to the back

of the room, miles from here, until the void sucked him in. The Nowhere was awful. He couldn't do this.

"Emil." Chávez had big brown eyes and she was biting her bottom lip in a funny little smile. This time, she put both hands on his shoulders. She was almost as tall as him. Lenny always called her a skyscraper. Emil would miss her if he died or got stuck on the other side—or worse, in between. Lenny and the others, too. "If you don't want to do this, you don't have to do this. Nobody will think less of you."

He'd think less of himself.

"I know how much you hate the Nowhere," Chávez said.

Emil didn't want anyone to know that about him. His private cowardice. But Chávez could tell and she still liked him. And Kit had seen it and Kit still... well. Emil couldn't say if Kit still liked him. Was Kit even still alive? He turned his attention to the back of the room. It was time to find out.

"I hate the thought of him stranded somewhere, dying," Emil said. He was wasting time here. "I'm going."

Chávez nodded. "Good luck."

She slipped out of the room and Jake slipped in, giving Emil a silent nod of acknowledgement. He stood guard as Emil crossed toward the other side of the room. The space changed unpredictably, stretched out in some places and shrunken in others, so his progress was uneven.

He was uncomfortable, but his discomfort stemmed from the experiments he'd subjected himself to and the unfinished experiment unfolding—in a strange, literal sense—all around him. It wasn't his usual, inside-out, upside-down and backwards discomfort with the Nowhere, although he was aware of the encroaching void. He couldn't normally sense it until someone had pulled him in, and then it was a horror show of being pushed and pulled in all directions, cracked open and squeezed shut. But now it was simply a pressure all around him. The sensation was neither pleasant nor unpleasant, merely a sense he'd never possessed before, a consciousness of this membrane that slid between all worlds.

How long had it been? He was still walking, but the white walls of Lange's lab faded into darkness. When he looked down, there was no floor, but a blackness that extended beyond his comprehension. He'd never conceived of the Nowhere like this. Before, its name had always seemed far too mundane to capture the sickening wrongness of it, but now he understood. For runners, it didn't feel like that. It was just a place between. A nothing space. Nowhere.

Emil was in the Nowhere alone. He hadn't, as far as he could tell, lost all sense of his human form and become whatever Solomon Lange was. He was just... floating. It was a miracle.

Unfortunately, one miracle wasn't enough. He'd gotten into the Nowhere, but now he needed to get *out*. And it had to be wherever Kit was, or this would all have been a waste. A vision of coming out the other side with a backpack full of Kit's ridiculous, brilliant wardrobe and no Kit went through him like a knife. He couldn't let that happen.

Emil wasn't sure *how* to get out, exactly, but he knew he couldn't do it until he was certain Kit was on the other side of the darkness. He'd stay in the void until he was dead sure, even if all his energy withered to nothing. Let the Nowhere spit him out in some desert or ocean or tundra, whatever unknown otherworldly wilderness, as long as he could pull that red sweater out of his pack and hand it to Kit.

20

A BAD DEAL

THE BEAST—THAT WAS THE ONLY THING KIT COULD THINK to call it, since it wasn't an animal he recognized—emerged from the darkness. It sauntered, moving in the casual way of a predator with nothing to fear. Kit, not feeling so confident, stayed very still.

It looked like a mammal, with striped light brown fur rippling all over its six-legged body. Like a wolf or a big cat, its eyes faced forward. Its snout was doglike, but it had pointed ears that angled back from its head. When it yawned, it revealed two terrifying rows of jagged teeth. Huge, the beast moved with a powerful grace, its long tail snapping behind it. Kit found it hard to connect this animal with the sound he'd heard—claws scratching loose rock—because its giant paws padded silently toward him.

Taking his eyes off the approaching beast was nearly impossible. Kit wasn't sure how he managed. But somehow, he saw three tiny pairs of eyes glinting in the darkness behind it.

Babies.

They'd been the ones making noise. Their mom knew better. So much for hoping she might just sniff him and decide he wasn't a threat. She could probably smell the fear coursing through his blood from where she was. Kit had no way to defend himself. There weren't even any rocks worth throwing— not that he wanted to take that risk.

Ten feet separated them. Kit had forgotten how to breathe. It would have been so much nicer to slip quietly into death rather than getting shredded. Maybe she'd rip his throat out and make it quick.

Emil appeared right next to him.

Kit must be fucking dreaming. This was some kind of end-of-life vision. Or maybe he'd already died? Emil couldn't be here, especially not alone. He wasn't a runner. And even if he was a runner, how would he have found Kit?

Kit's fantasies had taken a turn for the nerdy, apparently, since this dream version of Emil came equipped with a huge backpack. Was there food in there? It wouldn't matter to a dead version of himself, of course, but the thought made his heart leap. *Emil brought me food and heaven is real*, he thought, dazed to the point of laughing. This cave was a bargain-basement version of heaven, but he'd take what he could get.

There wouldn't be a fanged monster in heaven, though. Shit.

Emil—who was probably not a dream after all—took in Kit and the animal and the cave in one instant, and in the next, he was pulling a spray can from a holster at his waist. "Close your eyes and hold your breath," he said, and Kit did. He heard the hiss of something being sprayed into the cave, and then the beast roaring and kicking up gravel as it ran back into the darkness. Kit watched for a few long moments, but there were no more eyes glinting back there.

When Kit turned his attention to Emil, he'd holstered the spray. He gave Kit a slight smile, then swayed on his feet. His pupils, already large, dilated enormously and his expression went slack. He fainted.

He'd toppled face first and was now lying under his pack. Kit crawled over to him and tried to wake him. When Emil didn't rouse immediately, Kit tried pulling the pack off his shoulders. His fingers were frozen stiff but he managed it.

"Emil, wake up," he said, working the zipper. "I hope you brought something useful in here." He got the pack open and went through it like a raccoon through a garbage can, tipping its contents everywhere. There were clothes—Kit's clothes—and bottles of water and all kinds of food and medicine and and a few unrecognizable objects, plus way more knives than Kit expected. Kit even found little hand warmer packets. "Oh my God, Emil, I've never been so happy to see anyone in my life." Kit shook one until it heated up and then pressed it between his hands. He put on every piece of clothing he could find, which was difficult when his fingers were misbehaving, but worth every second spent on the effort.

Emil was still lying on the ground with his eyes closed. Kit shoved a protein bar into his own mouth then sat cross-legged next to Emil and pulled Emil into his lap so his head was pillowed on Kit's thigh instead of lying on the cave floor. "You're so heavy," he complained, chewing. "And I can't tell if I'm just really, really cold—well, I am, no doubt about that—but I think you might have a fever."

Kit laid his hand against Emil's forehead. Thank fuck, Emil's eyes opened a moment later. They were glassy. "Kit."

"Hi," Kit said. "I have a *lot* of questions, like what the fuck did you do to yourself to get here and how did you even find me and *why*, but maybe we should leave this cave before that thing comes back to snack on us. Can you get up?"

Emil reached up and touched Kit's face, his hand clumsy and imprecise, but warm.

It was sweet, and totally useless, and Kit rolled his eyes and huffed because he did not have time for whatever melty-gooey thing was happening near his heart. That beast could come back at any second. Death was still way, way too possible. "Emil," he chastised. "You've totally misunderstood our dynamic. *I'm* the useless one. You take care of me, because I'm always in trouble, and you're good at that kind of thing. You know, being authoritative and reassuring and unbearably gent—whatever, I mean, just —you know what the fuck you're doing. I don't. I have one skill in life and it's not functioning right now."

Emil didn't seem to have heard any of that, but he did sit up in response to Kit pushing at his shoulders. He surveyed the cave, the explosion of his pack, and turned to Kit to ask, "Why are we on the ground?"

"Great question," Kit said, maybe too brightly. It was a relief that Emil had said anything remotely coherent. "You fainted. After a pretty perfectly timed arrival-slash-rescue. Guess you were holding it together to save our lives and then once that thing was out of sight, you gave up the ghost."

Now that Emil wasn't leaning on him, Kit took this opportunity to repack everything. He managed to down a few more protein bars during the process.

"I went through the Nowhere," Emil said. It was hard to tell if he was watching Kit. His gaze was unfocused. "I don't feel good."

"Believe it or not, I had guessed both of those things," Kit said. He didn't know how to be comforting, especially not when he was scared. What would it take for someone as tough as Emil to admit he didn't feel good? What the hell had he done to himself to get here? Kit pushed the pack through the cave entrance, crawled out, then held his hand through the opening. Whatever was ailing Emil seemed to have broken his sarcasm detector, but he was able to take Kit's hand and crawl through.

Kit stood up and shouldered the pack, which was heavy and almost as big as he was, and nearly dropped back to the ground on the spot. He still had all his complaints—cold, hunger, fatigue—but the prospect of survival had given him some energy. And Emil wasn't in any shape to carry anything.

They set off in a random direction. The only thing that mattered was moving *away* from the monster. They'd find shelter somewhere else. Kit needed a few more hours of food and rest before he could contemplate making a run. And if Lange came after him again, he didn't know what he'd do.

He and Emil weren't setting any records, as slow as they were. But it was a lot more pleasant to walk through the snow in boots and warm clothes. If he weren't half-dead and afraid of being full dead, Kit could almost imagine how a person could do this for fun. Almost.

Emil had unzipped his jacket and wasn't even keeping his hands in his pockets. What did you even do with a person who had a fever? Kit stopped and rummaged through the pack. Water was probably a safe bet. And who knew if over-the-counter fever reducers would work on someone who'd just passed through the Nowhere, but they probably wouldn't hurt. Kit put a couple pills in Emil's palm. He accepted them, along with the water bottle.

Kit tugged on Emil's hand to get him walking again.

"I guess being delirious with a fever is as close as someone like you ever gets to getting high," Kit joked as they took off. He'd put on gloves that he'd found in the pack, but he could still feel how hot Emil's hand was.

Emil laughed, and the sound lightened the weight hanging over Kit.

"Guess this isn't a very good high, though. Not as much fun as those berries." That made Emil laugh harder. Suspicion took hold of Kit.

"I was saving them for science," Emil said, which Kit supposed was an explanation and an admission all at once.

"Somehow you coming here involved you eating those berries," Kit surmised. Which one of his team members had Emil made out with? Kit didn't *want* to care, but he couldn't shut off his thoughts. What did Emil like, exactly? Other than Kit in convenient circumstances, that is. Was he only into guys? That would narrow the field. Dax didn't seem like they were into anyone, anyway, and Chávez was probably a lesbian. If Emil was gay, he couldn't possibly be into that woman who'd pushed Kit against a wall, which was comforting. Lenny seemed straight, as did Jake. How high had Emil been? He'd been competent enough to come through the Nowhere and save Kit's life. Maybe he hadn't made out with anyone. Trying to keep his voice neutral, Kit asked, "How was it?"

"Chávez hugged me and it was nice," Emil said. Kit's relief lasted a nanosecond, because then Emil said, "It's not as much of a high as real."

Now it was Kit's turn to laugh. Carl Akins dealt real—also called "virt," both short for *virtual reality enhancement*—and Kit preferred not to know if it was in the packages he delivered for Carl. It was wildly dangerous and addictive. Junkies ended up totally severed from reality. Seeing a few of them had been enough to scare Kit off trying the stuff. "Right, because you've done enough real to know."

"Just two times," Emil said agreeably.

"What the fuck," Kit said. That didn't fit with his idea of Emil at all. He pulled Emil's hand up and rounded on him. "When? Do you know how dangerous that stuff is?"

"Not as dangerous as walking into the breach in Lange's lab," Emil said.

"Holy shit," Kit said. *That* was how Emil had crossed into the Nowhere? "Stupid and brave, but mostly stupid."

"But you're not dead," Emil pointed out, and for someone with a high-grade fever, he was making some pretty unassailable arguments.

"Right," Kit said. He dropped Emil's hand, which he'd been squeezing without intending to. The light had changed around them. It would be dark soon. "You must be feeling a little better. So now I need you to, you know, be Emil and look around here and tell me where we can find shelter."

"There's a tent," Emil said.

"Is this some kind of fever delusion?" Kit said, scanning the forest for any sign of habitation.

"In the pack."

"Oh." Kit wasn't at his sharpest, either. He thought back through everything he'd seen in the pack and realized that some of the unrecognizable items must be pieces of a tent. "Can you put it together?"

Emil nodded. Kit set the pack down. Emil searched through it and pulled out the tent. He didn't seem to need or want help, so Kit took the opportunity to plop down beside the pack, not caring about the snow. He ate as much as he could and watched as Emil constructed a tent from almost nothing. Once or twice, Emil had to pause to catch his breath or steady himself, but he seemed much better overall. And the tent impressed Kit a lot. There was even a sleeping bag. "I have never been excited about camping *ever* until right now," Kit said.

Emil laughed. "Do you ever think about what it would be like if we'd met in different circumstances?"

"We wouldn't have met," Kit said with certainty. He didn't talk to people he didn't know, not unless they were offering him a lot of money.

"Even by chance? You wouldn't have looked twice at me if we'd passed on the street?"

"Oh, I would have looked," Kit said. But if he'd met Emil in other circumstances, he wouldn't ever have had the courage to kiss him. "I would have enjoyed looking. But that's it. I keep moving. I don't introduce myself, especially not when someone is intimidatingly perfect."

For some reason, that made Emil frown. Kit had meant it as a compliment. But the frown passed as Emil examined his handiwork with the tent. He'd chosen a small, flat space among the trees. He unzipped the tent flap and crawled in. Kit handed him the pack and then made as if to follow.

"Kit," Emil said. "We haven't really... talked."

"I almost died and you're delirious. It's not a great time."

"I was out of it after crossing through the Nowhere, but I'm okay now," Emil said. "Still feverish and tired, but *compos mentis*, I promise. I just wanted to make sure you knew that before I said this." He took a breath. "I'm really sorry, Kit. I knew it was wrong to work for Quint and I did it anyway, because he offered me something I wanted. And you and your friends and who knows how many others got hurt in the process. I'm sorry. I'll keep trying to make it right."

"I know," Kit said.

Emil's eyes widened.

"I mean, apology accepted, or whatever I'm supposed to say," Kit said, putting a hand on Emil's before he got upset. He was still kneeling in the snow outside the tent, but saying this was more important than anything else, including moving inside where it might be warmer. "I figured you were sorry after you showed up here, having done whatever you did to yourself to survive jumping into that fucking skin-crawling breach. And..."

Emil said nothing into Kit's silence. Fuck, this part of apologies was hard.

"It occurred to me that I maybe shouldn't have been so pissed at you for working for someone evil," Kit said. "Since, uh, I do it all the time."

"Oh," Emil said. Kit could tell he wanted to ask questions and was trying hard not to. Good. Kit's career was a topic for another time.

"It's sort of my whole reputation. I make deliveries and I take no interest in what or who they're for. The money's all I care about. Or it was. But when I learned about what Quint thinks about runners, it felt personal," Kit explained.

"I get that. I really should have gotten it a lot sooner than I did," Emil said, tripping over himself to get the words out.

"Shh," Kit interrupted. "I'm trying to reveal some important shit about my life to you, like you wanted, and it's not just to trick you into having sex with me. Although come to think of it, if that's not the reason, I don't really know why I want to tell you any of this awful stuff."

"Do you want to come inside?" Emil asked, obviously biting back a smile. Kit crawled into the tent. "And for the record, I wouldn't need to be tricked. But anyway. I'll be quiet. Say what you want to say."

Kit took his boots off and stuck his legs into the sleeping bag, which spread out over a pad that Emil must have inflated while Kit wasn't paying attention. Kit took his time, and Emil watched him without saying anything. The sleeping bag was clearly meant for more than one person. Had Emil considered that when he'd packed? Kit didn't care either way. He patted the space next to him.

"I'm guessing I can't catch whatever it is you have."

"I don't think you can," Emil agreed. "You sure you're okay with this?"

"It'll be warmer with you in here," Kit said, which was pretty far off *I have a lot of feelings about you and not all of them are sexual and I don't know what to do about it,* but it had only just then occurred to him that he and Emil might live through this. What would he say to Emil when he dropped him back at

Facility 17—if that's where he wanted to go? "Bye, thanks for repeatedly saving my life and also sucking my dick that one time"? Kit didn't want to say that. Emil would be unhappy if Kit said, "Would you mind if I showed up in your bedroom sometimes?" Emil especially wouldn't like it if Kit specified that he wanted to show up in Emil's bed but never have any contact outside of that, so Kit wouldn't be in too deep in case Emil changed his mind. But that was all Kit knew how to do. How did other people—normal people—have relationships? Did you just... make yourself vulnerable and hope the other person wouldn't abandon you some day? Kit had spent his whole life armoring himself against that.

Emil slid in next to him, calming the torrent of thoughts in his brain. It felt so nice to settle his head on Emil's chest that Kit almost forgot he'd promised to tell Emil something important.

Well, that ruined the mood. Might as well get on with it.

"I never knew my biological family. I spent my childhood in a place called The Nashville Home for Wayward Youth," Kit said, his voice flat. "They kicked me out when I was eleven after I came back from my third run through the Nowhere. You know the first couple of times, I didn't even go anywhere? I just wanted so badly not to be where I was, lying in bed in the minutes before one of the caretakers would come in and make us get up for school—and suddenly I wasn't there. When I wanted it, I could disappear into the darkness and come back a second later. Reality had an escape hatch. They didn't catch me those first two times, slipping in and out of bed, but the third time, I vanished while I was getting scolded—for stealing from the kitchen, of course. For just a second, I showed up in someone else's kitchen. I have no idea where in the world it was or why I ended up there, but I remember the smell of chicken roasting in the oven. I thought I was dead or dreaming, and probably the woman in that kitchen thought the same. I panicked and went right back to where I had been, and they kicked me out three days later."

"That's terrible. I'm so sorry."

"You know why they kicked me out?" Kit asked. He didn't wait for an answer. "They said a few things about inappropriate behavior, but I overheard them whisper-arguing in the hall outside the kitchen, so I know the real reason."

"Adults don't like the idea of a kid with powers they can't control," Emil said.

"Yeah," Kit said. "There's that. But you know what I heard them saying? Runners are too expensive. We eat too much."

"They didn't want to feed you? That was it?"

"They talked about how they could take in three more kids —*normal children*, I remember that phrase clearly—for the same cost as keeping me," Kit said. He was glad he didn't have to look at Emil for this conversation. "I guess from a certain point of view, they were doing the right thing."

"They shouldn't have kicked you out! Is that even legal?"

"Laws don't have much to do with my life," Kit said, shrugging the shoulder that wasn't pressed against Emil. "And they didn't put me on the street. They found me an unofficial foster family, one that had contacted the Home looking to take in runners. Those were rare, like you pointed out—most people didn't want kid runners. Most people thought I'd go wild and they'd have no way to punish me. It was always in the news back then, you know, runners being unstoppable super criminals. Laila hadn't even robbed Franklin Station Bank at that point. They were worried all the same."

"I gather the foster family wasn't Zin."

Ha. "No, the Shaws weren't Zin. I don't know how they'd convinced anyone that they wanted a foster child. I guess maybe the Home didn't hold them to high standards. What they actually wanted was a free ticket to travel anywhere in the world. They didn't count on me, you know, being a person."

"A child."

Kit didn't want to talk about this anymore, but he was in it now. After a moment of silence, he forged ahead. "I wanted them to like me. To love me, I guess. I thought maybe they could be my family."

Emil squeezed him.

"At first, I did whatever they asked," Kit said. "The Grand Canyon, Inland New York. But there were three of them—Bob, Becky, and their son Nick. Taking all of them somewhere in one day was impossible. I had to spread it out over two or three days, and they hated that. But I was sure they would love me if I did better, so I never said no. I pushed myself. They never fed me enough, so I learned how to steal. I never had the energy to jump myself out of sight in those days, so I had to get good at it. At some point, over the course of months, I started to understand that they weren't ever going to love me or be my family. They just wanted to use me. I got scared then. What would happen if I said no? What would happen if my power failed me? I overheard them chatting about longer and longer jumps—Beijing, Johannesburg, the Amazon, Everest, the ruined coastal cities of the world—and I ran right then."

"Good," Emil said.

"I fantasized about dumping them somewhere far away—or maybe three separate destinations—and not going back for them," Kit admitted. "But in the end, I just left. I wasn't even twelve then. It had only been seven months."

"I'm so sorry, Kit," Emil said. "You must have met Zin soon after that."

"You went to see her," Kit said. He knew his wardrobe well enough to have figured that out.

"Yeah," Emil said. "Sorry about that, too. Feels like an intrusion."

Kit shrugged. "If it helped you save my life, I don't mind. And I found Zin and Louann because I was hiding in the alley behind the bar one day—I'd just stolen a bunch of candy bars—when I saw Louann's bike. I stopped to admire it, and Zin saw me and thought I looked hungry—she was right—and things just, you know, developed from there."

"I tried to pay her, you know. She fed me and I said 'where do you wanna go?' and Zin looked at me, like... I don't know. My whole life, nobody has ever looked at me like that. Like I was the best and the worst thing that ever happened to them all at once, like I'd broken her heart and put it back together again all in one sentence. And I'll never forget what she said. 'Sweetheart, I've already been everywhere.'"

Kit stopped. He hadn't meant to imitate Zin's slow, honeyed speech, but it was impossible to imagine that sentence in anyone else's voice. The words lingered in the darkness, their presence another kind of blanket.

After a moment, Kit continued, "I got worried right after she said it, because I knew I couldn't pay her any other way, but she just smiled and said, 'I'm happy right here. Are you happy?' and I was so stunned I don't even remember what I said, but I guess it was yes. I ended up staying there for years."

"I'm glad you found her," Emil said. "She didn't tell me that part of the story."

"She probably doesn't know it," Kit said. "I never told her how important it was to me. How important *she* was."

Emil's arm was a solid weight against him, giving him a firm hug. "She knows."

"Still," Kit said. "I couldn't stop thinking about it when I first got stranded here. That I was going to die without ever having said 'I love you' to Zin or Louann or... anyone."

If Emil noticed Kit's awkward pause, he was too polite to comment. "You'll get a chance to tell them."

"You know I've never taken them anywhere?" Kit asked. "Not Paris or London or Inland New York. They've never asked. Not even to see what it's like in the Nowhere."

"Maybe they'd rather not know," Emil said, sounding like he wished the same for himself. "And if they know how the Shaws treated you, I'm sure they'd never ask."

"I never told them. Only you."

"Like I said before," Emil said. "She knows."

Sweetheart, I've already been everywhere. Somehow, Zin had figured it out just from looking at him. He was so grateful he'd never had to tell her. Maybe he'd taken her perception for granted. Just because somebody already knew something didn't mean they didn't want to hear it said out loud.

"Thank you for telling me, Kit," Emil said. It was fully dark in their tent now.

"Thanks for... you know, jumping into an unknown rift in space to save my life, being stupidly brave, perfect, whatever," Kit said. Emil shifted beneath him, like something Kit had said made him uncomfortable. "It's a bad deal for you, really."

Emil squeezed him again and kissed the top of his head. "No," he said. "It's not."

21

NOT QUITE FAMILIAR

EMIL WOKE A FEW HOURS LATER TO KIT WHISPERING HIS name in his ear. They'd separated in their sleep and were now side by side.

"It's so cold," Kit complained, his voice sleepy and muffled. "Come back over here. I don't understand how I didn't die last night. Thought I was going to."

There was a thought more chilling than the air. Emil spooned him and Kit snuggled against him.

"You're perfect," Kit said, and Emil recoiled. That word again. "How come you flinch every time I call you perfect? It's not an insult."

"I'm not perfect," Emil said. "And my last two partners told me I was—just before they left me."

"Shit," Kit said. "Who would leave you? What was wrong with them?"

"According to them, something was wrong with me," Emil said. "They didn't think I loved them. Rose slept with someone else. And Lucas felt like I was choosing my career over our relationship. I think that was what drove Rose away, too—and it was a little bit true."

"I'm sorry."

"It's okay. It was a long time ago. I don't miss them, although sometimes I wish I could have explained to them why I am this way, but if they'd wanted to know, they'd both had years of living with me to find out." Emil stopped. Only a few days ago, Kit had been opposed to sharing their life stories. He'd divulged parts of his past earlier, but Emil didn't want to presume. It was hard enough to tell the story to someone who actually wanted to hear it.

"I want to know," Kit said after a pause. "If you want to tell me."

Emil let out a breath. He wanted to put a leash on his hopes and hold them back. He couldn't read too much into Kit wanting to hear one story. "I do want to tell you, but maybe some other time. You should rest. We're, uh, not out of the woods yet."

"Nerd," Kit said with what Emil hoped was affection. "You might as well tell me now. The suspense will keep me awake."

From the way Kit wriggled against him, if Emil didn't tell him the story, he might ask for a different kind of entertainment, and that was a far worse idea. They needed rest. Emil was amazed, after all he'd put himself through, that his body could even respond. Kit gave him all sorts of reckless impulses, from casual sex to risking his life.

His last reckless impulse was paying off so far, but he silenced that voice in his head. Kit had finally opened up about himself, and now he wanted to know something about Emil. Too bad that something would be a big disappointment.

"It's not much of a story," Emil warned.

"Good, it'll put me to sleep."

"When I was about thirteen, I drove my parents to desperation. I skipped school constantly—to shoplift and smoke weed and play video games. When I did go to school, I talked back and got detention. My grades were dismal. I figured out every possible way to sneak out of the house at night. Anything they didn't want me doing, I was determined to do."

"Thirteen-year-old you sounds *way* cooler than present you," Kit interrupted.

"He wasn't," Emil said, irritated.

"Alright, alright, keep telling the story," Kit said. "But wait—you had parents. Weren't they... involved?"

Kit didn't sound heartbroken, but that pause broke Emil's heart all the same. All of Kit's adolescent bad behavior had been driven by a need to survive. No one had been watching out for him. In contrast, everything in life had been handed to Emil, and he'd spit on it. He closed his eyes as if he could stave off the guilt. His poor parents. "They were involved. They didn't want to be strict with us, since their parents had been strict with them. They wanted us to have *dialogue*. In theory, it was a great idea. My adolescent self didn't want any part in it. Eventually, I forced them to impose rules on me, which I then applied all of my most determined efforts to breaking.

"Anyway, at that age, if I could have convinced anyone to have sex with me—or even kiss me—I'm sure I would have been doing that as often as possible. Probably not safely or wisely or even discreetly. But I hadn't had my growth spurt yet, or discovered personal hygiene, so it was a lost cause. Braces, pimples, bad facial hair, baby fat—you name it, I had it."

"Aww," Kit said. "I wish this story came with pictures."

"I don't."

"This is the most endearing thing you've ever told me, and it warms my heart to think of you as a chubby adolescent boy with authority problems."

"Stop."

Kit must have heard something in Emil's voice that alarmed him. "Okay."

"It gets a lot less endearing," Emil said. "I think part of the reason I was such a bad kid—and this isn't an excuse—is that I knew I could never live up to my sister, so it seemed better not to try."

Even when he'd decided to tell this story, even when he was committed, it was still hard. He paused. Kit was probably making the connection between this story and then moment in the kitchen when he'd asked Emil if he had any siblings. Emil had hesitated.

"Zora was good at school, good at sports, good at music, good at making everyone happy. She even loved *me*. She was a star and I was the family fuck-up—not just of the two of us, but out of all the cousins—and we still got along great. Zora made me feel like I was great company, just the way I was. She never said I had 'potential' or any of the other things my parents and teachers were always saying to try to turn me around in life. She just liked being with me. She didn't like to shoplift or steal, but she'd play Galaxy Race with me. I always won, and we'd laugh about how it was the only area of life where she came in second. That might sound like a mean joke to you, but it never felt that way between us.

"Anyway, around this time, my delinquent friends and I got into real."

"Holy shit, you weren't kidding," Kit said.

At last, Emil had managed to convince Kit that he'd been a true fuck-up. Real was a drug not even fearless Nowhere runners would mess with. "No," Emil said, shaking his head. "I wasn't. I took it twice, had a bad experience, and swore off it. But the dealer, a guy we all called Greens who was a few years older than me and who'd dropped out of school—he was good-looking. I don't know if I understood then why I wanted to be around him so much, but I did. And then one day when it was pouring rain and Greens was too busy to give me a ride, I messaged Zora to come pick me up. And they met."

"Oh," Kit said. "Shit."

"It's so stupid, you know? I remember being mad then, that Greens had seen my pretty sister and now he wasn't ever going to look at me again. As if I'd had a chance. And everybody loved Zora, so of course Greens loved her. I guess she was looking for an escape from something, because they started going out. Even though I was jealous, it was kind of awesome at first. My perfect, good-at-everything sister and her cool, older boyfriend were letting me hang out with them. I saw Zora smoke for the first time ever and it blew my little mind. That went on for a few months.

"And then one night, Zora drove Greens's car home. She got pulled over because one of the taillights was out, but the back-seat was full of his stash of real. When the cops called and said they were holding my sister, I remember feeling just... totally bewildered. My parents were, too. It was supposed to happen to me. I was the slacker, the screw-up, the one who ended up in jail. We went down to see her and I had to look at my sister through the glass and I burst into tears.

"You know what she told me over the phone? She said, 'You know what this means, right? I'm better at being the fuck-up than you. I win—first place in everything except Galaxy Race.' And I tried to laugh, but it came out like a sob. She kept right on talking. 'You have to be the good one now, Emil. Mom and Dad can't have two fuck-ups for kids.' God, I was so scared. Meanwhile, Zora was a seventeen-year-old in jail and she was just sitting there, calmly mentoring me. It was so lonely and strange at the house without her around. She wrote me letters while she was in there and I slowly pulled my shit together. All the energy I'd been spending on breaking rules, I applied elsewhere. My parents telling me to pay attention in school and make something of myself had never worked, but for some reason, my sister's letters and calls from prison did. She'd always wanted to go to space, but she'd never be selected with a criminal record, so I decided I'd go for her. I joined the Orbit Guard. For her. Can you imagine?"

"No," Kit said. "But the way you told the story, I'm glad she's only in jail and not a real addict on life support or dead in a ditch or something."

"She's not in jail anymore. She did two years, went back and got her high-school diploma, wrote dazzling college application essays about her time in jail, and became a biomedical researcher studying the effects of real on the brain. Meanwhile, I'm stranded in another reality and when we get home, I'll be out of a job."

"So she went to jail and you're *still* the fuck-up," Kit said, amused.

"She's prettier than me, too," Emil said.

"I'd like to know what kind of family this is where you're the ugly one," Kit said. "Actually, can I ask you a dumb question? I hate when people ask me about my name, or where I'm from, but I'm so curious. Emil Singh is an unusual combination of names. Why is your name Emil?"

"That's easy. My mom is a comparative literature professor. Zora and I are named after writers she loved," Emil said. "She wanted my name to be 'Émile' but my dad insisted they anglicize it. Honestly, I'm amazed she conceded even that much. Sometimes people ask me why she didn't pick famous Desi writers 'to go with the last name' but I've never known how to answer that."

He didn't ask a question, but it hung in the air.

"I don't know what name I was born with, or where I'm from," Kit said. "People at the orphanage always called me 'Kit' as a nickname, maybe because I've always been small, and it stuck. Zin calls me 'Christopher' as a joke sometimes, but that's not on any official documents. Not that I have any."

"So you were just... found? And nobody knew anything about you?"

Kit nodded. "They wrote my date of birth as January first, figuring I was maybe six months old when I was left at the Home in June. Obviously I don't remember any of it. Do you know how annoying it is when people ask 'no, but where are you *really* from?' and you genuinely don't know?"

"It's annoying even when you do know the answer, since nobody ever wants to believe me when I say Schaumburg, Illinois," Emil said. "So I guess it's worse for you."

"I always just say Nashville," Kit said. "But I'm not officially anything. I'm from nowhere."

Emil didn't comment on the pun, if it was one. "You're not American? I guess you did say you had no official documents."

"As you can imagine, the care at the Home wasn't that great. Some of us slipped through the cracks. It's sort of what I've spent my life doing, if you think about it," Kit said. "Zin and Louann pulled together what they could over the years, but mostly we learned to stay out of trouble and do things in an unofficial, cash-up-front kind of way."

"You haven't done a great job of staying out of trouble."

"Neither have you," Kit said.

"True," Emil said. "You know the thing you said, about being from nowhere... Lange has this theory about how runners are born. He thinks sometimes people cross through Nowhere by accident, end up in a reality that's not their own, and then somehow survive long enough to have a child with a local."

"And that kid grows up to be a runner," Kit guessed.

"He hypothesized that crossing through the Nowhere was hard on people who weren't runners, and that a lot of those people died young," Emil said, a note of apology in his voice. "Or possibly they crossed back through, and that's why so many runners don't know both of their parents."

"Laila's mom died when she was little," Kit said. "She remembers her, though. But she never knew her dad. And her mom had people in Detroit, you know, relatives and friends. And there are records of her. Her dad just…"

"Appeared out of nowhere?" Emil suggested.

"And then disappeared," Kit said. There was a beat of silence, and then he sighed. "It used to make me jealous. That she got to know her mom, at least."

"I'm sorry you never got to know yours," Emil said.

"Yeah," Kit said. He sighed again. "I guess one of my parents was from *really* far away, if this is true."

"Yeah. Not the kind of place you get on a plane to go visit for three weeks every summer," Emil said. "Although I guess in your case, you wouldn't need the plane."

"Do you think they were… human?"

"Yes," Emil said. "And so are you."

There was a pause, and then Kit said, "We should sleep. We have more trouble to get into." It was too dark to see, and Kit was facing away from him, but Emil was sure he was smiling. "How are we gonna get out of this?"

It was a funny moment to use *we*. This wasn't Kit's mess. *I'm not part of your team.* He wasn't obligated to clean up. And Emil didn't want him in danger, not when he'd already been through so much and Zin was probably crying over him right now. "You can get out as soon as we're back. You don't even have to take me back to Facility 17—it's too risky, anyway. You get us back to Nashville, I'll get myself to Quint Services, and whatever happens, I'll deal with it."

"Right," Kit said. A long time passed with no sound but the uncanny, not-quite-familiar rustle and trill of the forest at night.

EMIL HAD FELT BETTER. STILL, HE WAS ABLE TO GET OUT of bed, nudge Kit awake, and dismantle the tent. Compared to the threat of death, a little fatigue, an ache or two, and some dizziness was nothing much. Kit's eyes were ringed with shadows, and he'd groaned in complaint when Emil had woken him, but he was upright.

"You think we can make it back?" Emil asked.

"Depends more on Lange than on me," Kit said.

"Cross your fingers that Jake is distracting him," Emil said, and Kit didn't look enthusiastic about that. Emil checked their campsite, making sure they weren't leaving trash from another reality on the forest floor. With everything packed, he turned to Kit. "Ready when you are."

Kit had been quiet since they'd woken. It was a contrast to all that they'd shared last night. Maybe he regretted telling Emil about his childhood.

Emil's thoughts were cut off as Kit grabbed him and the void enveloped them. Emil had withstood the Nowhere yesterday thanks to a brief moment of having three different foldings of matter in his system, but the dimensional prion had done its work. He no longer had enough to make a difference. The Nowhere was as miserable and wrong as ever, stretching and restricting his body all at once, a mixing up of inside and outside that abstracted everything except pain.

The trip seemed longer than usual. He gasped for air when it was over, relishing the normal confines of his body and the space around it. Taking in his surroundings was the work of several long minutes. They were in a large, industrial space of some kind. Concrete floor, cinderblock walls, fluorescent light. There was a garage door behind Kit, and parked next to that was a motorcycle. Behind Emil, the corridor ended in double doors.

"Where are we?" he asked.

"Quint Services Headquarters," Kit said. "I guess you were unconscious for arrival and departure last time."

"You didn't have to bring me here," Emil said, dazed. He didn't want to take on Kristian Auer—or Quint himself—while still dealing with nausea from the Nowhere. Not to mention that given his preferences, he would have shaved, showered, and worn a suit. The winter coat he was wearing wasn't suited for a professional meeting or Tennessee's weather, and there was still otherworldly mud caked on his boots. "And you don't have to stay for whatever's next."

"My bike is here," Kit said, as if that justified everything.

"You could probably buy another bike for less trouble," Emil said. "I hear smuggling is pretty lucrative, I bet you're good for it."

"Shut up," Kit said, but there was no rancor in it.

"Being stupid and brave?" Emil asked. He'd wanted to protect Kit from the consequences of this, but now that Kit was here, gratitude overtook anger and concern. It was nice not to be alone.

"I'm here to make sure you're not being too much of either,"

Kit said. "You need a selfish person around to keep you reasonable."

"You being here isn't selfish."

"Sure it is. I want you alive for my own purposes."

That sounded suspiciously like a flirtation. "Oh?"

"Yeah. Don't get too stupid in this meeting," Kit said. "Let me negotiate."

"Oh, you're in charge now, is that it?"

"Yeah," Kit said decisively. "I've been working for evil pieces of shit for years. I know how to fend for myself. You're always thinking about other people. When we find that guy with his creep face and his helmet hair, he's going to sell you some bullshit about how you should do what he wants *for the good of your team* and you're gonna fall for it."

"You have a pretty low opinion of my negotiating skills," Emil observed.

Kit leveled a look at him, and Emil conceded the point from the force of his expression alone. Thinking back on it, Emil had never seen Kit back down from an argument. He'd done what Emil asked once, in the desert, but those had been unusual circumstances.

"Alright," Emil said, although it was clear by then that his agreement wasn't required, since Kit was already walking down the hall ahead of him. If Emil wasn't dressed for this meeting, Kit looked especially outlandish. He was wearing the teal pants he'd left on Emil's floor and a black winter coat, and the tail of his oversized red sweater was visible beneath it. His violet hair stuck out in all directions, stiff and dirty, serving to prove that Kit's hair did indeed look bad sometimes, but Emil was attracted to him anyway. Kit marched down the hall, not caring about any of this, his boots leaving wet prints.

"Think about what you want," Kit said over his shoulder.

"I don't really know," Emil said, which was true of so many

things. "I want Heath and Winslow removed from any position of power, of course, but... I'd hate to lose the opportunity to go on missions." *I want you to come with me*, he couldn't open his mouth and say. Kit wouldn't want that. Kit didn't like joining things and working with people. He didn't like going outside, either. If Emil had been looking at Kit's resume when he'd been choosing his team, he would have tossed it aside.

And yet Kit's abilities made him invaluable. And he was courageous and shrewd. He'd be an asset to the team.

And then there was the fact that Emil didn't want to go anywhere without him. That wasn't professional reasoning, though.

"Fine," Kit said. "I can work with that."

"Is there something you want from this?" Emil asked.

Kit kept his expression neutral. "I already told you. I'm here to make sure you don't do anything too stupid. But I want to make sure those assholes get punished, too."

That was a sensible, honest answer, and Emil had no right to feel disappointed in it. Kit had never indicated any desire to join his team. He'd been very careful not to suggest any sort of future for the two of them. It was best to change the subject. "Do you... know your way around?" Emil asked. As they'd walked down the hallway, they'd passed a few locked metal doors. Kit stopped in front of one marked "restricted."

Kit pulled on its handle and set an alarm blaring. Then he waved at a corner of the ceiling where there was a camera that Emil hadn't noticed. "They're gonna come to us."

"Do you really think this is a good—"

The alarm cut off. When Emil turned around to see what Kit was looking at, Kristian Auer was behind him in an identical black suit, his lips pursed. "Mr. Singh," he said. "Mr. Jackson. Follow me."

The conference room was indistinguishable from the one

where Emil had first seen Oswin Lewis Quint's face on the wall display. Emil couldn't tell if it was the same one. How many rooms were in this building? What did Quint Services do with all this space?

Auer didn't turn the display on. He sat down on the other side of the table and gestured for them to take their seats. At least no one had handcuffed them yet.

"I assume there's something you want to tell me," Auer said.

It was better than Emil had expected to be treated.

"Dr. Heath and Dr. Winslow were conducting an illegal and unethical experiment in a secret room in Facility 17," Kit said. "We discovered the experiment and stopped its progress."

"I'm aware," Auer said, and it wasn't clear if he meant he was aware that they'd taken control of Facility 17 or if he was admitting knowledge of the experiment. "The kidnapping of Dr. Heath and Dr. Winslow will result in the termination of Mr. Singh's entire team. Criminal charges will be brought against both of you."

Emil had expected as much, but his stomach still dropped. "Don't charge Kit—" he started, but Kit held a hand out under the table where it was only visible to Emil.

"Bullshit," Kit said. "That's not what you want."

"Mr. Singh's team is replaceable."

"Not if you want to keep that facility and all the research in it a secret," Kit said, "which I know you do. In fact, because you want Quint Services to continue to exist, you will remove Heath and Winslow from their positions, you will see them prosecuted by the justice system, and you will not punish anyone involved in uncovering their crimes. You will restore Mr. Singh to his position, you will grant him and his team a say in the hiring of all future personnel, and you will give them all a five-percent raise. You will offer both victims compensation for physical and psychological damage incurred. And you will pay me triple my fee for last week's delivery."

Emil tried to keep his expression from showing his thoughts, or rather, *thought*, singular: *holy fuck, the balls on this kid.* It was a gamble. How did Kit know someone higher up at Quint Services—maybe even Auer himself—hadn't authorized Heath and Winslow's experiment? Someone had built that secret room.

"And why would I do that?"

"We have proof," Kit said. "Victims, witnesses, documents, physical evidence. If you don't want it all over the media, you'll do what I said."

"Your demands conflict with your threat. If Heath and Winslow are prosecuted, this will all be out in the open," Auer said.

"We both know Quint Services has ways around that," Kit said. "You get them convicted of something else if you have to. Fraud. Plagiarism. Something that stops them from working again."

Auer smiled and it was a horrifying sight. "Yes," he said. "So you see why I'm not troubled by this threat of exposure."

"Well," Kit said. "That was my best offer. The other option is I dump you in the Arctic Ocean and shake this place up until Oswin Lewis Quint falls out, and then I'll take it up with him."

Auer stopped smiling.

"You know you couldn't stop me," Kit continued, a new edge in his voice. "Quint is right to be afraid. Every fearful thing people say about runners is true about me. I exist outside the law. I'm a criminal. I'm from Nowhere. I am loyal only to myself. I'm sure you've seen those bumper stickers and ads —*the only thing that stops a runner is a bullet.* You don't have a gun."

Emil struggled to keep his mouth closed. When Kit had

offered to negotiate, he hadn't expected it to involve threatening the lives of executives at a multi-billion-dollar corporation.

"An interesting proposal," Auer said. "But I do have a gun."

Emil shot out of his seat and shoved his way in front of Kit.

"Unnecessary, Mr. Singh. I was speaking figuratively. Your infamous associates, Ms. Njeim and Mr. Blackwood, were given an experimental treatment that should soon render them unable to access the Nowhere. One dose would do the same to you, Mr. Jackson."

Shit. Travis had told him as much, and Emil had forgotten to tell Kit. Auer had failed to mention the antidote, though.

There was a knock on the door, and when Emil turned, the door was already open and Quint himself was leaning against the doorframe. With his blond hair, salesman's smile, and tailored grey suit, he looked far more approachable than Auer. "Kristian is being overzealous," Quint said. He sauntered into the room—Emil's mind shot back to the predatory beast in the cave—and sat down in the chair next to Auer. He leaned back, taking up as much space as possible. "There's no need to resort to threats. I'm sure we can come to an arrangement that suits all of us. You're an impressive young man, Kit. I'd like to have you on my team."

Quint leaned forward, offering a hand to Kit.

Kit didn't move. He locked eyes with Quint until he retracted his hand.

"Understandable," Quint said, still unsettlingly affable. "We've gotten off to a bad start and I've done nothing to make it up to you. I'm sure you've heard about my former views of runners, which I now know were offensive and misguided. I assure you I've changed."

"Uh huh," Kit said. Those two syllables captured Emil's feelings exactly.

"Let me try again," Quint said. "You probably know, based

on my reputation, that I am a driven and competitive man. I want Quint Services to be the first to explore other realities. That, above all else, is my priority. You're the first runner we know of to cross through the Nowhere into other realities. That makes you valuable to me."

"So you're willing to put aside your bigotry for potential profit," Kit said. "That's more like it."

"That's not how I would put it," Quint said. The best way Emil could think of to describe him was *glossy*. He was attractive and friendly, almost impossibly so. Nothing about him seemed real. "As I said before, my former views were reprehensible and I do apologize for them. But I understand if you find it hard to trust me. You're not wrong—I stand to gain financially from the explorations at Facility 17. If you can't trust me, trust the money. Having you on my side is worth a lot to me. I know you work well with Emil and his team and I think you could do more with them in the future."

"It hasn't even been 72 hours since we got Laila and Aidan out of that cell, so you can cut the shit about how you've changed," Kit said. "Tell me what you're prepared to do to prove it."

"I did encourage Dr. Heath and Dr. Winslow to create a drug that could disable runners, but I swear to you I knew nothing of their methods," Quint said. "I am appalled and will do everything in my power to prosecute them. I'm prepared to fulfill all your demands—justice for Laila and Aidan, more transparency here at Quint Services, more independence for Emil's team, and of course compensation. Additionally, if you'll work with us, I can offer you a salary that I'm sure you'll find more than satisfactory."

Emil expected Kit to spit on the table. Instead, he said, "I have more demands."

"Yes?"

"You fix Laila and Aidan," Kit said. "And you stop research and production on whatever it is you gave them."

"And Travis," Emil said. He saw Kit restrain his surprise. Emil wasn't sure Travis deserved a cure the way that Laila and Aidan did, since he'd been the one to abduct them, but he'd been mistreated by Quint Services himself. And he'd helped Emil. "Travis Alvey requires a cure, too."

"Quint Services will devote every possible resource to restoring your friends to their former state," Quint said. "But you understand why I can't possibly agree to your second demand. Runners exist outside our legal system. We need a way to curtail the abilities of those who would abuse them."

Kit was silent. Emil didn't trust Quint for an instant, but he could see the man's point. There were a few infamous instances of runners committing violent crimes. The drug represented a non-violent solution for bringing such criminals to justice— provided it was used ethically. Its development in secret, on innocents who hadn't consented to the experiment, didn't inspire much confidence. Emil didn't know what to say.

"Quint Services will redirect all funding from that project into repairing the breach in the Nowhere at Facility 17, rescuing Solomon Lange, and restoring Laila Njeim and Aidan Blackwood to their former state," Kit said. He swallowed. "And Travis Alvey, if he can be found. Until those things are accomplished, all research and production of that drug will remain on hold."

"An excellent compromise," Quint said smoothly. "Those will absolutely be our priorities. Is there anything else?"

"There will be no further research on subjects who don't consent," Kit said.

"Of course," Quint said. "We'll review the ethics of all ongoing research projects. I'll even send you a list that you can discuss with Emil and his team. Full transparency."

Emil had hardly said a word, and neither had Auer. He glanced at the other man, who sat ramrod straight in the chair next to Quint, expressionless. It was an effective routine, he had to admit. But Quint and Auer doubtless had experience bullying and cajoling people into what they wanted. Emil couldn't tell what he wanted. He didn't trust them at all, and yet he found himself tempted. It was just like before. He'd always had his hesitations about Quint Services, but he'd told himself he could do good from the inside. That whole time, he'd been living with Heath and Winslow while they committed atrocities in secret.

But maybe it would be different. This time, he'd know not to trust them. This time, he'd have Kit.

"You know how to get in touch," Kit said to Quint, standing and moving so close to Emil that when Emil stood, there was no space between them. "Send me a contract." Then he wrapped his arm around Emil's waist and they disappeared.

They were only briefly in the Nowhere, and when they reappeared in the loading dock next to Kit's bike, Kit moved quickly to roll it toward the garage door. The door rose as they approached, a silent sign that Auer and Quint were still watching them. Kit mounted the bike and gestured for Emil to join him, and it wasn't until they were miles away that he relaxed—*sagged* was the better word—against Emil. That last jump, an impractical and aggressive show of power, had cost him. On their long ride back to Zin's, Emil tried to suss out whether any of that had been worth it.

[23]

FLAWS

KIT AND EMIL PULLED INTO THE ALLEY BEHIND ZINNIA'S
an hour and a half later.

Zin cried, of course. She gave him an extravagantly long hug
and a monologue about how worried she'd been. Louann said
"Hey, Kit," smiled, and gave him what constituted an extravagantly long hug for her, which had nothing on Zin's version, but
still made him tear up. They loved him and he'd been such an
asshole.

The bar was supposed to open in an hour, but as soon as Zin
had hustled Kit and Emil from the back alley through the
kitchen, Louann walked to the front, put up the *closed* sign and
locked the door. The eccentric clientele of Zinnia's wouldn't be
surprised to find their favorite dive unexpectedly shut, but
they'd be loudly disgruntled about it next time they came in. Zin
would tell them she had to close the bar on a whim sometimes
because she was still a spoiled pop princess at heart and she had
to let the world know *somehow*. They'd grumble. Secretly
charmed, they'd all come back.

Kit knew all that because he'd lived here for ten years. He'd
washed thousands of dishes and poured even more beers. He'd

rolled his eyes at everyone who'd asked him for a specialty cocktail or a photo with Zin. More importantly, for the past decade, he'd eaten breakfast, lunch and dinner—and most of the meals in addition to that—in Zin and Louann's kitchen in their apartment upstairs or in the bar itself. Because it was home. They were his family.

Zin and Louann made them sit in a booth in the bar. Then, because they were both angels, Zin called for pizza and Louann went to pick it up. That made Kit smile. Louann had never paid for delivery once in her life and she wasn't about to start now.

While they waited, Emil sent a message to his team to say they'd made it back alive and he'd be in touch soon. They didn't talk about anything else until Louann came back.

Kit let Emil tell the story. He was happy to have someone else do the talking so he could eat. Zin asked a lot of questions, and eventually she moved away from questions about Quint Services, the Nowhere, and other realities, and started asking Emil where he grew up, what his family was like, and what else he loved in life other than her discography.

It dawned on Kit that Emil was meeting his... parents. At their home. Over dinner.

They were on a date.

While Zin was asking Emil about what kind of plants she should grow on the roof, Kit made panicked eye contact with Louann and she gave him a knowing smile. In the past day, he'd nearly been eaten by an alien predator and had threatened the life of a Quint Services executive, but somehow this—sitting in the booth next to Emil and watching him chat with Zin—was the interaction that made his heart rate spike.

Why was he so scared?

It's not like any of them were discussing anything awful. Zin was being perfectly pleasant and charming, keeping her conversation to safe topics. Louann had been positively extroverted when the conversation had turned to gardening, which meant she must *really* like Emil. Kit managed to add a sentence or two to the conversation over the next half an hour, but that was all. Hopefully the others would ascribe it to tiredness. Then the meal was over and Louann was clearing the table and shooing him upstairs and the fog of panic broke when Emil caught him and slid Kit's hand between both of his.

"Are you okay?"

"Yeah."

Emil didn't buy that. "Can we talk? Somewhere private?"

Kit nodded and made for the stairs before his brain caught up: *Emil has nowhere to sleep tonight. Last time he was here you made him stay on Zin's couch.* That was a stupid thing to worry about. He worried anyway.

Kit sat down on his mattress. Emil joined him after carefully closing the door, but he left some space between them.

"Hey," Emil said gently. "We've been through a lot—and you've been through more than me—in the past few days, and you just got a very strange offer from Quint, and I just want you to know that you don't have to do anything you don't want to do. I won't pressure you about that or... anything else."

Great. Now Emil was being all mature and experienced and nice. And Kit was so tired and mixed up, he sort of wanted to cry. He brought his knees up, wrapped his arms around them, and hid his face.

"You saved me," Kit said. "You risked your life to do it."

"I didn't do it so you'd owe me back," Emil said. "It wasn't a transaction."

"I don't know how to do this, Emil."

"What do you mean, 'this'? Are you worried about Quint—"

"Have a relationship like a real person!" Kit said, lifting his head and looking Emil in the eye. "I don't know how."

"You're smart—and you've been watching Zin and Louann

for ten years. You'll figure it out. It doesn't have to be right now and it doesn't have to be with me." There was a little hitch in his voice in the middle of that last sentence, impossible to miss.

"You just... let somebody know everything about you, let them become an important, essential part of your life, and then... trust that neither of you will fuck it up?"

Emil smiled. "Something like that. Except I think it's more like—when one of you fucks it up, you talk about it. I haven't always been great at that part."

"Can't we just have sex?" Kit said.

Emil's smile faded. "I told you I don't—I'd prefer—I can't—" He stopped abruptly instead of trailing off. Then he said, "I'm in love with you, Kit."

Kit nodded slowly. It wasn't a surprise. Emil showing up to save him, having experimented on himself and walked through the breach, was as good as a declaration. Kit could see now that it was cruel to ask Emil to limit things to sex. Emil wasn't Travis. He didn't want a transaction, like he'd said. Emil had feelings for Kit. He probably wouldn't have been able to find Kit on the edge of Nowhere if he didn't.

If Kit was honest, he had feelings for Emil, too. How could he not? Emil was heroic and beautiful and kind and transcendently good in bed, plus he kept saving Kit's life. And he loved his team and his family and he'd helped save Laila and Aidan. Worst of all, he couldn't dress for shit and he was a huge nerd who liked camping and he idolized Zinnia Jackson's pop career, and those things just made Kit love him *more*.

Kit had been quiet for too long now and Emil was having a hard time looking at him, which probably meant he felt rejected and Kit had already ruined everything before they'd even started. So Kit said, "If you leave, or die, it's gonna fucking kill me."

He meant *it's already too late for me*. He meant *I love you*.

Being plunged into the ocean or dropped from the sky had been less terrifying. At least when those things had happened to him, he'd been able to jump into the Nowhere and save himself. There was no running from this.

Emil blinked. Maybe he didn't understand. Or he was thinking of what to say. Whatever it was, Kit figured it was a good time to kiss him. Eager, anxious, needing to convey what he'd failed to, he put his hands on Emil's face and moved in fast. It was a hard kiss, Kit gripping Emil and chasing down the taste of him, and Emil met him with equal force. Kit kissed and kissed and didn't let go until there was no breath left in his lungs and his lips were swollen and scraped from Emil's stubble.

Emil's hands were still in his hair. Emil leaned his forehead against Kit's. "Remember what you said to me the night you almost drowned? *The question is—do you want to?*"

"Are you asking to fuck me? Of course I want to."

"I'm not talking about sex," Emil said, and Kit couldn't help the flutter of disappointment that went through him. "But the context is similar, right? That night, you were afraid you might die. The future seemed uncertain. So the only thing left to do was... whatever you wanted. This is just like that. We can't ever know what's going to happen. We might hurt each other. We might break up. One of us might die. Eventually, both of us will die and there's nothing we can do about that. But right now, we can love each other. If you want to."

"I do," Kit said quietly. "I'm just not as brave as you are."

"Or as stupid, I hear," Emil said, which made him smile. "Although I saw a few things in that conference room this afternoon that made me wonder."

"We're not talking about that now," Kit said.

"What are we talking about instead?"

"A shower," Kit said. "With you in it."

"Are you saying I smell?"

"Yeah," Kit said, shoving playfully at Emil's shoulder, then pushing off him to stand up. He offered his hand down to Emil, who stood up and followed him to the bathroom. Kit's shower wasn't really big enough for two people, especially not when one of them was Emil, but he didn't let that get in his way. Besides, after watching Emil strip every layer of clothing off his sculpted brown body, Kit couldn't imagine having an inch of space between them. He must have taken his own clothes off at some point, but he didn't remember anything that happened between his first sight of Emil naked and the moment they pressed their bodies together under the hot spray of the shower.

"I didn't get to see you naked last time," Kit said. He soaped up a loofah and began to rub it over Emil, although they were standing so close that the lather got all over both of them. "I was missing out." He trailed his hand through the hair on Emil's chest and over planes of his abdomen, then traced the angle of his hipbone and the thickness of his thigh, and back up again. He lingered over Emil's hip, where there were a few faint lines in his skin. "Hm, look at that. Stretch marks. Not perfect after all."

Emil laughed. "When I told you I was uncomfortable being called perfect, I didn't intend for you to make a list of my flaws."

"That's too bad because I have such a good one going," Kit said.

"You don't have to share," Emil said. "I can already tell it starts 'stupid and brave' and probably goes on to include 'huge nerd with terrible taste.'"

"Oh, definitely," Kit said, putting the loofah back on its hook while the shower rinsed them both clean. "And then there's this," he continued, trailing his fingers through the dark hair below Emil's navel, "which is extremely distracting, and as soon as I saw it that first day, I wanted to know where it led, and it's been plaguing my thoughts for a week, which is unfair."

Kit let his fingers travel lower until his hand was hovering next to Emil's erection, hard and thick and pointing straight up between their bodies. "And this," he said, taking hold of it. "Which is just obscene, and obviously way, way too big."

"Ah," Emil said, more strangled gasp than word, which was how Kit liked it.

Kit slid his hand down to the base. "I mean, just think how long you're going to have to spend fingering me before you can fuck me. You're going to have to go so slow, slicking your fingers up and working them into me until I'm writhing and begging for your cock, it's gonna be torture for both us. And then when you finally do fuck me, think of how tight the fit will be. You'll want to come right then, but you can't. Not after all that work. You have to make it last."

They were standing so close that Kit could feel the shiver that ran through Emil's body. He kept stroking his cock, then said contemplatively, "Are we going in the wrong order? Should we have had dinner and a movie first?" He paused in his movements.

"Kit," Emil complained. His pupils were huge and dark and his expression was soft with that sleepy, lust-dazed air. Kit had never seen anything so gorgeous.

"Just checking," Kit said, smiling. He picked up the pace again. He stretched up to kiss Emil, who obligingly bent his head down. Then Kit said, "So anyway, as I was saying, this thing is obscene. I'm not sure how I'll ever focus on anything else again. It's a danger to my health. I can't even look at it anymore."

Then he dropped to his knees and took Emil's cock into his mouth. He wasn't as genius at this as Emil was, he didn't think, but he liked the taste of it and the weight against his tongue. And the sound Emil let out shot straight to his dick and made Kit want to practice until he was a goddamn world-class expert at cocksucking. He locked his lips around the shaft and then experimented until he found the right tempo, which in this case, after lots of teasing, was fast. Kit reached up to cup Emil's balls and then a second later, Emil fisted a hand in his hair and came in his mouth.

Emil pulled him up afterward and reached down to touch his cock, but Kit moved his hand away. He was close. A touch might set him off. "I told you what I wanted," he said. "Were you not listening? Because if so, that's going on my list of flaws."

"I listened," Emil said in a voice that sent a thrill down Kit's spine.

They got out of the shower, toweled off, and made it to the bedroom somehow—Kit was only paying attention to Emil's hands and lips, which seemed to be all over his body, every-where at once. Then they were in bed, with Kit on his back with his knees bent and Emil sitting between them. "It's over there," Kit said, jerking his thumb toward a corner of the room behind him. "Under the pile of clothes."

Emil went to sort through Kit's mess, which was just enough time for Kit's nerves to get the better of him. He tried to sound lighthearted as he said, "You know, the first time I tried this with Travis, we were in his room and I freaked out and jumped by accident. It was really embarrassing. I showed up in a doctor's office waiting room—naked—then came back to my room and hid for hours. I hadn't jumped with no control like that in years. Like getting a boner in front of your crush in middle school, except... the opposite."

Emil froze, still kneeling in the corner, the bottle of lube in his right hand. "Shit, Kit, I'm so sorry. I had no idea this was your first—"

"No, no, stop. You're being all serious. Laugh!" Kit sat halfway up, propping himself on his elbows. "You were supposed to laugh. It was funny. It was a joke." He smiled at

Emil as if he could change Emil's expression by changing his own.

Emil didn't laugh or smile. A number of expressions crossed his face like he was trying them on and rejecting them. He looked like he wanted to say something but wasn't sure what.

"You worry too much," Kit said.

"Given the week we've had, I'm beginning to think I don't worry enough," Emil said dryly, coming to sit next to Kit on the mattress. He set the bottle of lube on the floor. "But we were talking about *you*. Are you sure you want to do this, Kit?"

Kit glanced pointedly down at his erection, which had lasted throughout this decidedly unsexy conversation. Emil was still sitting on his bed naked, after all. "Emil. Stop worrying. It's not going to happen again." When that didn't satisfy Emil, he said, "I didn't trust Travis. I trust you. I love you."

Emil did smile then, and while Kit was trying to say, "And in case it wasn't already clear, I really, really want you to f—" Emil grabbed him by the shoulders and pulled him up into a scorching kiss. The heat of it rolled all the way through him and he let Emil lay him back down on the bed and then move to sit between his legs.

"You know," Emil said, a little too casually. "If you ever want to try this the other way, I like to bottom."

"Is that so," Kit said, his heart fit to burst at the mere suggestion of a *next time*, a strange and novel feeling. Maybe having a relationship was a better idea than he'd thought. They hadn't even finished this time and Emil was making him want more. However long they could make their time together last, Kit wanted every second of it.

As Emil was opening the bottle of lube, he said, "And as for that thing you said earlier about whether we're doing things in the wrong order, I think surviving two different alien wildernesses and the berserk ghost of one of my colleagues together counts for a few dates."

"Whatever weird mental accounting you need to do," Kit said agreeably. "As long as it gets you to fuck me."

"I would like to take you to dinner and a movie sometime," Emil said. "Or, you know, some other kind of date. Something normal where nothing tries to kill us."

"Sure," Kit said, and anything else he'd been planning to say was blotted out of his thoughts as Emil touched him, one warm, dry hand steadying his thigh and the first gentle, circling touch of his slippery fingertips.

"I want to spend time with you," Emil said. "Get to know you. Talk about our pasts, our futures, our *feelings*."

"Oh my God," Kit said, squeezing his eyes shut, because Emil—the fucking sap—was torturing him and his fingers felt so good that Kit would agree to anything right now. When Kit opened his eyes again, Emil was smirking.

"You can't tease me and expect not to get teased in return."

"Fair," Kit said. His voice came out breathy. "And yet it's going on my list of flaws anyway."

"Uh huh," Emil murmured. The slow, methodical stroke of his fingers gradually undid Kit until their conversation was no longer in words but in gasps and sighs. The pressure inside him was unexpectedly sweet and he couldn't help but flick his hips, chasing some sensation. He'd never been treated like this—cherished—as though his pleasure was an experience to be savored rather than rushed through. How long had it been? He wanted it to last forever and he wanted to go careening over the edge. Happy and desperate all at once, he could feel his aching cock dripping onto his stomach.

"Fuck me," Kit said.

Even in his current haze of lust, he expected some sort of

measured "are you sure?" concern from Emil, but instead, Emil just smiled and said, "Alright."

Kit spread his legs. There was a moment of emptiness and then overwhelming fullness as Emil replaced his fingers with his cock. As with everything else, Emil was careful and tender, letting Kit relax before he pushed any further. It was intense, the stretch and the pressure of it, but it was also hot and slippery and wonderful, and even as he knew he was taking as much as he could, he wanted more. When Emil finally buried himself inside, Kit squirmed against him, thrilled by the feel of it. He'd never been so close to anyone.

"Now," he urged. "Fuck me."

Emil laughed. "Oh, you're not satisfied? You have some constructive criticism to share?"

He shifted until he was leaning forward between Kit's legs, supporting himself on his arms, and Kit could rise up to kiss him. He thrust his tongue into Emil's mouth, hoping to inspire him, and then was caught off-guard when Emil slid out and plunged back into him. It felt like every nerve in his body lit up at once—an explosion of sensation that left him writhing for more. And more came an instant later, and then again, and again.

"Holy fuck," Kit whispered.

Emil only smiled at him, black hair falling into his eyes and his lower lip caught between his teeth as he kept up his efforts. Kit was in awe. A sheen of sweat covered him. He moved with such grace and force. Kit watched their bodies meeting then drawing apart and couldn't help but move with him. He'd curved one hand around Emil's neck when they were kissing and he kept it there, hanging on, while his other hand skated down his body to wrap around his cock. He was reluctant to touch himself, since it was an admission that they were approaching the end, but it felt so unspeakably, incomprehensibly good. He was so close. It was nothing to slide his hand from the head to the base, slicking down the shaft.

Emil's gaze had followed his hand down and there was a little hitch in his rhythm as he watched Kit stroke himself. Fuck, that was hot. Kit bit his lip and met Emil's eyes. Emil leaned down to kiss him and Kit's orgasm shot through him. He moaned, spilling onto his hand and his belly. Emil came after him, a few, fast, stuttering thrusts behind, and then he laid down on top of Kit and pressed his nose into the side of Kit's neck.

"So good," Kit said, stroking his free hand through Emil's hair.

"Mm," Emil said, nipping Kit's neck.

"We can do that again sometime," Kit said, and even to himself, he sounded wrecked. Now that the glow was fading, his body reminded him that he'd spent the past week hungry and exhausted and fearing for his life. Luckily, he was already in bed.

"Yeah?" Emil asked. "Not going on the list of my flaws?"

"I don't know what you're talking about. What list?" Kit said, kissing the top of Emil's head. "What flaws?"

Emil extricated himself from Kit. "Come on," he said. "Another quick shower and then we can fall asleep."

"Ugh," Kit said. "I remembered the list and this is going on it. Too much energy." But he took Emil's hand and let himself be pulled into the bathroom.

Emil turned on the shower and stuck his hand under the spray. "So it was good?"

Kit couldn't imagine how he could possibly need any more confirmation. But Emil looked genuinely uncertain, and that was adorable. He took Emil's face between his hands. "So good. Really good. Amazing. Magnificent." He paused. "But not perfect."

"No?"

Kit shook his head. "Nope. You'll just have to try again next time. Lucky for you, I was serious about doing it again. You won't even have to buy me dinner first."

"What if I want to?"

Kit grinned and stepped past Emil into the shower. "Well, you should know I can eat a lot."

[24]

SPEND SOME TIME

EMIL WOKE UP WITH KIT IN HIS ARMS AND PASSED A blissful instant before he remembered that yesterday Kit had risked his own life and livelihood in some devil's bargain with Quint. They'd have to return to Facility 17 to sort out the mess with Lange and the breach in the Nowhere sooner rather than later. His team would have questions. He sighed and closed his eyes, wishing he were asleep again.

Kit stirred against him.

Being awake had its advantages. "Good morning," Emil murmured. "How are you feeling?"

In answer, Kit grabbed Emil's hand and dragged it down to his hard-on. Everything else—and in their case, that meant the fabric of reality—could wait. Their morning sex might not have been as revelatory as the night before, but it was warm and easy and suffused with sleepy affection. It felt like the kind of thing he could wake up to every day, which was its own kind of revelation.

"I really do have to get up," Emil said. "I expect Quint and Auer got in touch with the team yesterday after our meeting, but they'll have questions for me... and you, I suppose, if you're staying."

"I'll have to read the contract," Kit said. He sat up and stretched, treating Emil to a view of his naked back. Then he began to pull on clothes, picking things up from his piles and then discarding them. "But I'm coming with you either way."

Emil stayed on his back in bed, watching the show. "Are you sure about this—working for Quint, I mean?"

Kit finally settled on an outfit. It involved the least tasteful and respectable three-piece suit Emil had ever seen in his life. The tailoring made him want to stare, but the multi-colored print, which shifted from floral to abstract under his gaze, made him dizzy. It was already excessive, so naturally Kit added jewelry, eyeliner, and a scarf around his neck. Emil stared, transfixed by the hideous grandeur of it all. He would relish removing it later.

Kit pulled on a pair of black boots, startlingly utilitarian in contrast to the rest of him. He messed up his hair with his fingers, then turned toward Emil and put his hands on his hips. "Of course not. I don't trust that asshole at all. But I've been working for evil people and watching out for myself my whole life, so I figure it's not that much of a change. And Laila is up there, and I can't let her down again. I don't know what it's like to have a sister, but... I think she's my best friend."

Emil nodded. He got out of bed and dressed with far less enthusiasm, since he had only the clothes he'd been wearing yesterday. It wasn't like he could fit into anything Kit owned— and even if he could, he wasn't sure he possessed either the particular courage necessary to dress like a drunk alien peacock or the swagger to pull it off. He smiled to himself at how Kit and Zin shared their outlandish fashion sense, and from what he'd seen of Laila, she fit right into their found family.

Emil thought of Zora and his parents and how he should

have called them on Sunday. They'd be worried, just like his team. He couldn't tell his family the details of what had happened, but his team would be angry. They already were. Unlike Kit, they wouldn't be content to work for Quint Services once everything was out in the open. "Just so you know, there's a chance we'll end up doing this alone. I don't think my team will be happy with this arrangement."

"They will," Kit said. He was already out the door and heading down the stairs and Emil followed him. "When you tell them we're going to figure out a way to take Quint for everything he's got."

"What?" Emil said, pausing in the landing, so stunned the word came out half-laugh, half-gasp. Kit had threatened Auer's life yesterday, but that had been blunt. Destroying Oswin Lewis Quint would require a far more subtle scheme.

"I haven't worked out the details yet," Kit said. "But your friends are smart. And as you know, Laila used to rob banks. And Aidan's up there, and it's gotta be his life-long dream to ruin a billionaire. They'll help. And there's other reasons for me to stay in Facility 17, you know, saving Lange and fixing the breach. I'm the only one who's successfully rescued a living thing trapped in the Nowhere. And you, of course."

"And me?" Emil walked down until he was on the same step as Kit. He knew what Kit meant, but he still wanted to hear it. Logically, he should be asking questions about Kit's nascent revenge plot, but he had his priorities.

"Well, you live and work up there, and it's dangerous, so someone has to make sure you don't do anything too stupid," Kit said, putting the tip of his index finger to the center of Emil's chest. "I can't trust your team to do that, since they facilitated you poisoning yourself and walking into the breach to find me."

"You're welcome," Emil said dryly.

"Plus, I want to see you again," Kit said. He dropped his

hand, shrugged and looked away. "Because I'm in love with you or whatever."

"Or whatever," Emil repeated, raising a brow.

"Don't push it," Kit said, continuing down the stairs. But he looked over his shoulder and beamed at Emil, and that was good enough.

They ate breakfast in Zin and Louann's narrow kitchen. Emil had been to another reality—or multiple other realities—but part of him still couldn't get over that he was drinking tea and eating yogurt with Zinnia fucking Jackson. Kit informed them that he was planning to spend some time with Emil. He didn't say "live on a secret base inside an asteroid" or "work for Quint Services" or "save the known universe from unfolding." He said *spend some time with Emil*. It was foolish to think about it that way, but it was foolish to take on any of it, so Emil supposed he shouldn't nitpick. He focused instead on the way it made him feel when Kit said his name like that. And when Zin and Louann nodded like Kit was making a great choice.

And then when Emil went to the counter to refill his mug, Kit leaned toward Zin and said, "Zin, um..." and in the long pause that followed, Emil decided to walk across the living room with his mug of tea and become very interested in looking down at the street. Even as hard as he was trying to give them some privacy, he still heard the chairs scrape the floor as they got up to hug, and Zin exclaiming "oh, baby," and when he eventually walked back in, all three of them were wiping their eyes.

"You be careful now," Zin said, and Kit kissed her cheek.

Then it was time to go. They packed up and left directly from Kit's room, right after Emil messaged Jake to say that if he could find a way to draw Lange into the lab, now would be a good time. It must have worked, since their trip was uneventful —or as uneventful as a trip through the Nowhere could be for Emil, since it still felt like pure misery.

They appeared in Emil's room. It took some time to gather everyone after that, but Emil managed to get them all into the kitchen. Laila and Aidan were already somewhat improved, and Lenny walked in leaning on Chávez's shoulder.

"Hi everyone," Emil said. "You all know Kit. He's joining the team."

———

Hours passed before they could be alone again. Kit crawled into Emil's bed and said, "You need a bigger bed."

"You can have your own room if you want," Emil said. "There are empty ones."

"Fine," Kit said. He could use it to hoard clothes and snacks. "But that's not what I asked for."

Emil laughed. He squeezed into the bed, proving Kit's point. "Okay. How good are you at transporting beds?"

"Not great. I could do it with Laila once she's better," Kit said, staring at the ceiling. "But maybe it's too dangerous for her."

"Well, we'll figure it out," Emil said. "We have time."

"I was thinking about this relationship thing," Kit said. He turned toward Emil. "Since you said you wanted to go on a normal date."

"Just something that doesn't get us killed."

"Where do you want to go?" Kit asked. "I'd say Paris or something, but I guess you're more likely to want to go somewhere with trees and dirt."

"Well, you've got me there. I do love trees and dirt," Emil said. "You know, I'm not Zin—I haven't already been everywhere—but I don't want you to feel like you have to do that for me. Take me places."

"I know," Kit said. He laid his head on Emil's chest. "But maybe I want to."

"I'd like that."

"So where should it be, then?"

"Well, I would say the places I most want to go are places nobody else has been yet," Emil said. "But I've had enough of that for this week. So... dinner with Zora and my parents?"

"Fuck, you always go right for the scariest option," Kit said. Visiting someone else's family sounded just like traveling to an alternate reality. But maybe hanging around Emil was making him stupider and braver, because Kit kind of wanted to meet Zora. And Chávez and Lenny had a lot to say about the care packages from Emil's family. Maybe it would be nice.

Emil laughed. "We can wait. I don't want to rush you. As much as I'd love to see them more often than I do, I'm also happy to stay right here."

"Yeah," Kit said, curling up against him. "Me too."

The series continues with *Out of Nowhere*. Turn the page for a sneak peek!

Aidan dropped the notebook, the rustle of pages and the click of its metal spine against the lab bench resounding in the silence of the room. He'd had to turn on the overhead light to take photos. Even lit up, dread haunted the lab.

The notebook splayed open to a random page of observations with neat handwriting in blue ink. It was dated September 20, 2093—six days ago—and the first line said *Subject No. 1 resistant, still unable to access the Nowhere.*

Damn right he'd been resistant.

Aidan picked up the tablet he'd set aside, snapped a picture, and sent it. He'd already sent dozens of other photos like it, plus a written account of what had happened to him, to his contacts in the Runners' Union. The first news articles about the experiments Quint Services had performed on Laila and Aidan had already surfaced. It wasn't enough. Oswin Lewis Quint wasn't in prison yet.

Shoving aside his revulsion, Aidan lifted the page and flipped it. The scientist who'd written these notes was already serving time. Not for hurting him or Laila, but for fraud. A false charge. Whatever else you could say of Heath and her collaborator Winslow—cruel, greedy assholes, both of them—they'd done their own experiments.

Their careers were over. They'd never do this to anyone again. But Heath and Winslow were lackeys. None of it had touched Quint, that slimy piece of shit. Aidan snapped another picture and sent it. A fucking cover-up. He intended to uncover it.

As long as Quint was out there, unspeakably rich and powerful, no runners would ever be safe. He'd figure out some new impossible prison to hide them in, and then somebody else would get strapped down and starved.

The page in his hand ripped.

"Aidan? What are you doing in here? It's the middle of the night."

Caleb. Better him than anyone else who might have caught Aidan here. He unclenched his hand from the crumpled page but didn't turn around. "We're in space, it's always the middle of the night."

Caleb didn't laugh. "Aidan."

It was concern coloring Caleb's voice, but it felt like a rebuke. Aidan was supposed to be resting, not secretly gathering evidence. "I couldn't sleep," he said, which was true. It had been true for days.

"So you broke into Heath's lab to photograph her notes? What are you doing with those, anyway?" Caleb paused and Aidan heard him walk closer. Caleb yawned. "Is that my tablet?"

Of course it was Caleb's tablet. Aidan didn't have any personal possessions at Facility 17 because he'd arrived here by getting fucking *kidnapped*. It was Caleb's clothes hanging off his even-scrawnier-than-usual body. He was barefoot because neither of them had thought to grab his shoes out of the cell before blowing it the fuck up. Where else would he have gotten a tablet?

Instead of saying any of that, Aidan said, "I didn't break in. The door was unlocked."

It had been deprogrammed after Heath and Winslow had been escorted from the premises three days ago. No one at Facility 17 had had time to go through the labs yet—except Aidan. He had to record this stuff before it was all swept under the rug.

"Hey," Caleb said, and there was no way his hand could possibly be that hot even through the sleeve of Aidan's t-shirt. Aidan must have taken a chill in the lab. He hadn't noticed until now. "Look at me."

If Aidan did that, it would be his undoing. He could withstand Caleb's worried voice and even his careful touches, but not his expression. They'd been friends so long that Aidan knew it by heart without looking: the pleading eyes, the strained twist of his mouth.

Aidan didn't have time to fall apart. He had to put Quint in prison.

Caleb reached across the lab bench and flipped the notebook shut. "It's four in the morning. We should both be asleep."

Aidan stared down at Caleb's hand pinning the notebook closed. It was a nice hand, broad and long-fingered with clean, blunt-tipped nails. That was the problem. Caleb's hand was attached to a nice forearm, warm beige skin lightly furred with dark brown hair, and a nice bicep, and a nice shoulder, and an even nicer face.

Fuck. He hadn't meant to look. Now not only was he magnetized by Caleb's ridiculously, offensively blue eyes, but worse, Caleb could see him. Aidan was mostly bones and under-eye shadows. He'd last combed the nest of black hair on his head three or maybe four days ago, something he only thought about when Caleb was regarding him with his perfect eyebrows drawn together like that. Rage was the only thing keeping Aidan upright, and he couldn't feel it with that much concern beamed directly at his face.

His shoulders sagged.

Caleb caught him in a hug. His scent was a comfort: clean laundry and a hint of sweat, the only soft thing in the lab's dry, recycled air. He'd been asleep before he came here; his cheek was marred by a pillow crease and his hair mussed. Caleb was only a couple inches taller. He didn't used to seem so much bigger. Aidan couldn't dwell on that, not when Caleb was enveloping him in warmth, not when Caleb's touch was making it possible to forget the smoking wreck of his life.

Shit. He had fires to put out. Aidan pushed Caleb away, the air cool where they no longer touched. "I just have to finish this."

"I woke up and you were gone," Caleb said, obviously still troubled.

Since the rescue six days ago, Aidan had been convalescing in Caleb's bed, and Caleb had been using an extra mattress that took up most of the remaining floor space in his room. Inconvenient, but familiar. Aidan had spent his vagabond adulthood shuffling from one shared room—or couch, or floor—to another. He'd spent his childhood with Caleb. No doubt this temporary arrangement was more pleasant than whatever came next.

"I'll be done soon," Aidan said. He had no way of knowing that. He could photograph every last pen stroke in this laboratory and Quint still might get away.

"You never said what you were doing. Is it Union business?"

Caleb always carefully respected the secrecy of the Runners' Union. He wasn't a runner, but for the first few years, he'd helped Aidan talk people into joining.

"I'm exposing Quint." Might as well be truthful. Caleb had

caught him, and anyway, he wasn't working on behalf of the Union. This was personal. "Or trying, anyway. I've been sending evidence for days and it's still barely making the news."

"Can I help?"

"No, it's fine, go back to bed."

"You should come with me. To sleep, I mean, not—you know what I mean."

A dull flush crept up his neck. It must be the late hour making Caleb trip over his tongue. He usually treated their closeness as something unquestionably platonic, as though the possibility of sex had never occurred to him. Aidan should know, since he had to put in years' worth of work to keep his end of that bargain. The possibility occurred to him all the time.

"I worry about you," Caleb added unnecessarily. "You know this could wait for a more normal hour. You could sleep now and then come back to this."

"They'll clean this lab out and then what evidence will I have, besides my testimony and Laila's?"

"Emil and his team wouldn't do that, not if they knew what you were working on. They'd want to help you."

Aidan grimaced. Caleb might trust them, but they were strangers to him. No, worse than strangers: they were people who'd signed up to work for Quint. Aidan could only trust the Union. "I have help. And I'll sleep when I'm done."

Caleb searched him with a look, then bit his lip like he was biting back protests, and withdrew. By the time Aidan came to their room, Caleb was asleep. The brush of Aidan's fingertips against his own skin as he undressed was cold enough to make him shiver.

———

THE BUZZ of the tablet woke Caleb. He reached over the edge of his mattress, groping in the dark until his hand hit it. The screen lit up with a message from Deb—*answer my texts you jerk*, typical little-sister stuff. Caleb unlocked it.

She'd texted him *l'shanah tovah* on Monday, six days ago. Must have been Rosh Hashanah. Caleb had missed the holiday and Deb's message, as well as several subsequent messages, because he'd been busy rescuing Aidan.

Aidan, who was—thank fuck—currently asleep in his bed. Whatever he'd been doing in Heath's lab in the middle of the night, he'd finished.

Sorry, Caleb wrote back. He'd been saying that a lot for the past few months. Nobody had been happy with his decision to take a job with Quint Services, and Caleb couldn't tell his family he'd done it to spy on the company. They'd been even less thrilled with his transfer to space.

But he'd found Aidan, and now the two of them could go home.

Back down to the surface, back down to the city where he and Aidan had grown up, where Deb still lived. She was in college now, and his parents had retired to warmer climes, so *home* no longer meant the second-floor of the old brownstone where the three of them had been teenagers together. For a moment, he wished it did.

Happy new year to you too, he wrote to Deb. *Talk soon, I promise.*

Caleb didn't know what he was going to tell her. If Aidan's plan worked, the whole story would be in the news soon enough.

There was no need to keep a strict schedule since Emil's team had seized control of Facility 17, but Caleb was awake now so he might as well get up. He could check on Laila, who'd been in the cell with Aidan, and Lenny, who'd been wounded during the rescue. Both of them had been more receptive to care than Aidan.

Caleb kept the lights at ten percent while he got dressed, letting Aidan sleep.

He picked up his tablet again and went through the rest of his messages. It wasn't snooping. The damn thing belonged to him. No new photos. No record of new sent messages, either. Finding nothing made him feel worse for looking in the first place. Guilt and disappointment twisted in his stomach. He just wanted to help.

Being Aidan's best friend didn't come with a high enough security clearance for that, apparently. Neither did saving his extremely frustrating life.

Caleb carried the tablet with him to the brightly lit industrial kitchen, which was bustling as though nothing had changed. It smelled like coffee, and he could hear butter sizzling in a skillet. The routine was a comfort, especially since no one knew what to do now that Heath and Winslow were in prison. Caleb wasn't sure who was in charge, other than Emil. The other top scientist at Facility 17, a physicist named Solomon Lange, had disappeared in a lab accident before Caleb's arrival. Not died. Vanished into the Nowhere.

The team was still working on a plan to locate and, if possible, revive him. Discovering the secret prison cell where Aidan and Laila had been tortured had interrupted them, but now that they had a measure of control over the facility, Caleb was confident they'd solve that problem and any others that cropped up.

Emil, the team leader, an intimidatingly handsome guy of Indian descent, was seated at the long metal table in the room with a cup of tea and his own tablet in front of him. He smiled at Caleb. "Good morning."

Caleb smiled back and said good morning to all of them in turn. He liked these people, but he wasn't one of them. Insinuating himself into social groups, at least superficially, was never hard. People were primed to like him because he was youthful, halfway fit, and blandly symmetrical. He made good on that advantage by smiling a lot and remembering names and personal details for small talk. It felt calculating to think about it in those terms, but he'd had to. Charming his way into a post at Quint Services' most secret research facility had been a lot of work.

Caleb hadn't needed to charm Emil's team into rescuing Aidan, which was a relief. They'd done it because it was the right thing to do.

He didn't see the violet-haired runner, Kit, who'd been instrumental in discovering the secret cell. Kit must not be a morning person.

Caleb grabbed a couple pieces of toast, sat, searched for Quint Services on the tablet, and sorted the results by most recent. It took several minutes to find any mention of the experiments, and the articles only implicated Heath and Winslow, not Quint himself. None of them were from major news sources. No wonder Aidan was disappointed. A story like that ought to be in the headlines. It ought to have spurred a massive criminal investigation.

Quint had to be burying the articles. That piece of shit.

"Do you think Quint will ever see consequences for what he did up here?" Caleb asked, setting the tablet down.

"Well, Kit vowed to destroy him," Emil said, as neutrally as if he was reporting the weather. He took a sip of tea. Caleb supposed it was bad form to be openly pessimistic about your boyfriend's chances of ruining a man with a net worth of 11 trillion dollars. It did seem like a long shot, even if said boyfriend could teleport.

"Are you asking because Aidan's been leaking sensitive information to the press?" Dax asked. The team's pale, redheaded physicist was methodically peeling the liner from their blueberry muffin, and they'd spoken without looking up from the task.

The question still gave Caleb pause. He wasn't here to snitch.

"I'm not mad," Dax clarified. "No one here cares. But I did notice."

"How?" Caleb asked. "It's barely made the news."

"I keep weird hours and I saw the lights on in Heath's lab in the middle of the night. Wasn't hard to put it together after that," Dax said. "It's good that he's trying, but he should be prepared for failure. Quint has a history of crushing journalists or outlets that report negative stuff about him."

"Yeah," Caleb said, dismayed. When Aidan had said *I'll sleep when I'm done*, he hadn't been talking about documenting evidence. He'd been talking about ruining Quint.

The conversation moved on, but Caleb didn't pay attention. He finished eating and put his plate in the dishwasher. Leaving after so little clean-up was definitely shirking, but no one called him on it.

The facility operated by having everyone who worked there take a hand in its maintenance. In his transfer interview, Caleb had claimed to be very handy, fabricating an anecdote about fixing a leaky faucet in his apartment. Any potentially leaky faucets in the facility would just have to keep dripping. There were bigger problems. If Aidan was awake when he got back to the room, Caleb would ask if he wanted breakfast. Then they'd discuss Quint.

He didn't know what he'd say. There were only so many variations on *please let me help you*, and none had worked so far. He came to the door of his own room too quickly. Kept walking.

The facility, carved inside of an asteroid, was far larger than it initially seemed and almost all on a single level. The kitchen and the greenhouse were clustered together at one end and there were labs and medical exam rooms at the other.

This hallway passed by a lab with caution tape on the door. There had once been windows permitting outsider to peer in, but an accident had shattered them and now there was brown paper blocking the view. Inside this space—Dr. Lange's former lab—was something the team had taken to calling *the breach*. Dr. Lange had designed a machine meant to open a door into the Nowhere, and in a way, he'd succeeded. The problem was that nobody could close it.

Caleb knew this space disturbed runners. He'd witnessed Kit's reaction to it. But he couldn't feel anything wrong with it. The papered-over windows and the caution tape on the door were enough to keep him out, though. He turned the corner.

He ran straight into himself.

It took him a full two minutes to realize that. At first he was only aware of having run into another person, one about the same size as him. How had that happened? He'd been thinking, sure, but his eyes had been open. It was as if the person had materialized right in front of him. A runner?

They both grunted and began to apologize and disentangle themselves, and that was when Caleb began to take stock of the guy. A white man, about the same build as him, dressed in grey and black, with brown hair and blue eyes and—*holy fucking shit*.

That was his face.

Backwards—no, not backwards, just not a mirror image— and with two days' scruff on his cheeks, but that was his mouth and those were his cheekbones. That was the angle of his nose and the surprised arch of his eyebrows. Caleb had an absurd moment of thinking *wow, handsome*, and then he blinked it away and said, "What the fuck."

Caleb was wearing blue scrubs and sneakers because habit was a powerful force. His double was dressed for some other purpose, way less friendly—boots, a utilitarian black jacket, black jeans, and a gun holstered around his thigh. Panic stabbed through Caleb's chest. He checked the man's face again. *I wouldn't shoot anyone*, he thought, as though he could will this other man's body like it was his own.

"Like what you see?"

This motherfucker even had his voice. It was as disconcerting as the gun. The double didn't reach for the gun, though. He put his hands on Caleb's shoulders as if to steady him—or to size him up. His grip was heavy but loose, almost lazy. Not a touch intended to force Caleb in any particular direction. Between two people who knew each other, it would have been affection; between two strangers, an advance. Between him and his double, Caleb had no idea.

The sound of his double's question echoed in his mind. Caleb would use that voice if he was flirting. But why would he flirt with himself? Sure, Caleb wanted people to like him, enjoyed making people giggle and blush, but he'd never been so overtly sexual with another man.

His double was smirking. Caleb had never looked that smug in his life. As for his own face, he wished he could muster an expression other than bewildered. "Who are you? Where did you come from?"

His double pulled him close and kissed Caleb on the mouth.

Stubble scraped Caleb's skin, a tongue plunged between his lips, and fingers threaded through his hair before he could collect any thoughts. Panic strobed through his brain, flashes of fear and arousal accelerating his pulse. When the kiss continued past its rude beginning, smoothing into something steadier, but still commanding, Caleb leaned into it.

No, that couldn't be right. He'd meant to back away.

The heat of the kiss melted his resolve and all his common

sense. His hands fisted in the thick material of his double's jacket.

Caleb had kissed a lot of people, none of whom had been men, or total strangers, or identical to him. This wasn't normal, and he should think carefully—and *that* was an arm around his back, tugging him closer. A very forceful arm. None of the people Caleb had kissed had ever been this aggressive. He'd never been pressed so close to another man.

He *liked* it.

It was the best explanation for why he hadn't squirmed away yet. The magnitude of the realization shook him. Had he really lived his whole life until now without knowing that? What did it mean?

Before he had time to consider it, something pinched the side of his neck and he passed out.

ACKNOWLEDGMENTS

I wrote *Edge of Nowhere* as a fun distraction while I was stuck in the middle of another book. It was a rush in all senses—a thrill, a hurry—and I published it not long after writing. Its original 2018 publication did not contain an acknowledgments section, which was an oversight borne of haste. In March 2021, I am correcting the record.

The made-up science in this novel owes a great deal to my beloved Science Consultant, who excels at asking all the right questions about my ideas. I still remember shouting "Dimensional prions!" while we were sitting in bed and then frantically hunting for my phone or a pad or any kind of writing implement. Whatever feels thorough and thoughtful about my sci-fi should be credited to the Science Consultant, while the blame for all nonsense can be laid at my feet.

I'm also grateful to my friends and family for their love and support, especially my fellow writers Valentine Wheeler and K.R. Collins, and the online communities that brought us together.

Thornfruit (The Gardener's Hand, Book 1)

The sun never sets in Laalvur, and children born with magic keep disappearing into the city's shadows. Alizhan, a mind-reading thief, uncovers part of this plot and nearly gets killed for it. Another young woman rescues her, and they both end up entangled in a conspiracy and fighting to save their city—and each other.

———

Praise for *Thornfruit*

"The world-building is excellent, the prose is gorgeous, and the characters and their relationships are phenomenal." — *Smart Bitches, Trashy Books*

"[Thornfruit] is well-written, original and diverse, and definitely one I would recommend." — *Strange Horizons*

"Thoughtful world-building with an underlying hard sf spin that hit the spot for me. Ev and Alizhan are rounded and believable, and their relationship to each other is utterly endearing. The antagonists are complex with too-understandable reasons for their decisions. I also really appreciated the excellent integration of a neurodivergent character's perspectives. I can't wait to read the next book and find out more about where the story is headed." — Bisexual Book Awards, 2018 finalist for Best Speculative Fiction

———

Nightvine (The Gardener's Hand, Book 2)

Alizhan and her companion Ev leave the constant sun of their homeland to sail for the Nightward coast. They pin their hopes on His Highness Prince Ilyr of Nalitzva, a man rumored to understand any language, even one he's never encountered. But Ilyr is not who he claims to be, and danger lurks in the glittering court.

Shadebloom (The Gardener's Hand, Book 3)

The conclusion to the trilogy, available now!

ABOUT THE AUTHOR

Felicia Davin is the author of five novels, including the queer fantasy trilogy *The Gardener's Hand* and the sci-fi romance *Edge of Nowhere*, which was a finalist for Best Bisexual Romance in the 2018 Bisexual Book Awards. Her short fiction has been featured in *Lightspeed*, *Nature*, and *Heiresses of Russ 2016: The Year's Best Lesbian Speculative Fiction*.

She lives in Massachusetts with her partner and their cat. When not writing and reading fiction, she teaches and translates French. She loves linguistics, singing, and baking. She is bisexual, but not ambidextrous.

She writes a weekly email newsletter about words and books called *Word Suitcase* (feliciadavin.com/word-suitcase). You can find her on Twitter @FeliciaDavin or at feliciadavin.com.

CPSIA information can be obtained
at www.ICGtesting.com
Printed in the USA
LVHW111157190621
690661LV00001B/187